Bomb

A Gho

by Simon Leighton-Porter

ISBN 978-1-80440-420-1

Silver Quill Publishing

Also by the same author:

The Seven Stars

The Minerva System

Death to Bankers

The Manhattan Deception

This book is respectfully dedicated to the memory of the men of Bomber Command, over 55,000 of whom lost their lives during the Second World War.

Chapter One

My eyesight is fading – just like the rest of me. Darkness is closing in, its fingers pulling me ever deeper; so deep that no one will ever see or hear me again. Even writing these words is draining what little strength remains to me. No more access to a computer, just the agony of pushing a pencil stub across the pages of yet another exercise book. How many books on the pile now? Too many to count, but the fact that you are reading this means that someone has found and transcribed what I have written. Too late for me of course, but at least the truth will now be told. Not just my story – my passing won't even make the footnotes of history – but the story of men who died for something they cared about, something that those who came after seem to have forgotten.

If this sounds like I am talking in riddles I quite understand. A few months ago I would have felt the same way. Logic, common sense and science tell us such things cannot happen. That's what I thought too, until it happened to me.

Let me explain so that you can avoid the same fate as me.

My name is Bill Price and I am a journalist – or rather I used to be. The last time I saw a copy, The Lincoln Post had become a free sheet with a few pages of news bought in from an agency and the rest taken up by advertising. My former editor retired to spend more time with his drinks cabinet and most of the staff are on the dole – one is trying to write a book and the rest are driving taxis or stacking shelves until something better turns up. Lincolnshire's like that these days. Unless you're willing to compete with the eastern Europeans for farm labouring jobs there isn't much choice.

It hasn't always been like that, not for me, anyway. I came back here, stayed here really, for a very simple reason. It was a place where I'd been happy. I'm a Londoner by birth and until I joined the Royal Air Force, venturing outside the M25 meant visiting a strange, unknown land of mud, cowpats and shops that didn't sell anything you wanted.

After university I went to RAF Cranwell for Officer Training and basic flying training, stayed there to do the multi-engine conversion course and was then posted up the road to RAF Waddington, only a stone's throw from the city of Lincoln itself. That's where I met Amy. We married and a few years later, our daughter Julia was born. The usual round of postings followed, including three years of living death, walled up in the Ministry of Defence Main Building in Whitehall. 'It's good for your career, Bill,' they kept saying. 'You'll make Wing Commander before you're forty.' Trouble is, I didn't want to be a Wing Commander. Flying a desk, or "mahogany bomber" as they're known, didn't appeal. I was happy flying aeroplanes, so that's what I did. I stayed a Squadron Leader and went back to Cranwell as a flying instructor, put on weight, took up golf and watched Julia grow into an inquisitive and happy child. No heroics, no wars, no medals – but I was content with my lot. More importantly, we were happy as a family. I miss that terribly. The passage of time has never healed the wound, not for one moment.

In my second year of instructing at Cranwell I

applied for my dream job. The Battle of Britain Memorial Flight – usually shortened to *BBMF* – at RAF Coningsby has one of the world's few remaining airworthy Lancasters and at any one time there are three pilots qualified to fly it. All three have full-time flying jobs elsewhere in the Royal Air Force but volunteer to share display duties during the summer months. One of them, an old friend who had taught me to fly on Jet Provosts when I'd first joined the Service, was retiring and now the trawl was out for volunteers to take his place. I applied and along with the other half-dozen hopefuls went through a series of check rides: first in the Chipmunk, and then in the BBMF's 1940s-vintage Dakota, to see how we managed the unfamiliar challenge – for those of us who'd only flown tricycle-undercarriage aircraft – of flying what are known in the trade as tail-draggers. I must have done something right because I got the job.

That summer was one of the happiest of my professional life. Although it meant more nights away from home, particularly at weekends, the chance to fly the Lancaster, to be entrusted with such a precious and special aircraft was every Service pilot's dream come true. Not only that, but I had the privilege to meet some of the surviving veterans of Bomber Command.

A few months later, everything I held dear was snatched away from me.

***

Friday evening. Happy hour at RAF Coningsby and a last drink with friends and colleagues before the Christmas break. My mobile rang. 'Have you seen the weather?' I could hear the anxiety in Amy's voice.

Clamping the phone to my ear to blot out the roar of a hundred beery voices, I moved out into the corridor, leaving behind the alcoholic fug of the Officers' Mess bar. 'I can't hear you properly, darling. Did you say something about the weather?' I did my best to enunciate properly, but I knew that after all these years together Amy could tell to the exact pint how much I'd had.

'Take a look outside,' she said. 'It's chucking it down with snow.'

I wandered through into the deserted foyer and peered out into the December gloom. 'Just a few flakes here,' I replied. 'But if you're worried about driving in the snow, why don't you come and get me now before it settles?'

'You *know* I hate driving in snow, Bill. Can you do the drive back?'

'Sorry, no. I've already had four pints.'

I heard her swear under her breath. We rarely argued or fell out, but I knew her well enough to expect long periods of chilly silence for the rest of the evening.

Twenty minutes later I climbed into the rear passenger seat of our old BMW and did up my seatbelt. Julia sat in the front next to her mother, chattering excitedly about her part in the Guide troop's Christmas pantomime. Amy said nothing but stared grimly ahead, tense, her back held away slightly from the seat, hands gripping the wheel as though it were a lifebelt. I remember looking back as we turned out of the main gate towards Coningsby village. Snow had begun to settle on the road and was already covering our tyre tracks as Amy slowly eased the car up to twenty mph.

4

Tyre tracks and snow lit yellow by the sodium lights dotted along the security fence. Those were the last things I remember.

Then cold, desperate cold all over and a man's voice talking into a radio. Blue flashing lights reflecting in the snow. Sitting on the verge with a blanket round my shoulders and a desperate longing to curl up in the snow and sleep for ever. Then someone shone a light in my eyes, piercing, bright and painful, adding to the agonising throbbing in my head. A mumble of voices. People talking about me, but not to me. Then nothing.

They call it an artificially induced coma. I found that out after they woke me two weeks later. Tubes, pain from the developing pressure sores and a terrible throbbing that felt like my head was about to explode. 'Hello? William? Mr Price? Can you hear me? Say something, please.' Nobody's ever called me William, not even my parents when I was little. Who were these people? Why would I want to say anything to them? All I wanted was to go back to sleep.

Slowly, the world swam into view. Blurry at first. Lots of white and a hum of voices. I understood this had something to do with me, but couldn't work out what I was supposed to do or say. Some of the white detached itself and moved towards me. Another light shone in my eyes. A disembodied voice said, 'Good papillary light reflex.' Then, 'How many fingers am I holding up, Mr Price?'

I blinked and squinted. It was a stupid question, I couldn't see any fingers, just a blur. 'No idea.' Speaking was painful and my voice sounded slurry and drunk. My throat was dry and hurt in a way that made me want to retch.

The moving blur of white gradually coalesced into the form of an earnest young doctor, peering at me over the top of her half-moon glasses. To me she looked barely older than Julia. With a huge effort I managed to force the words out. 'I'm in hospital, aren't I?' It wasn't my voice, but that of an elderly wino, slurring and croaking on the edge of incoherence.

'Yes, Mr Price. You've had an accident. You've been very ill.'

'Does my wife know I'm here? She'll be worried sick.' I saw the doctor look away. Neither of the nurses by the bedside would make eye contact. I half guessed what was coming next although my mind wouldn't entertain it as reality.

'I'm afraid your wife and daughter are dead, Mr Price.'

***

The weeks that followed passed in a haze of misery and pain. Not only could I remember nothing of the accident, but it became clear to me, if not to those treating me, that there were huge holes in my memory. It didn't really hit me until I received my first visitors. Two strangers were shown into the side ward that I shared with three other "head cases", as we had christened ourselves. A man and a woman, smartly dressed, both in their mid-forties, a few years younger than me, smiling and calling me by my first name. 'We're so sorry about Amy and Julia, Bill,' said the woman, placing a hand on my forearm, just below where the drips were attached. The young doctor with the half-moon glasses hovered nervously in the background.

The man stepped forward and placed a hand gingerly on my shoulder as though afraid I might break. 'We're all so sorry, Bill. Just glad you're in one piece.'

It was too much. I tried to choke back the tears, but without success. Now the woman was speaking again. 'We're so sorry, Bill. You know, if there's anything we can do…'

'No, it's not that… Well yes it is that but…' still the slurry, borrowed voice, not mine.

'But what, Bill?' she said, dabbing away the tears for me.

'I don't know who you are,' I sobbed. 'It's clear I should, but I don't know who you are. I can't remember.'

They shot a nervous look at the doctor who stepped forward. 'I did warn you this was possible,' she said.

Then the stranger stepped forward, introducing himself as my commanding officer from Cranwell; in reality a man whom I'd known and respected for the last three years, but whose existence had been wiped from my memory. He then introduced his wife who apparently had been a close friend of Amy's and a regular visitor to our home.

That night I lay awake, staring at the ceiling and listening to the bedlam chorus of howling from the geriatric ward further along the corridor. However hard I tried I had no recollection of ever meeting my two visitors before. With time, people around me got used to my patchy memory, but it embarrassed me enormously.

***

Cranial trauma, they call it. Cognitive impairment is another term they use. 'Why don't you just be honest and tell me I've got brain damage?' I asked them, but never got a satisfactory answer. 'Will I get better? How long would it take?' Again, their non-committal evasion and lack of eye contact told me all I needed to know.

Then, a day before I was due to be allowed up to start physiotherapy came nature's cruellest twist of all. It was in the sleepless watches of the early hours that it happened. A figure stopped in front of the frosted glass door separating the side ward from the corridor, silhouetted by the dim night-lights illuminating the nurses' station. Without opening the door the figure moved through the solid glass and into the room. I screwed my eyes shut and then reopened them but the figure was still there, its outline less blurred as it began, to my addled mind, to take on familiar human form. This wasn't possible. It was too dark to make out the face but the shape was unmistakeable. 'Amy!' I screamed. 'Amy!' and tried to sit up, nearly tearing the catheters from my right arm. I cried out in pain and turned to try and disentangle them so I could go to her, but when I looked back, the vision had gone. The sound of running feet in the corridor and then the door burst open. I don't remember what I said or did and all I can recall is the sharp stab of the needle in my right hip as they sedated me.

The following day a jolly little Scottish neurologist came to see me. Tufts of red hair sprouted from everywhere. His ears, nose, his shiny head, completely bald on top, and his forearms were covered in a thick mat of it. He took the best part of an hour and used a series of very long words to describe what had happened to my brain. Even in my fuddled state I could summarise it as, "major bang on the head, brain damage, might get better, might not, no idea which bits will work and which will stay off-line for good." His version explained that damage to my temporal lobes, brain stem and a bleed affecting my hippocampus, were all going to take a long time to heal. He warned me that while the brain was sorting out the rewiring process, hallucinations such as my visit from Amy were likely to occur at any time. *Peduncular Hallucinosis* he called it, but the way he spoke he might have been discussing an annoying bout of hiccups. However, to me, the vision had been horribly real and I was terrified. I ached to see Amy again, but at the same time knew that wasn't possible – I've always been the world's biggest sceptic when it comes to ghosts and the paranormal – what I'd seen was a result of my own mind playing cruel tricks on me and I wanted it to stop.

The staff at the neurological unit did their best, but my progress was frustratingly slow. I've no patience at the best of times, but this was torture of the cruellest kind. The random gaps in my recall of the past were a constant source of frustration – I could remember infants' school, but not my primary school, bits of my time at university, but next to nothing of my degree course. Oddly, my short-term memory didn't seem to have been affected.

Part of my problem was motivation. The other patients had visitors; parents, husbands, wives, children and friends to help jolly them along. I had visitors too. Lots of them at first – Amy's parents were regulars. My parents are no longer alive and I saw no point in dragging my older brother all the way back from Vancouver just to sit at my bedside. Cousins and other relatives are thin on the ground – procreation doesn't seem to be high on the Prices' list of priorities. The visits I looked forward to most were from my RAF colleagues – noisy, good-natured, flirting and bantering with the nurses. Looking back, I suppose I recognised about half the people who came to see me and had to explain to the others that the bang on the head from the car crash had randomly wiped parts of my memory – just like a faulty hard disk. No one took offence but I was conscious of one thing in all of them – knowing what to say to the recently bereaved doesn't come easily to the British, and the embarrassment of trying to find the right thing to say about Amy was a constant problem that kept down the numbers coming to my bedside.

The embarrassment and the fact that people have their own lives to live meant that the stream of visitors dwindled to a trickle over time – I've no complaints. They did their best, but none of them could take away the terrible void left by the death of Amy and Julia. With them gone my motivation to get better was close to zero. What was the point? Who was I doing this for?

Next came the coroner's inquest. Unable to walk properly I was wheeled into court, a tartan rug over my knees like some octogenarian invalid. I sat through the proceedings in a daze of disbelief, an unwilling spectator at a play that I neither understood nor wanted to see or hear. That the people being discussed were my wife and daughter was horribly surreal.

***

After a year of rehabilitation, endless tests, a daily diet of pills, plus two more operations on what was left of my brain, I was declared well enough to live independently once more. My neighbours in Lincoln kept an eye on me in a very British way, hoping I wouldn't notice their little acts of kindness and cause embarrassment by thanking them, but I did.

The hallucinations still came and went and it got to a point where they became just a fact of life to which I paid no heed. The nib of a pen would suddenly detach from the page and bend through ninety degrees while I was writing. I could still feel its pressure against the paper and the words would appear correctly, but it was disconcerting none the less. Sometimes my coffee cup would seem to float around the room. I worked on the rather eccentric premise that it was attention-seeking and that if I took no notice, it would return to the table. It always did.

Then there were the voices – nothing I could make out, more like the hubbub of a cocktail party in the next room. Just like the errant coffee cup, I found that if I ignored them long enough, normality would eventually resume and the voices would go away. Although Amy appeared to have stopped haunting my waking hours, both she and Julia haunted my dreams – always fit and well, fully recovered, saying there'd been a mistake, they weren't dead, no car crash, the coroner had got it wrong and they were coming home.

One of my unexplained visitors during waking hours was a ginger cat that made a habit of walking along the kitchen worktop only to disappear through the wall next to the microwave and out of sight. In a funny way, I looked forward to his visits as a form of company.

Levitating coffee cups and white walls that turned from purple to green and back to white again were alarming, but somehow the cat seemed less threatening.

As expected, my medical discharge came through from the RAF. Everything was handled with sympathy and efficiency – the RAF gets a lot wrong, but when it comes to this kind of thing, you see them at their best – and the disability pension after nearly thirty years' service gave me enough to live on.

However, I was bored. I needed something to do, and that's how I ended up working as a journalist, freelance at first, but then on the staff of the Lincoln Post. The pay was awful but I enjoyed the job, even when it meant covering tedious village fêtes and school sports days. Nothing much ever happens in and around Lincoln anyway, or at least that's what everybody seemed to think until the Leckonby story broke.

Chapter Two

RAF Leckonby is a disused airfield to the east of Lincoln, tucked away in a remote spot where the soft curves of the Wolds swell up from the billiard table monotony of the fens. In its heyday, it was one of the many busy bomber bases of RAF Lincolnshire, operating Wellingtons, and then, from late 1942, Lancasters. Like many of the stations built during the war, the facilities were spartan and Leckonby was earmarked for closure in the autumn of 1945.

It's not any easy place to get to and its location has saved it from the worst ravages of vandals and thieves. However, as with so many other disused airfields in Bomber County, the place is gradually fading back into the landscape. Two hangars remain and now serve as grain stores. Other buildings, including what was the Officers' Mess, are used by a farmer to store machinery and chemicals. Rows of chicken sheds take up the first hundred yards of what was once Leckonby's south-westerly runway, and the old control tower was used by local youths to smoke dope and drink away the boredom of rural adolescence on smuggled extra-strong lager bought from the eastern European farm workers. There were several raves and the police were called – many of the better-heeled residents declared it the end of civilisation. The young tend to avoid the place now. One of them, no doubt under the influence of terrestrially produced spirits, claimed to have been chased by the ghostly figure of a wartime airman, so instead they now congregate around the bus shelter by the council estate on the edge of the village.

Any relief that the blue-rinse set may have felt at the ending of night-time noise and disturbance was shattered by what became known as the Leckonby Master Plan. The Master Plan was simple. The former airfield would become a "fully sustainable eco-town" with an obligatory proportion of affordable and social housing. The future inhabitants' energy needs would be met by a new wind-farm built on the summit of the Wolds, a few miles further east.

Local opinion of the Master Plan divided along very clear lines. First came the landowners who stood to gain from selling up. They were all in favour, as were a second group, those who saw the chance of moving to a bigger house that otherwise would have been beyond their means. Last of all came a more vociferous group – NIMBYs to some, preservers of the English countryside to others – loudly opposed to the Master Plan. They set up a collective shudder at the thought of ugly, noisy wind turbines and, although they were at pains not to say so out loud, were horrified at the influx of council tenants whose presence they feared would devalue their houses and generally 'lower the tone'.

The battle lines were drawn. I lived in Lincoln, and not being directly affected, tried to consider each side's point of view, with what I hoped was professional detachment. If I'm honest, my good intentions didn't last very long. I have a thing for disused airfields, there's something intensely poignant about them, a sense of walking on hallowed ground – the same awe and sensation of being spotlighted under history's gaze that I get from walking up the nave of Lincoln Cathedral. I try to imagine what it must have been like for those thousands of young men who so desperately wanted to live, but passed each waking moment facing the ghastly odds that within weeks, if not days, the Reaper would claim them, screaming as the flames filled their cockpits and turrets, or pinned them, immobilised by the g-forces as their stricken aircraft plummeted, out of control, down through the icy night skies over Germany. Two thousand five hundred Bomber Command aircrew died in January 1944 alone and I tried to imagine the courage that drove them – many still in their teens – to volunteer. Not only Britons, but young men from the Dominions who crossed the world from the cattle stations of Australia and from the prairies and forests of Canada to face a 60% chance of death during the thirty missions that made up an operational tour.

The gut-wrenching wait to hear whether ops were on tonight and then the false jollity shared with the rest of their crew, joshing and bantering in the blue, cigarette fug of the briefing room, dreading the moment when the curtain would be drawn back to show the red ribbon stretching far across the map of Europe to show tonight's target. Code name *Whitebait*. The Big City. Berlin. All hopes of an easier op – somewhere nearer in Northern Germany or maybe a factory town in occupied France – now dashed. Fucking Berlin. Then the silent prayer – please let it not be me tonight, Lord. Please let it be some other crew falling in a ball of flames, incendiaries and target markers lighting their funeral pyre with a red and green firework display. To face this ordeal once would have been more than most people could stand – probably me among them, if I'm honest – but to face it night after night with only a scant chance of coming through a tour alive, defied imagination.

Such intense emotions – the unspoken fear of dying, the joy for the lucky few of defeating the odds, the beer-soaked oblivion they sought when not on ops – seem to penetrate the very fabric of these now forgotten airfields, and that's why when I scrunch over the broken glass and push my way through the nettles and brambles to reach an old dispersal hut, the place feels alive with the presence of that doomed generation.

I have always believed we cannot relive the past, nor should we try to inhabit the minds of the dead, so although building houses on the disused airfield at Leckonby made sense, I hope you can understand why I felt more than a hint of sacrilege at the prospect. Utterly illogical of course, but as I've explained, the atmosphere that goes with these decaying monuments affects me very strongly.

***

As strength began its slow return I found walking to be a great solace. In my head, I'd describe what I saw to Amy, sharing with her the beauty of a hawthorn in bloom or a field full of spring lambs, bounding and leaping, quivering their silly tails just for the fun of it. So it was, that a few weeks after the announcement of the Leckonby Master Plan, I decided to swap the cabin fever of a suicide-grey Sunday afternoon for a walk at the disused airfield. Parking on one of the old dispersal areas which bordered the road, I pulled on my boots and set off, following the perimeter track towards what had been the bomb dump. Cold air, spilling down from the Wolds on a damp easterly wind, was condensing out into mist, reducing the visibility to a few hundred yards.

Hands in pockets, head down and thinking about Amy, I felt cocooned by the mist which, rather than spoiling the view, merely added to the atmosphere. From the gloom in front of me, a grass-covered bank rose up – one of the earth blast walls surrounding the buildings that had once held the airfield's stock of bombs and ammunition – and with feet skidding on the wet grass, I scrambled to the top. I had only gone a few yards when I felt something wet against my hand. I spun round in surprise, only to be greeted by the happy face and wagging tail of a black Labrador.

'Snipe, dammit, leave the man alone will you.' The dog's owner loomed up out of the mist. Clad in a thick tweed suit, and with a battered brown trilby on his head he looked as though he had come straight from the shooting field. 'I'm awfully sorry about that,' he said, in clipped, no-nonsense tones. As he drew closer I could see that he was older than I had first thought – at least seventy, but ramrod straight and brisk in his movements.

'That's all right,' I said, patting the dog, who treated me to another lick. 'He just gave me a surprise that's all. Didn't hear him coming, I'm a bit deaf in one ear.'

The old man fixed me with his pale blue, almost colourless eyes. I wasn't sure whether they signalled approval or suspicion. 'Not sure we've met. Not from round here, are you?'

'No,' I replied, a little taken aback by his abrupt manner. 'I live in Lincoln – I'm a reporter for the Lincoln Post.'

'Are you indeed? Well, you can tell your editor from me that covering perfectly good land in concrete is the height of stupidity. Needs to be on the front page every day.' The way he put it sounded more like a direct order than a rhetorical complaint. 'There's backhanders and greasing of palms going on. That's what they're up to. You mark my words.'

This was interesting. The solitude of my walk had been broken and, even if the old man's story did turn out to be just the usual conspiracy theory of dodgy councillors on the take from big developers, my journalist's nose caught the whiff of a story. 'Do you have any proof?' I asked.

His lined features flushed bright red and I thought he was going to explode like an angry colonel in a Bateman cartoon. 'Proof? Dammit, man, of course I have. Letters, photographs too. I'll show you. Then you can print it in that paper of yours. That'll settle their hash.'

The sheer incongruity of the conversation made it hard for me to hide a smile. Two grown men, standing on a bank in the fog on the edge of a disused airfield, discussing the relative merits of old, broken wartime concrete versus modern concrete, was beyond surreal. 'Listen,' he said, looking over his shoulder as though anyone else would be mad enough to be out walking in this weather, let alone eavesdrop on our conversation. He fumbled in his pocket, drew out a flat silver case and opened the lid. 'Here's my card. Come for tea tomorrow – three o'clock sharp, don't be late, can't stand people who are late – and I'll show you just what they're up to.'

I examined the card – expensive, printed on good quality stiff paper, embossed letters, very old school. I read, "Lieutenant Colonel AWP Cavendish, Hobbs End Hall, Leckonby, Lincs". So he was a colonel after all. The card bore no post code, no phone number, no e-mail

– his disdain for the modern world was plain to see. I patted my pockets. 'Sorry, I don't have any cards on me. I'm Bill Price, by the way.' I offered my hand.

He shook it firmly. 'Aubrey Cavendish. How d'you do?'

'So where exactly is Hobbs End Hall?' I asked.

'Can't miss it,' he said. 'Follow the Horncastle road out of the village and it's about a mile on the right. Now don't be late, mind. Three o'clock sharp.' With that, he turned away and with the dog gambolling at his heels, disappeared into the mist.

The following day I set off from Lincoln for my appointment with Colonel Cavendish. Strictly speaking, I should never have started driving again, but I had told the doctor that the hallucinations had stopped and only ever affected me at night when I was dozy and about to fall asleep. In reality they were getting steadily worse as the little Scottish neurologist had warned me they might. I was on a course of Levetipine tablets which he explained were dopamine and D2-specific receptor agonists. Whatever they were, just as he predicted, their effectiveness was wearing off. My visits from the non-existent ginger cat and the hubbub of voices from the next room had become more frequent. On one occasion, I swerved the car to avoid a red letterbox which wandered out into the road in front of me. Luckily, there was nothing coming the other way and when I got out to investigate, the box was firmly embedded in the grass verge where it had been ever since – according to the embossed crest on the door – the reign of George VIth.

You would think I would have had the common sense, particularly given what had happened to me, to take road safety more seriously, but I'm ashamed to say that my selfish need to get around under my own steam rather than rely on public transport, overrode my consideration for my fellow road-users.

***

The mists of the previous day had given way to leaden skies from which fell a fine drizzle, the kind of soaking rain that forces its way into every corner and seems to dampen everything in its path. The streets of Leckonby village were deserted and a dark, grey day which had imperceptibly lightened around noon, had already given up the unequal struggle and agreed surrender terms with dusk well before mid-afternoon.

Just as Cavendish had said, after about a mile, an imposing pile of a house, built in red brick, loomed up out of the dripping gloom on the right hand side of the road. A large, freshly-painted sign, spotlit from below, announced Hobbs End Hall to be a retirement home. He had seemed far too sprightly to be a resident in a place like this and I tried to picture him, sitting in a circle of the demented and the dying, tunelessly bashing at a tambourine while an earnest young care assistant tried to jolly the inmates into a sing-song. I shuddered. Just like death or road accidents, ending up in places like this was something that happened to other people.

Parking outside the entrance, I hurried into the welcome shelter of the porch and pushed open the double doors, trying not to leave finger marks on the highly-polished brass handles. Clearly Hobbs End Hall was doing well financially, as it had none of the end-of-the-pier shabbiness that these places usually exude. Inside, the heat nearly bowled me over. I had forgotten how sensitive the elderly are to the cold.

A smiling blonde receptionist greeted me in an eastern European accent. I gave her my name and told her I had been invited for tea with Lieutenant Colonel Cavendish at three o'clock. At once, the smile evaporated and her face went the colour of putty. 'Cavendish? You're sure about that name, Mr Price?'

This seemed very odd. Maybe she was new or didn't understand what I'd said. 'Yes, absolutely. Aubrey Cavendish. Tall, pale blue eyes. Has a Labrador called Snipe.'

She clasped her hand to her mouth and ran out from behind the desk. I thought for a moment she was going to be sick. With tears in her eyes, she ran across the expensive carpet and, without knocking, disappeared into the manager's office. A few moments later, the door opened, and, dressed in a well-cut suit, more fitting for the City than a provincial retirement home, the manager appeared. I would have put him in his early forties, hints of grey at the temples and with a broad, open face that was clearly trying to hide the emotion he felt. He turned to the receptionist who followed a few paces behind him. 'Don't worry, Magda,' he said. 'Take the rest of the afternoon off. I'll deal with this.'

She sniffed, wiped her eyes with the back of her hand and ran to get her coat. I introduced myself to the manager. 'I'm sorry,' I said. 'It looks as though I've upset your colleague.'

'Don't worry, Mr Price, it's not your fault,' he replied.

The penny dropped and I clasped my hand to my forehead. 'Oh God, I'm awfully sorry. I take it the Colonel has passed away?'

'It's a little more complicated than that,' he said, ushering me into his office and offering me a seat. Without speaking he took a key from his desk drawer and opened a wooden cabinet that stood against the wall. From it he took out what looked like an old photo album. Flicking through the pages, he opened it and passed it to me, his finger resting on a photograph about eight inches by six. 'Is that the gentleman who invited you for tea?'

Although it was in black and white, there was no doubt as to the identity of the subject. Tall, late sixties or early seventies, upright, tweed suit and with a dark trilby slightly pulled down over his right eye. Next to him, sat a black Labrador looking adoringly up at its master. Underneath, in a precise copperplate hand, was written, *Aubrey with Snipe.* 'Yes, that's him, absolutely no doubt…' but then my voice trailed away as I re-read it and saw the date – *Aubrey with Snipe, October 1938.* 'But that's not possible. It must be his son or his grandson that I met.'

The manager shook his head. 'Don't worry, Mr Price, you're not the first person this has happened to. We thought it had stopped, but the row about the new town on the airfield seems to have, how shall I put this? …disturbed things again. Magda has seen him too. You gave her a bit of a fright I'm afraid.'

For a moment I was speechless. Here was a grown man telling me I'd just had a conversation with a man who would by now be about a hundred and fifty years old. I knew a leg-pull when I saw one. 'Hold on a minute,' I said, tapping the photo with my finger. 'Are you suggesting this is the same man who invited me here yesterday? And he was seventy-odd in 1938?

Somebody's having a laugh.'

The manager spread his hands out as if to say he didn't know what was going on. 'I can't explain it either, Mr Price, but I can tell you what I've managed to find out. There have been Cavendishes at Hobbs End Hall since the middle ages. Then the land was requisitioned in 1941 to build the airfield...'

I interrupted. 'That would explain what he said about covering perfectly good land in concrete.'

'Yes', he said. 'From some of the letters I've seen, Aubrey Cavendish was livid about it. He certainly didn't live long afterwards.'

'Interesting. What else do you know about him?'

'I haven't found much. He was a colonel in the Lincolns during the First World War. When he left the army he went back to running the farm and died in 1942. His widow moved to a smaller house on the estate. That's all we know. There were no children. By 1942, the airfield was completed and Hobbs End Hall became a military hospital. It reverted to the family after the war but they had to sell it in 1946 to pay death duties. It was a school for a while – that went bust in the nineties – and then it became a retirement home which it remains to this day. The photo album and other family papers were found in the loft when we refurbished the place.'

This was all very odd. 'So no son, no grandson, then who the hell did I meet yesterday?' I asked. 'A ghost?'

The manager's expression remained non-committal. 'That seems to be what a lot of people who've met him believe,' he said with a shrug.

'And what about those of us who don't believe in ghosts?'

'I presume they come up with other explanations.'

23

'From that I take it you fall into the camp of the believers?' I asked, hoping to get some sort of reaction from him.

'Like you, Mr Price, I was a sceptic. But, also like you, I've met Colonel Cavendish, and now… now, well, let's say my scepticism isn't quite as solid as it was.'

I made no reply and carried on leafing through the photographs. Whatever the truth of my meeting yesterday, the album was a fascinating glimpse into a bygone era, a last look at a world where upstairs was divided from downstairs by the green baize door. As I turned the pages, a bookmark fell out and I leant forward from my chair to pick it up. It was a calling card, exactly the same as the one Cavendish had given me on the airfield the day before. With trembling fingers I slid it back between the pages and closed the book. The citadel of my logic was in danger of crumbling.

By the time I left Hobbs End Hall it was almost dark. Instead of heading straight home, I turned right in the village and made for the spot where I had parked the previous day. Cramming my waterproof waxed-cotton hat onto my head – Amy hated that hat and said it made me look like a child-molester – I turned up my coat collar against the slanting drizzle and retraced my route towards the dark whaleback of the blast wall which stood out on the horizon against the fading twilight. Scrambling to the top, I gazed across the airfield towards the outline of the ruined control tower which stuck up like a black, decayed molar.

By now, rain was trickling down the back of my collar and I decided to turn back. Then, something caught my eye. At first I thought it was a car's headlights, but squinting into the twilight I realised that couldn't be possible. The light seemed to be coming from the base of the control tower, faint at first and then flickering as though someone was using a torch to find their way around. There had been plenty of reports of unexplained lights on the airfield before. To me they were perfectly easy to explain. Kids usually, scaring themselves silly by getting into places they weren't supposed to – I'd done as much myself at their age – and as I squinted into the mist and rain, permitted myself an indulgent smile at the memory.

The light seemed to be climbing now, following the wall of the tower as it rose. That made sense because the concrete steps leading to what had been the visual control room at the top, ran up the outside of the building. Now it was inside, and the skeletal remains of the controllers' greenhouse were silhouetted like the ribs of some long-extinct creature. I was about to turn away when I heard a muffled pop, borne on the south-westerly wind, and a red Very flare arced into the night sky, tracing a livid parabola, bouncing twice on the remains of the concrete taxiway before going out. I stared, open-mouthed, not able to believe what I had seen. I knew from studying the history of bomber operations that this was the signal to the waiting crews that operations were cancelled for the night. A green flare was the instruction to start engines.

Then the light in the tower snapped off and I stood rubbing my eyes in disbelief. It had to be one of my hallucinations, but normally I get a bit of warning – headache, flickering in my left eye with a slight loss of peripheral vision, that sort of thing. I reached into my coat pocket and levered the lid off the pill bottle, swallowing one of the blue and white capsules, just as the doctor had instructed. For a moment, I stood watching the tower, waiting for the light to reappear, but all was black once more, leaving me with only the sighing of the wind and the gentle pattering of the rain for company.

If someone was trying to frighten me they had picked on the wrong man. Stumbling over the tussocky grass in the dark, I made my way back to the car and fetched my own torch from the glove box. The batteries were past their best and gave a weak, yellow beam but it was enough to keep me from falling down the potholes which pocked the old taxiway that ran past the control tower.

Crunching over a carpet of rubble and broken glass I went through what had once been a doorway into the shell of the building. Inside, the smell of damp, mould and urine was foul, and, as I shone my torch around the interior, I noticed without surprise that the walls were covered with the usual graffiti and the floor strewn with cans, broken bottles, and the twisted remnants of old metal window frames.

I snapped off the torch, listening for any sound that might betray the presence of whoever had fired the flare, but all was silent and black as the tomb. Then, an uncomfortable feeling of being watched came over me. I gave an involuntary shiver and immediately cursed myself for being feeble. Not like me to get the wind up in the dark. Even so, I quickly turned the torch back on, thankful for its comforting glow, and made my way round to the concrete steps leading up the outside of the building. The treads were worn and in some places had crumbled away so I hesitated before going up. If I fell and hurt myself, it might be days or even weeks before anyone found me. Worse still, I was on my own, and a nagging inner voice kept asking what if someone was lying in wait for me up there – not ghosts born of someone's over-fertile imagination, but real-life flesh and blood with no desire to have their silly games revealed for what they were?

Common sense too told me not to go up. So did the cold feeling in the pit of my stomach – fear was a better name for it. So, being the stubborn cuss I am, the need to prove to myself that I wasn't really frightened drove me up the wet, slippery steps.

Level with the first floor of the control tower, a black oblong marked a doorway. I shone the torch. Inside were only the remains of the concrete floor joists. Continuing up to what had been the controllers' eyrie, I stopped on a broad terrace which ran round the top floor. The presence of the metal balustrade which was still in place took away some of my fear of falling. Although I spent most of my professional life as a pilot, I've never had much of a head for heights.

Then I heard it. My blood froze. A tapping sound, footsteps on the concrete. Two voices, one male, one female, indistinct, but close at hand. The wind picked up again and the voices disappeared, leaving the steady tap, tap, tap that had set my nerves jangling. I fumbled with the torch and it dropped to the concrete at my feet, its beam extinguished. Frantic now, I fell to my knees and scrabbled in the wet. The cap had come off allowing one of the batteries to drop out. Tap, tap, tap. Louder now, it seemed to be getting closer. Come on, it has to be here, it has to be, but the second battery still eluded me. I made to stand up but stumbled and half fell, putting my hand down in a filthy puddle that soaked me to halfway up my forearm. Crawling, incoherent with fear, away towards the greasy, three storey drop that were the steps I'd so recently climbed, my knee bumped against something. It rolled away and I grabbed it. The battery. Thank Christ for that. With fumbling hands, I pushed it back into the barrel of the torch and jammed the lens cap back on. It cross-threaded. Tap, tap, tap: louder still. Come on, work, damn you. This time, the welcome yellow beam sprang back to life and I swung it around me, desperate to see in which direction the danger lay. A gust of wind. Tap, tap, tap. Coming from behind me. In a sweat of fear, I spun round and pointed the torch in the direction of the sound.

The beam revealed a scene of decay and devastation similar to the ground floor – rubble, broken glass and graffiti. Worryingly, there was no sign of the owners of the voices, just the intermittent tap, tap, tap. Trying to take the initiative, I called out. 'Come on out. Stop mucking about. Who are you?' I had meant to sound confident, masterful, the man in charge. Instead, my voice was reedy, the piping sound of my younger self whistling in the dark. Clambering over a pile of broken concrete on legs rubbery with fright, I focused the light into what had been the corner of the visual control room. Hanging from one rusted hinge was a metal window frame, boarded up long ago with plywood and flapping about in the wind, banging against the brickwork with each gust. Tap, tap, tap. Thank God for that, I thought.

My relief was short-lived. There were the voices again. A man and a woman, laughing, but no longer close to. Moving as fast as I could over the piles of bricks and twisted metal, I found my way back out onto the balcony and shone the torch into the rain-swept gloom below. Whoever it was must have got past me and down the steps while I was looking for the battery. Then I saw them – two indistinct forms, laughing and running across the grass towards what had been RAF Leckonby's operations block. They stopped and looked back at me. I could just make out two pale, upturned faces before they vanished through the black rectangle of a doorway and into the building itself. Whoever it was had led me a merry dance and I cursed myself for falling into their trap so easily.

I turned to retrace my steps and it was then that I saw it, glinting in the torchlight, lying on the ground near the top of the stairs. I must have walked right over it without noticing. Bending to pick it up I knew at once what it was – a cartridge case. From my limited knowledge of these things, it looked too big to be from a shotgun. It had a brass base and seemed to be made out of reinforced cardboard rather than plastic. If it was indeed from a Very flare pistol, it would prove that what I had seen was real and not, as I had feared, one of my hallucinations. I put it in my coat pocket and, keeping as close to the wall as I could, heart thumping, slithered and scrabbled back down the steps.

Still fizzing with adrenalin and angry at having been taken for an idiot I decided to have one last look for my tormentors. A concrete path, cracked and overgrown with weeds, led from the base of the control tower across to the operations block, straight to the doorway through which they had vanished. The entrance was protected from the elements by a small concrete porch from which hung the lopsided carcass of an enamel lampshade. I shone my torch into the recess. What had once been a doorway was now bricked up with breeze

29

blocks, completely impassable. Once more I doubted myself but my hand in my coat pocket closed around the solid, tangible evidence that was the Very flare cartridge. Someone was clearly going to a lot of trouble to frighten me. I hated to admit it, but for a while they had succeeded.

By now I was wet through. My trousers were soaked from crawling around looking for the torch and my sleeve clung to my arm, clammy and cold from its immersion in the puddle. As I walked to the perimeter track to head back to the car, the wet grass wrapped itself insistently around my legs, soaking me still further, so when I finally reached it my mood was foul. Starting the engine and putting the heater on full, I turned into the lane, heading back towards the village to pick up the Lincoln road – the other direction is a dead-end, leading to the halt at Leckonby Junction. The station has been closed since the Beeching cuts of the 1960s. However, it seemed that my misfiring brain hadn't finished with me for the evening, because as I rounded a corner I came face-to-face with a single-decker coach of the kind I had only seen at vintage car rallies. Bracing against the inevitable impact, I stamped on the brakes and swerved up onto the verge, the looming bodywork flashing inches past my right ear. As my car slithered to a halt, I seemed to get a glimpse of blackout masks on the coach's headlights and a white stencilled serial number on the side of the bonnet.

Hyperventilating with shock I turned to look back down the lane in the direction of the station, but there was nothing but blackness between the tall hedgerows. The coach had vanished. My hands shook as I grasped the wheel. What I had seen on the airfield was real. This simply couldn't be. Perhaps it was time to come clean to my GP about how much worse the hallucinations had got even if it did mean losing my licence.

Chapter Three

About a week or so later I was at my desk, writing a story for the Lincoln Post about a charity rowing event on the River Witham. At first, I put the headache down to tiredness and the eyestrain that comes with spending too long staring at a PC screen. Then the symptoms became more familiar and I realised that I could no longer read what I had written. A temporal lobe seizure the doctors call it – for me it heralded the onset of one of my hallucinations. I gripped the side of the desk, hoping no one would notice what a state I was in.

The letters started dancing and changing places at will. As ever I offered up the same silent prayer to the void, a mute scream of anguish. Please no, not again, but the symptoms were nauseatingly familiar. From something that happened every six weeks or so, this was the third attack in almost as many days. Pain nagged at my temples and the screen slid in and out of focus. With fingers that felt fatter than marrows I tried to type once more, but my hands fell silent on the keyboard as the words in front of me dissolved into a meaningless blur. I was aware of the letters so I suppose they formed some kind of image on my retina, but it penetrated no further into my consciousness. With these fingers borrowed from a clumsy giant, I fumbled to lever the top off the pill bottle, washing down two capsules with a gulp of water. I closed my eyes and waited, counting slowly to myself. Ninety-nine, one hundred... I opened one eye. The frame of my PC screen shimmered, turned purple and multiplied itself around the walls of my office cubicle like electronic wallpaper. It wasn't real, it would pass, it always did and I once more screwed my eyes tight shut, cursing, but the dancing oblongs were still there. A deep breath, the sound of my own blood thudding in my head and a rising wave of panic. Try to control your breathing, the doctor had said, hyperventilating will only make it worse – something about carbon dioxide levels. Bugger carbon dioxide, just make it go away. I put my head in my hands and waited. An hour? Minutes? A lifetime? Time itself seemed to bend and stretch as I waited for normality to return, hating this thing that had taken over my life and the accident that had taken away my family.

Tentatively, I opened one eye. The patterns returned to grey and now sat as shimmering outlines round the screen, slowly fading one by one. I opened the other eye. Almost back to normal now and the pain in my head yielded its place to a dull ache like the last dregs of a whisky hangover. Through a grey mist of nausea I tried once more to concentrate on the article. Young farmers pulling a tractor along a high street for charity, that was it. No, hang on, that was before lunch. I read what I had written as though seeing it for the first time.

The peripheral vision doesn't work very well in my left eye, so I didn't notice his arrival until he was almost in front of me. I looked up from the screen. My editor's features had all gathered in the middle of his pudgy face, clustering around his boozer's nose. From experience I knew this wasn't a good sign.

'Are you all right, Bill? Give me a break and please don't die at your desk, I couldn't face the bloody paperwork.' I'd heard it a million times before and tried to smile at the gallows humour, but even smiling hurt. He continued. 'Got something right up your street, my lad. Your old mob have been causing trouble again.'

I looked away and briefly closed my eyes. On reopening them, to my disappointment, Derek Bennett, editor of the Lincoln Post was still there, features puckered into what always reminded me of a pug's arse.

'Which old mob, Derek?' I asked.

'The RAF, Wing Commander, old boy,' he replied, attempting to mimic my southern accent and twirling an imaginary moustache.

I tried to smile. 'I was a Squadron Leader. It's very kind of you to promote me, but I think it's a bit late. Anyway, what've they done?'

Bennett consulted his notepad. 'The Battle of Britain Memorial Flight Lancaster nearly took out an Anglia Airways flight coming in to Humberside Airport yesterday afternoon. Couple of passengers hurt by falling luggage and a stewardess with a broken collar bone.'

My head cleared a little. Bennett had his facts wrong. 'A Lancaster? That's not possible. The BBMF don't fly during winter.'

He shrugged. 'That's what the RAF are saying too, but the airline reckon they're telling porkies. Both pilots got a very close look at it. Too bloody close by the sound of it.'

I shook my head. 'Still doesn't make sense. Everybody knows the Lanc spends the winter in bits while they get it ready for the display season.'

Bennett shrugged. 'Well someone's either telling fibs or they've got something to hide. Whatever it is, I'm sure there's good copy to be had.'

'Where do you want me to start?' I asked.

He handed over a printed sheet. 'You all right to

34

drive these days?'

'Fine now, thanks,' I lied, taking the piece of paper and pretending to read the words which stubbornly refused to stay in focus. 'The doc's got me on a new line of happy pills.'

'Good. Get down to RAF Coningsby and check the BBMF's version of events. See if the Lancaster looks like it's being serviced or whether they just started taking it apart this morning.' I stood up to leave but the editor called me back. 'Have a word with the Anglia Airways people too. They've got times, positions, heights and so on. Even got the Lancaster's serial number. They seem pretty sure of their facts.'

Bennett waddled off, leaving me in peace. Gradually, my head began to clear and the printed words became readable once more. The crew of the Anglia Airlines turboprop had certainly got a good look at the aircraft that had nearly hit theirs. Their report described it as an Avro Lancaster bomber with squadron letters CD-O on the side of the fuselage and serial HK807 stencilled in smaller writing near the tail. Out of curiosity I looked on the web and found that CD were the battle letters of 362 Squadron, based at RAF Leckonby, and that HK807, O-Orange had been lost on operations in March 1944.

I made a few calls and managed to track down the airline crew. We arranged to meet at Humberside airport the following afternoon. I also put in a call to my old friend, Squadron Leader Harry Riggs, commanding officer of the Battle of Britain Memorial Flight at RAF Coningsby.

***

'There's your suspect.' Harry Riggs turned to me and smiled. With two of its four engines removed and the front turret mounted on a stand in the corner of the hangar, it was clear that the BBMF's Lancaster was in the midst of its usual winter overhaul. On its black flanks it carried the battle letters AJ-G, the markings of the aircraft used by 617 Squadron's most famous commander, Guy Gibson, on the Dams Raid in May 1943.

'Looks like a pretty good alibi to me,' I said, breathing in the familiar atmosphere of the BBMF hangar. It was as though I'd never been away, but until now I had avoided all invitations to go back to Coningsby since the accident. My motives for staying away were a jumble of reason and irrationality, ranging from a wish to remember the happy times and a fear that going back would turn the knife in the wound by showing me just how much I had lost.

Riggs is one of those canny Yorkshiremen who doesn't say much but never misses a thing. He stood beside me, reading my thoughts no doubt, keeping quiet for fear of intruding on the cascade of emotions that flowed through my mind. Seeing the dear old Lanc again was like being reunited with a long-lost friend. Even stripped down for servicing, surrounded by scaffolding and access ladders, and perched on a series of trestles and tree-trunk sized screw jacks, it had lost none of its elegance.

Riggs folded his arms across the front of his flying suit and gazed at the Lancaster like a proud father. 'Nothing's changed since you were here, Bill. The display season still runs from April to October and we use the winter period for servicing. She had new props and magnetos last year and this time we're working on the hydraulics. Some of the actuators are getting a bit long in the tooth so we're changing them.' Riggs ducked under the barrier delimiting the public viewing area and indicated to me to follow. An RAF corporal was working on the starboard rudder and nodded his assent to Riggs' request to show the visitor around. We climbed the short aluminium ladder to the door in the rear fuselage, ducking into the narrow space which was lit by a row of lights clipped to the fuselage frames. At once, my nostrils filled with the unmistakable smell of old aircraft – a cocktail of aviation fuel, oil, hydraulic fluid, old electrical wiring and leather. For an instant I felt happy once more – something that rarely happens these days – but then came reality's bucket of cold slops. This wasn't part of my life any more. I was nothing more than a ghost, haunting the byways of my past. It was the same feeling I got whenever I visited the suburb of London where I grew up – a place of familiar names, but where the old bricks have been replaced by new concrete and the once familiar streets now throng with hurrying strangers.

Savouring the atmosphere, I followed him into the belly of the whale, climbing onto the walkway above the bomb bay, then sliding over the wing spar covers into the forward crew compartment. We squeezed past the navigator's station into the cockpit. 'Go on, take a seat,' Riggs said with a smile. 'I think you know the way.'

For a moment I was speechless. Although the view through the Perspex was of the inside of a hangar rather than the green fields of Lincolnshire, I felt a surge of joy, an emotion I had thought completely lost to me.

'Thank you, Harry. You've no idea what it means to be back,' was all I could manage without choking up.

'I thought you might like it. Sit there as long as you like,' Riggs said.

'Careful, I'll be here till the display season starts,' I replied, swinging myself down from the seat and following him back down the narrow green tunnel to the door. I paused in the hatchway, looking aft towards the rear gun turret. 'That must've been a horribly lonely place to die,' I said.

Riggs shook his head in admiration. 'God only knows how those blokes did it, night after night, getting shot up, seeing aircraft going down in flames all around them, but still going back for more.'

We made our way back across the hangar to Riggs' office and he closed the door. His face was serious now. 'So what's going on?' he asked.

'What do you mean?'

'Come on, Bill, don't give me that. You of all people must be in the know. This is something to do with the new town at Leckonby, isn't it?'

'I think it must be. Someone's going to a lot of effort to scare people off buying houses there. They've even had a go at putting the frighteners on me.'

Riggs leaned forward, I could see I had caught his imagination. 'Go on, what did they do?'

'Well, you know that people say the place is haunted?'

He gave a derisive snort. 'Yes, lights, strange apparitions, things going bump in the night. Load of old cock if you ask me.'

'Couldn't have put it better myself. But if they, whoever *they* are, can convince enough people the place

38

is haunted, no one will want to live there.' I told him about the meeting with Colonel Aubrey Cavendish and my visit to Hobbs End Hall.

'And this Cavendish, he shook your hand, you say? Doesn't sound like a ghost to me.'

'Nor me,' I replied. 'At the time I didn't know what to think. You see, it's a bit embarrassing really, but since the accident, I've been having hallucinations and I thought at first Cavendish was one of them. But he was solid flesh and blood. So was his dog, it even licked my hand.'

'And the manager at the old folks' home with his conveniently long-lost photo album?' Riggs asked, eyebrows raised.

I shrugged. 'Could be all part of the game. I'm guessing he probably lives nearby and doesn't want a bloody great housing estate on his doorstep any more than the other locals do.' Then I remembered and reached into my coat pocket. 'You know what I said about the Very flare? Well I found this.' I laid the cartridge case on the desk between us.

Riggs examined it for a moment. 'I don't know anything about these, but I know a man who does.' He picked up the telephone and dialled. Moments later there was a knock on the door and a Flight Sergeant, clad in blue overalls, came into the office. 'This is Flight Sergeant Harris,' Riggs said. 'Better known as "Bomber". One of our armourers, if he doesn't recognise it, nobody will. Here you go, Bomber.'

Harris picked up the cartridge, closed his eyes and smiled, mimicking the tones of a fortune-teller. 'I'm seeing red. Am I right, sir?' he asked me, opening his eyes once more.

'Yes, how did you know?' I asked.

He handed it back to me. 'Feel the metal base. It's milled all the way round. That means it's a red flare. No milling means green. Half-milled is white and quarter-milled is yellow. The tops were different too. All so you'd know which flare was which in the dark – the system started during the First World War.'

'Can you tell me anything else about it? Like where the people who fired it might've got it from.'

He examined the cartridge carefully. 'You say this was fired recently, sir?'

'Yes, last week. Why?'

He smiled, 'Talk about past its sell-by date. It's a wonder it didn't misfire. This is a museum piece.'

'How old is it?' I asked.

He pointed to a series of numbers and letters stamped in black on the side. 'This shows it was made in October 1943, the code here is for the manufacturer – Schermuly in this case – and finally, we can see it came from their factory in Surrey – Newdigate to be precise. Where they found an antique like this is anybody's guess – it's illegal to buy flare cartridges without a permit so it's not something you'd pick up at a boot sale.'

After the Flight Sergeant had left I told Riggs about the voices I'd heard from the Leckonby air traffic control tower and the people running towards the ops block. I skipped over the inconvenient vanishing trick they seemed to have pulled by passing through a solid wall. I also kept quiet about the old bus that had forced me off the road. For now, I would mark those up as among my more vivid hallucinations.

'I think you're right, Bill,' Riggs said. Someone's

going to a lot of time and effort over this. Still seems a strange tack to take though. You know, ghosts and all that. Especially in this day and age.'

'So how do you explain what the airline crew saw?' I asked him. 'Getting hold of vintage flare cartridges is difficult, but not impossible. But a Lancaster? The only airworthy one in Europe is sitting out there being serviced.'

Riggs paused, deep in thought. 'No other explanation,' he said at last. 'They're in on it too.'

'Who are?' I asked.

'The Anglia Airways crew. Stand the aircraft on its ear, frighten the passengers, then log an *Airprox* report against an aircraft that couldn't possibly be there.'

The penny dropped. 'Of course. I must be getting slow in my old age. If it couldn't possibly be there, then it must be a ghost.'

'Precisely,' Riggs replied. 'And in the markings of a Leckonby-based aircraft. What a coincidence.'

'But why? *Cui bono*?'

His face creased into a rare smile. 'No idea. That's for you to find out, old lad. You're the ace news-hound. Questions like that are out of my pay grade.'

***

The following day I drove to Humberside airport. I got there a few minutes early so I drove past the signs to the terminal car park before turning left off the main road towards Kirmington village. Just before the church, I stopped the car and got out to look at the memorial to the aircrew of 166 Squadron, killed on operations while flying from what was then RAF Kirmington. In a small, neatly-tended square of grass and trees stood the simple stone plinth with its metal plaque, and behind it, a single blade from a Lancaster propeller. As I often do when standing in silent contemplation in front of one of these monuments, I wondered what the men they commemorate would make of the modern world. I hoped they wouldn't think their sacrifice had been in vain.

The Anglia Airways crew were waiting for me in the airline's offices. The captain, a bull of a man with a shock of dark curls overshadowing a square-chinned face, towered over his younger first officer who to me looked barely out of his teens. I introduced myself and handed each of them a business card. Neither man made eye contact and I sensed a strong atmosphere of tension in the room as we each took a seat.

My feelings were confirmed when the captain spoke. A vein stood out on his forehead and his voice was almost a shout. 'They reckon we're making it up,' he said.

'Who do?' I asked.

'The Civil Aviation Authority. Air traffic. The Anglia Airways management, that's who,' he replied. His first officer flinched

'And you're sure it was a Lancaster?'

'Course I'm sure. And before you tell me, yes, I know the only airworthy Lancaster on this side of the Atlantic is sitting in a hangar at RAF Coningsby being serviced. But we both saw it, didn't we?' he said, turning to glare at the first officer, who nodded his assent, eager to please.

'Anything on the radar trace?' I asked.

'Just us, that's what's so bloody annoying.' He

handed me a copy of the radar print-out. 'Here, keep this one if you like.' I spread it out on the desk and he jabbed a beefy finger at the line indicating the track of his aircraft. 'This is where we began our descent to two thousand feet for an RNAV approach to runway 02. And here,' down came the finger again, 'just before we levelled off is when we came out of cloud and saw the Lancaster. It was at the same height as us, crossing right-left and bloody close.'

'And I understand you had to take pretty severe avoiding action,' I said, remembering what I had read in the CAA report.

'Ninety degrees of bank and four g.' It was the first time the first officer had spoken. 'One of the cabin crew fell and broke her collarbone, and all the overhead lockers came open so lots of passengers got hit by luggage.'

I wrote this down. 'What's the g-limit of the aircraft?'

'Two point five,' he replied.

'You were lucky not to pull the wings off. Did you get another look at it after that?' I asked him, but before he could reply, the captain butted in again.

'Bloody right we did. I wanted to make sure I got a good look at the idiot's registration before we lost him in the murk again. The visibility wasn't great.'

I looked down at my notes. 'Battle letters CD-O and HK807 by the tail. You're both agreed on that?'

They nodded. I then took a half-million scale topographical aviation chart from my bag and together we transcribed the track of the airliner onto it, together with the assumed trajectory of the Lancaster.

Then, trying to make the question seem as innocent

43

as possible I asked each of them where they lived. The first officer, like me, lived in Lincoln, but it was the captain's answer that seemed to confirm my suspicions. His address at Lingate Heath was no more than a mile from the village of Leckonby. 'So what do you think about the new town and the wind farm?' I asked him.

'It'll mean a lot of construction traffic for a year or so. But if the appeal against the planning permission fails, I suppose we'll have to live with it.'

The captain's answer took me by surprise. I had been expecting a full-scale rant. I tried another tack. 'You do realise the markings of your Lancaster make it a Leckonby-based aircraft?'

'Yes, I looked it up. Funny coincidence that,' he replied, still without any trace of emotion.

I had a last try. 'They say the airfield's haunted. You don't think the appearance of the Lancaster could have a supernatural origin?'

He gave a derisive snort. I half expected him to paw the ground and charge at me. 'Supernatural? Nothing supernatural about what we saw. It was solid all right and so were the crew inside the cockpit. We got one hell of a bump when we went through its slipstream too. And before you ask, no, it couldn't have been a model. We nearly hit a full-size Lancaster, no mistake. Sorry if that spoils a good story, Mr Price.'

***

During the drive back to Lincoln I tried to make sense of what I'd heard. At first, the answer had seemed obvious. Take one large, aggressive captain whose house was about to be blighted by a new housing development and unsightly wind turbines. Add a biddable, timid young co-pilot, willing to back a claim that they had nearly hit an aircraft that couldn't possibly be real. Then throw in an overenthusiastic attempt to avoid the "collision" during which they'd overstressed the aircraft, injured one of their cabin crew and battered their passengers with a shower of falling luggage. It was the most plausible answer and certainly would have explained the tension I had sensed between the two men. The trouble was, I couldn't shake off the feeling that they were telling the truth. Yet at the same time, my mind kept going back to the more logical explanation that this was all part of the attempt to sell a wholly fictitious ghost story to a credulous public.

Chapter Four

The airline captain's fears were realised. The latest appeals against the planning process by the "Leckonby Action Group", or "*The Lags*", as they liked to call themselves, had failed, and work began on the airfield.

Demolition and building always seem to attract those with an eye for a quick turn and for making off with other people's property. A group of traveller caravans now huddled on a section of concrete near the old shooting butts, giving "*The Lags*" something else to worry about.

The small museum on the airfield was broken into and a World War Two parachute stolen. Other buildings were ransacked for copper piping and several houses in Leckonby village lost the expensive wooden gates to their drives. Inevitably, the travellers got the blame and the curtains of Leckonby twitched frantically every time one of their number was spotted in the village.

As for me, my story in the Lincoln Post about the phantom Lancaster had its fifteen minutes of fame – it even made national TV – and attracted the usual cast of conspiracy theorists, UFO-spotters and the deranged, until, like its subject, it faded from view.

On several nights, lights were seen on the airfield and worried "*Lags*" called the police. After the third late-night call-out, the police lost interest and persuaded the building company to put up security cameras. Blurry images of people moving about in the dark were recorded, logged and duly ignored. The travellers denied all responsibility, but nobody in Leckonby believed them.

Then came an event that even an old sceptic like me couldn't explain. Opposite the entrance to the RAF Leckonby site stands a memorial to the airfield's bomber crews who lost their lives during the war. On a base of Portland limestone, the bronze figure of an airman in flying gear stands looking towards the eastern horizon, with one hand raised to shield his eyes from the rising sun.

The report I got from the police went something like this – at about four in the morning, the owner of one of the houses on the edge of the village was woken by the sound of a man screaming. 'Like a soul in torment,' he described it.

After a second 999 call, the police finally arrived in the village to find one of the gypsies, lying in the gutter in the foetal position, incoherent and babbling, tears streaming down his face and his clothes soaked by the rain. Over and again he repeated the same words. 'It's the statue. It's the statue.' The police patrol called an ambulance to take care of him, and when it arrived, drove on towards the airfield. Lying in the middle of the road opposite the memorial, the figure of a man was lit up by their headlights. His neck lay twisted at a grotesque angle and the dull sheen of his sightless eyes showed that he had been dead some time. In the road next to him was a powerful disc cutter, itself badly battered.

By the time I arrived at Leckonby later that morning, there was little sign of the previous night's drama, and the overnight rain had been replaced by a watery November sun. As far as the police were concerned, it was a simple case of two men trying to steal what to them was merely a valuable lump of bronze. A line of new, bare metal on the airman's leg showed where they had started cutting. The dead man had obviously slipped from the wet plinth and broken his neck in the fall. The stolen ladder they had used to get up to the statue lay in the wet grass by the roadside.

I confess that at first I found it hard to feel too sorry for him. Then I realised that somewhere, probably in one of the caravans huddled on the cracked concrete on the other side of the airfield, a family was now mourning, and I rebuked myself for being so callous.

The young policeman guarding the crime scene shared none of my concerns. I introduced myself and showed him my press card. He looked around to make sure no one was listening. 'Don't for Christ's sake quote me on this, mate, but I reckon that's one-nil to Darwin,' he said, giving me a surreptitious thumbs-up. 'They've taken his mate off to the funny farm. S'pose that's two less pikeys to make a nuisance of themselves.'

I pressed him for more details. He laughed. 'This is hilarious, you'll love it.' He lowered his voice. 'The pikey the night shift boys found in the village had completely gone off his nut. Pissed himself with fright, the silly bugger. He reckons he was holding the ladder while his oppo started cutting into the leg of the statue and then, guess what?'

'He fell off?' I ventured.

'Nah. Better than that. He reckons the statue knocked the cutter out of his mate's hands, then leant down, swiped him one and broke his neck. Then, get this, it jumps down from the plinth thingy and chases him down the road. The statue, I mean. Couldn't make it up, could you?'

'It doesn't sound very plausible, I must admit.' He

seemed a little disappointed at my reply, obviously expecting me to find the tale as hilarious as he did. However, after the Lancaster incident, I'd had my fill of weird stories for one week. I took out my camera. 'Do you mind if I take a couple of pictures?' I nodded towards the ladder. 'I'd like to get a close-up of the damage.'

He treated me to a broad wink. 'More than my job's worth, mate. Look, I'm going to nip round the corner for a crafty smoke – not supposed to light up in uniform, you see – and I'll be gone at least five minutes. So if you want to use the ladder, that's up to you. Mind the statue doesn't give you a bash though.' Laughing, at his own joke, he sauntered off, shaking a cigarette out of its packet and cupping the match flame with his hands.

Propping the ladder against the plinth I scrambled up, trying not to look down. Even climbing the six feet or so to the base of the statue I could feel my hands becoming slippery with sweat. I managed to take all the pictures I needed and was about to climb down when something made me glance up. What I saw made me blink in disbelief but I had to get a closer look. By holding on to part of the statue's parachute harness, I pulled myself up so that I was standing right next to the bronze figure, which was slightly larger than life-size. The ground seemed a horribly long way down and I fought a rising tide of nausea. I looked again at what had caught my attention. There was no mistake. I reached up to the gloved hand that the airman held up to shield his eyes. Between the first two fingers was wedged a broken piece of hard, red plastic. At the second attempt I managed to work it loose and shove it into my pocket. Another look down and I felt my head start to swim – if

I wasn't careful, the police would have a second corpse to deal with – but I managed to get first one foot and then the other onto the safety of the rungs.

Once more back on solid ground, and having laid the ladder down in the same spot from where I had taken it, I examined my find. It was about four inches long and bore a series of letters picked out in embossed white capitals. This simply was not possible. I gave an involuntary shudder at the only possible explanation of what I had just found, and shoved it back into my coat pocket.

The young policeman returned, refreshed by his nicotine hit. 'Get all your pictures?' he asked.

'Yes, thanks. Really appreciate your help,' I replied, trying to sound matter-of-fact.

'Don't mention it, and if there's anything else I can do, just say the word.'

I hesitated. I wasn't even sure I wanted to hear his answer. 'There is one thing. I know this is going to sound like a silly question, but do you know what make of angle grinder the dead man was using?'

'Yeah, course I do. It was a Hilti. Top of the range gear that – my brother's in the building trade. He swears by their stuff – German, you see. The pikeys nicked a whole bunch of power tools from a delivery van in Brigg last week. That'll be where they got it.'

'Thanks,' I said, hoping my voice wouldn't betray the fear that had seized me.

Once back at the car, with trembling hands I took out the piece of plastic. The white letters spelled out "ILTI", with the jagged edge cutting the first "I" in half. The missing letter was obviously an "H". This simply could not be. The man who had been cutting the statue's leg would probably have been standing on the ladder while he worked, yet the fragment of disc cutter was wedged about seven feet above the cut. But how had it got there? There was only one explanation, but my mind could not, would not, allow me to face it. Statues do not hit people. But then again, Lancaster bombers that crashed in 1944 do not suddenly fill the windscreens of airliners in the winter skies over twenty-first century Lincolnshire. I had to know more.

**

"*The Lags*" had created their own website, which, on its home page, showed computer-generated images of the new town, and the forest of pylons that would carry the electricity generated by the giant turbines on the days when the wind blew. The site carried details of the next meeting, to be held in two days' time at the Rose and Crown in Leckonby. I rang the 'contact us' number, told them I was a journalist and asked if I could attend. The enthusiasm with which they said "yes" smacked of desperation, a hunch that proved to be correct.

There were about a dozen of them. Not the blazered old buffers I had expected, but instead, a normal enough looking group of people, some of whom were quite young. The mood I detected was one of baffled disappointment, rather than of foam-flecked outrage. The meeting was due to start at 7:30 but they all waited, looking expectantly at the pub door, hoping more of the faithful would show up. The chairman, Martin Watson, a man in his late sixties, whose grey hair and tall stooping frame gave him the mournful air of a heron that has just missed the last fish, explained. 'We normally get a better turn out than this, but there's the England match on telly tonight.'

'That's the only reason why I'm here,' said a round-faced woman standing next to him. 'Can't get a word out of my old man when the football's on.' The laughter seemed to ease the tension a little and we followed Watson into the function room at the back of the pub. It had been set out for at least fifty people, and our little group, which barely filled the first row, looked pathetically small. As the chairman stood up to speak, the door opened and a slim young man wearing a heavy tweed overcoat hurried in. He apologised for being late and asked if the seat next to mine was free. A little inner demon nearly tempted me to say no, and that the third seat from the left in the back row was the only one not taken, but I resisted. He was out of breath as though he had been running, and he brushed away a fringe of dark hair that flopped over his pale features. I noticed that his shoes and the bottom of his trousers were soaking wet.

In a careworn monotone, Watson began his address. He covered the progress of the latest appeal against the planning application. The news for *The Lags* wasn't good. Head down and reading from his notes, he spoke without interruption for about twenty minutes. To me it was a new language – called-in planning applications, the Town and Country Planning (General Development Procedure) Order 2009 were only the start. By the time he got to the possible advantages of Section 79(1) of the Town and Country Planning Act 1990, my eyes had glazed over. From what I could work out, *The Lags'* appeal against the development had been rejected and they were now all that was left of the opposition to the plan. The local farmers were delighted at the price the developers had offered. The really lucky ones were those set to receive huge rents from having wind turbines on their land. Looking to local government for help was a non-starter too. The Labour-controlled local Council were already counting the votes of the new 'social housing' tenants. As for the rest of the inhabitants of Leckonby, their silence had been bought by the prospect of the new retail park, which would save a long drive into Lincoln for their weekly shopping. Finally, he looked up. 'Anyone got any questions or good ideas?'

'Newts,' somebody suggested. 'Or rare butterflies. They managed to get the Newbury bypass moved because of butterflies, I think.'

Watson shook his head and fished in his briefcase for a document. 'Newbury was snails. The planners have got wise to that one,' he said, holding up a thick document bound in expensive-looking glossy paper. 'This is the "Leckonby eco-Town Environmental Impact Survey". Nothing rarer than foxes and mice, I'm afraid. And no unexploded bombs, heavy metals or toxic waste either.'

'When are they going to get rid of the gyppos?' asked the lady who ran the airfield museum. 'They tried to break in again on Monday.'

Another shake of the grey head. 'Apparently the police can't move them on because of the one who died trying to pinch the statue.' He made the inverted commas sign with his fingers. 'Because of the "trauma suffered by the traveller community," as they put it, it would be a breach of their human rights to force them to leave.'

A ripple of angry muttering ran through the little

gathering. 'What about our rights not to have our stuff pinched?' asked one.

'And when are they going to stop them doing their number twos in our gardens?' added another.

'I don't think you'll be having any further trouble with them.' The voice came from the young man sitting next to me. 'They've gone.'

'What? The gyppos?' At once the meeting came alive.

'Yes, the police are there now and I saw the last caravan leave. That's why I was late.'

'I wonder what made the police change their mind,' said Watson.

'Oh, it wasn't the police,' replied the young man. 'They left of their own accord.'

'That's wonderful news,' said the round-faced football widow. 'But why now? Did the police say?'

'Oh, yes,' he replied. 'Someone shot up one of the caravans and set fire to it. Luckily – or unluckily, depending on your point of view – no one was inside, but it certainly put the fear of God into them. The police seem to think it's something to do with a feud between gypsy gangs.'

'Well, at least they can't blame *The Lags* this time,' said Watson, casting a sideways glance at me. My article in the Lincoln Post about the Lancaster and the airliner had mentioned the Leckonby Action Group, but not in the favourable light he had evidently been hoping for.

I said, 'Unless one of your other members nipped out and did it at half time during the England match.'

The joke fell flat. Watson pulled a heron sucking a lemon face and looked away. 'We'll still get the blame,' he said to nobody in particular.

At this, everyone began talking at once. I could just make out Watson's voice over the general hubbub. 'Well, if those wretched gypsies have gone, that at least calls for a drink.' We followed him back into the bar.

Some of *The Lags* went straight home, leaving about six of us clustered round a corner table. I was torn between getting to the bottom of their involvement in the incidents at the airfield versus the more tempting prospect of hurrying off to see what had happened to the gypsy caravan.

The Rose and Crown had been popular with RAF Leckonby crews during the war. Its walls were adorned with a jumble of photos showing Wellingtons, Lancasters and the faces of their crews, some smiling because the scythe only took the other fellow, others who knew better, smiling to hide their fear. How many managed to dodge the Reaper? I wondered.

Inevitably, the discussion turned to the attempt by the gypsies to steal the statue of the airman for its scrap value. From there it was only a short conversational hop to wondering aloud what it must have been like for the flesh and blood young airmen who faced death on a nightly basis. Watson looked up at the grainy photograph on the wall next to him – seven young men in front of a Lancaster bomber. 'I wonder what happened to that crew, probably all dead by now.'

'They died in March 1944, actually.' This was the young man's first contribution to the conversation and he spoke with a rather stilted voice as though reading someone else's words aloud. 'That's Wing Commander Preston's crew – "Press-on Preston" they used to call him – he was CO of 362 Squadron. They were shot down by a night fighter near Cologne. No survivors. If Preston had only got the chop earlier, a lot more crews might've finished their thirty ops.'

'You seem very knowledgeable,' said the lady who ran the airfield museum. I detected a note of pique in her voice that somebody else knew more about her pet topic than she did.

'Oh, it's purely personal,' he replied. If this was meant to be a joke, his pale features showed no trace of a smile. 'Anyway, must dash. Do please excuse me. Big show on tonight. Wouldn't do to be late.' He rose to his feet and made to leave. Then he stopped, fixing me with a gaze that made me feel strangely uneasy. 'This is for you,' he said, pressing what felt like a small metal cylinder into my hand.

Without another word he went to the door and disappeared into the night. For me, there was something that didn't ring true about him. The stilted diction, the consciously old-fashioned haircut and clothes all spoke of an elaborately contrived performance. Maybe that was it. After all, he had just mentioned "a show" so perhaps he was an actor.

I turned to Watson. 'Interesting chap. One of your more active members?' I asked, puzzled by what could have attracted such an eccentric to the company of *The Lags*.

'No, never seen him before in my life,' he replied. 'Thought he was with you – theatre critic, arts correspondent or something. Seemed an odd chap to bring along to a meeting like this, but I didn't want to say anything, given that you're kindly doing an article on us.'

I ignored the hint. 'Believe me, the Lincoln Post

doesn't have an arts correspondent, or an anything correspondent, come to that. It's me, the editor, a couple of freelancers and the rest we buy in from the press agencies. I thought he was one of your members.'

'Certainly knows his stuff about 362 Squadron,' said one of the others, provoking another scowl from the custodian of the museum.

Keeping my hand under the table I sneaked a look at what he had given me. I recognised it at once – a rifle cartridge. He had obviously picked it up at the gypsy camp, and his over-dramatised way of handing it over fitted neatly with my assessment of him as an actor manqué. I showed it to the group before putting it back in my pocket.

After thanking Watson and *The Lags* for letting me attend their meeting, I made to leave. 'You will show us as rational, sensible people, won't you?' he asked, almost pleading. 'I hope you now realise we're not behind any of the nonsense that's supposedly been going on at the airfield.'

I didn't know what to say. As a hack reporter on a paper with a circulation in free-fall from an already low base, I wasn't used to being anyone's last hope. However, the look on his sad heron's face told me that's just what I was. I said, 'Listen, I don't usually do this, but I'll e-mail you the article before it goes to press. If there are any mistakes in it, you tell me and I promise I'll correct them.'

'Thank you, Mr Price,' he said and shook my hand.

The rain had stopped in what felt like the first time in months, and as I walked to my car, a keen north-westerly chased scudding clouds across the face of a thin crescent moon. The encounter in the pub had left me feeling ill at ease and I had the unpleasant feeling of being watched by many pairs of eyes. Despite telling myself not to be ridiculous, I couldn't help hurrying across the car park to the sanctuary of my waiting car.

Safely inside, I switched on the interior light and put on my reading glasses to get a closer look at the cartridge case. From its size, it looked like a NATO 7.62mm round – during my time in the RAF I must have fired thousands of them on the 25-metre range. I was about to put it back in my pocket when I remembered the Very cartridge and the letters stamped into the base; maybe this one had similar markings. Holding it up to the light I peered at it more closely. For once, my memory held. Instead of having a groove round the base of the cartridge, the one in my hand had a protruding flange. It was an old .303 cartridge, and I hadn't seen one of those since I was in the cadet corps at school. Hurriedly, I copied the inscription on its base into my notebook.

As I drove up the lane towards the airfield I puzzled over the odd statements of the uninvited visitor to the meeting. What had he meant about his interest in a long-dead CO of 362 Squadron being "purely personal"? The hammy nonsense about "a big show" I could just about fathom. But then why had he given me the cartridge? Why not hand it to the police? However, what bothered me most was the fact that his face seemed familiar. I had long since learned not to trust my ragged memory, but the strong feeling that I knew him from somewhere refused to go away.

The clouds had covered the timid face of the moon and, with the few street lights of Leckonby behind me, the lane from the village was pitch black. Turning into the Louth road I saw on the horizon a vivid pool of light. As I drew closer, I saw it was populated with scurrying, pale figures whose shadows seemed to be dancing a crazy gavotte on the old airfield – under dazzling floodlights, white-suited forensic specialists floated like ghosts across a cracked concrete dance floor. Other policemen paid out rolls of blue and white tape to cordon off the area around the still smouldering carcass of what had once been a caravan. I pulled into a lay-by and parked behind a fire engine. Its blue flashing lights added to the show and I began to wonder if I was having one of my hallucinations.

As I approached the tape one of the police came to shoo me away, but I had already spotted a friendly face. I showed my press pass and asked to speak to Inspector Grimes. With bad grace, the policeman went to fetch him.

Grimes, bear-like and shambling, wandered over. 'Hello, Bill,' he said, shaking my hand which disappeared into his vast paw. 'News travels fast. Who put you onto this one then?'

'A bloke down the pub,' I replied.

He threw his head back and laughed, then lifted up the tape for me to duck underneath. 'Ask a silly question. Anyway, come and have a look. It's all bloody odd.'

'So what did they do?' I thought it best to play the innocent.

'Only put about a hundred or so rounds of .303 through that caravan. According to the Scene of Crime boys, some were incendiary bullets.' He jerked a thumb at where two firemen were still playing a hose on the charred remains. 'Lucky there was no one inside.'

'And you reckon it was other gypsies?'

'Can't think of anyone else, can you?' Grimes said. 'Unless it was the old codgers from the Leckonby Action Group.'

I told him about *The Lags* meeting in the pub, omitting the episode of the eccentric stranger. I said, 'I can just about imagine them trying to frighten people off with ghost stories and shining torches on the airfield at night. But loosing off hundreds of rounds of rifle ammunition? Not a chance.'

I tried to catch his eye, but sheepishly, he looked away as he replied. 'Not rifles, Bill. Whoever did this used automatic weapons. At least two, possibly more.'

'And where would a bunch of gypsies get hold of hardware like that?' I asked. 'Shotguns or maybe pistols. But machine guns? You're pulling my leg.'

He steered me by the arm out of earshot of his colleagues. 'Look, Bill, I need to have a word with you in private. We've known each other a long time and I've given you some good stories.'

Here it comes, I thought. As Grimes continued, my suspicions that he was after a favour were confirmed. 'Bill, there's been some bloody funny stuff going on here for quite some time. You don't know the half of it.'

'Try me,' I said.

'The gyppo we found dead in the street last week.'

'The one who fell off the statue, you mean?'

'Yeah, him. Well, we've had the pathologist's report. Cause of death was a broken neck.'

'And?'

'And the injury wasn't consistent with a fall. And it wasn't consistent with the disc cutter kicking either. It's got an anti-kick clutch which was in perfect working order.'

'So his mate was right and the statue did it after all? Don't tell me. You've taken him in for questioning but he isn't talking.' Trying to hide my fears about the incident and a conclusion my mind would not accept, I forced a laugh at my own joke. From the wounded look on Grimes' big, amiable face, bleached white under the arc lights, I wished I hadn't.

'Please don't, Bill. I've had all that and worse from my Superintendent. He's got the chairman of the local council and that fucking idiot of a Police Commissioner all over him. If the Leckonby development gets held up, someone's head's going to roll. At the moment, it looks like mine.'

'So how can I help?' I asked.

'Write your story. I know I can't stop you, but please, don't go into details about the weapons. And particularly not the ammunition.' Grimes looked at me imploringly.

I thought for a moment. 'How about a drug-related revenge attack with shotguns and petrol bombs? Police treating it as attempted murder.'

'Perfect. Bill, you're a star. Give me a call tomorrow and I'll clue you in on what we've got.'

'Not so fast,' I said. 'What really happened here tonight? Somebody must've seen or heard something, or you boys would still be sipping tea back at the station.'

'One of the pikeys – sorry, one of the "traveller community" – called us.' The inverted commas in his tone were almost visible.

'Christ, that must be a first.'

'Quite. Said he heard a noise like somebody tearing

cloth, only much louder. Lasted about a second or so, he reckons. Then a bloody great bang when the cooking gas bottles went off.'

No wonder Grimes wanted this kept quiet. One hundred rounds in one second. I did a bit of quick mental arithmetic. 'And what do your Scene of Crime boys reckon can fire 6,000 or so .303 rounds per minute?'

'They don't know, Bill, but come and have a look at this.' He led me back towards the police van where two white-suited figures were kneeling, intently studying something on the ground in front of them. As we got closer I saw what they were looking at; two small mounds, five feet or so apart, shining brightly under the floodlights. 'Brass cartridge cases,' he said. 'Two weapons.'

I thought for a moment. 'That's still 3,000 rounds per minute. You'd need something multi-barrelled to get that rate of fire. Or maybe…' my voice trailed away to a whisper. 'Four Brownings…' I heard myself say. No, that was preposterous. Impossible. The feeling of being watched came over me again.

'Maybe what?' he asked.

'Nothing, just thinking aloud. Ignore me.' Quickly changing the subject, I asked, 'So apart from the gypsy hearing a noise, did anyone see anything?'

Grimes looked shifty again. Good job you're a copper, I thought. You'd make a lousy criminal. 'Not at the time,' he said at last.

I pressed him further. 'Meaning what, precisely?'

'One of my lads saw something just after we got here. But that doesn't make sense either.'

'Go on,' I said.

'Listen, Bill,' he steered me away by the arm once

more. 'This is between you and me, right? If you so much as breathe a word of this, I'll kill you.'

'I promise. Scout's Honour.'

'All right. Well, one of my lads was over by the hedge, securing the site, when he saw this bloke poking around in the pile of cartridge cases. Now, he's a good copper. Level-headed as they come. Not one for making up stories. Anyway, the bloke stands up, starts walking towards him and, according to my young PC, as he gets closer he sees he's dressed in old-fashioned flying kit. You know, sheepskin jacket, parachute harness, the works. Course, he thought the bloke was having a laugh, but when he went to speak to him, he just vanished into thin air.'

I felt a chill run down my spine. Half afraid to ask, I stammered out the question anyway. 'Did he get a look at his face?'

I could see at once that Grimes realised why I had asked. 'Christ, don't say you've seen him too? I'm surrounded by fruitcakes tonight.' He called the constable over. 'Right, my lad. Your vanishing airman. Our resident newshound here wants to know if you got a look at his face.'

I saw the PC give an involuntary shudder. 'Yes I did, sir. Youngish – early twenties at a guess. Really pale face, skin almost white. Very dark hair –'

I interrupted him. 'Parted on the right with a long floppy fringe.'

'You see, sir,' he said, turning to Grimes. 'Told you I wasn't making it up. This gentleman saw him too.'

Grimes tutted in disbelief. 'Bill, please tell me you're having a laugh.'

I shook my head. 'Sorry, no. I only wish I was.'

He dismissed the young PC to his duties and then rounded on me. Grimes the friendly bear was replaced by Grimes the angry copper. 'Listen, Bill,' he said. 'If you're withholding information relevant to this case, I can and will nick you.' Half a head taller than me, he put his hands on his hips and glared. 'You can start by telling me who put you on to this.'

'I told you. A bloke down the pub.'

'And does he have a name, this bloke of yours?'

'Probably, but he didn't introduce himself.'

Another glare. 'What did he look like?'

'Like your PC just told you,' I replied. 'Early twenties, very pale, dark hair parted on the right with a floppy fringe.'

'Bill, so help me, I will nick you if you don't stop wasting my time – '

'Here, take this,' I said, interrupting him. I tore the page from my notebook with the details of the cartridge case and passed it to him. 'Give it to your SOC boys. They'll know what it is. Then if you still think I'm wasting Police time, give me a call tomorrow and I'll come down to the station and turn myself in.'

As I drove home, I couldn't stop looking in the rear-view mirror. I've no idea what I expected to see, but I couldn't shake off the feeling of being watched, even at 60 mph on a straight, well-lit road. My jitters subsided once I had got home and turned the lights on. Later, I managed to find distraction by filing my story for the following day's edition of the Lincoln Post. I kept it deliberately low key and had it tucked away in the bottom left-hand corner of an inner page.

By ten thirty I was in bed, but the events of the evening came crowding back, turning somersaults in my mind and chasing sleep away. The young man at *The Lags* meeting had been real flesh and blood, and the cartridge case, now sitting on the kitchen worktop, was solid enough too. Yet something told me beyond doubt that he was the spectral airman seen by the young Constable at Leckonby. Every logical ounce of my mind fought against admitting the existence of such things, but just like the episode with the gypsy and the statue, the only explanation happened to be an impossible one.

Sleep would not come. Turning on the light, I rolled out of bed and put on my dressing gown. I shuffled over to my desk, started the PC, clicked on the icon for the satellite mapping software and zoomed in on the airfield at Leckonby, centring on the hardstanding where the gypsy caravans had been. Then I went to the airfield museum's website and looked at the 1943 plan of the airfield that I had already bookmarked. There could be no further doubt. The gypsies had unknowingly parked their vans on the site of the old shooting butts where the bombers' guns were test-fired and harmonised.

Next, I found a photo of a Lancaster rear turret – quite why I bothered, I don't know, it wasn't as if I hadn't seen the BBMF aircraft hundreds of times. It confirmed what I already knew. The two chutes for spent cartridges, one either side of the turret, were about five feet apart. That explained the two piles of spent cases that the SOC teams were so interested in. None of this was possible, yet it had happened. I shut down the PC, but still could not sleep. Insidiously, like a gas seeping under the door, the fear was back. Its tendrils closed around me.

I shut my eyes and tried counting sheep, but even against my closed lids, geometric patterns began to appear, like a time-lapse film of ice crystals forming, white against a background of shimmering blue. Cursing, I swung my feet to the floor and put on the bedside light. My pills were in the bathroom and I caught an unwelcome glimpse of my jowly, grey features in the mirror over the sink as I washed down the two blue and white capsules. I padded into the kitchen to make myself a cup of tea – tea always helps me sleep – and as I filled the kettle from the tap, I caught a movement to my right. It was the ginger cat and I knew that I was in for at least ten minutes of hallucinations before the medication took effect. As usual, the animal sauntered along the worktop, oblivious to my presence, and continued towards the wall. However, this time it did something different. It stopped, turned to look at me and then, with one of its front paws, playfully swiped the cartridge case onto the floor. Seeming satisfied with its night's work, and with a flick of its tail, it continued its promenade past the microwave and disappeared through the wall.

Hallucinations have become such a part of my life that at first I thought nothing of the incident. It was only a few moments later that the enormity of what I had just witnessed sent cold fingers down my spine. Apart from the odd occasion when the hallucination is plausible for a few seconds, I am always able to tell the difference between what is real and what isn't. So how could a non-existent cat with a penchant for walking through walls, conjured into being by a misfiring tangle of my own synapses, possibly interact with solid matter? After an evening of trying to reason away the impossible, this was the final straw. Sleep was even further away so I resorted to sleeping pills. I hate the wretched things.

They always leave me feeling hung-over and useless the next day.

Once more I shut my eyes, willing the geometric patterns to stop their dance across my retinas. They did nothing of the sort, and the sleeping pills left me feeling dry-mouthed but still no nearer the oblivion I craved. Then I heard it. At first I thought it was the wind blowing fallen leaves around on the terrace. But no, it was in the house and getting closer to my bed. I swore aloud and, screwing my eyes tighter shut, shouted at the hallucination to leave me alone.

'It's all right, it's only me.' I recognised the voice. Amy.

'No, leave me alone. Don't bloody do this to me,' I screamed, curling into a ball of misery. This was cruelty beyond measure, and the torturer was my own mind.

Then, the rustling noise again and something brushing against my cheek. I opened my eyes and wished I hadn't. In the dark of the bedroom I could make out the blacker outline of something solid – a human form leaning over me. I tried to shout for help but no sound came. My hand flailed for the bedside lamp, but all I did was knock it onto the floor together with my water glass and the book I had been reading. With the duvet wrapping itself around my legs, trying to hold me back as though in league with this nightmare, I half fell, half crawled out of bed, groping in terror for the elusive lamp.

'Bill, don't worry, I won't hurt you. Come to me, Bill, come to me.' The form was definitely Amy's, and getting closer. At last, my trembling fingers closed round the stem of the lamp and light flooded the room. Yet she was still there. Solid, living flesh, her shadow stark against the white of the bedroom wall. Delicate fingers closed over mine. I looked into her face. Sadness in those familiar brown eyes, and then the faint trace of a smile as she held one finger to her lips to silence my attempt to speak. Taking her hand, I pressed it to my mouth and kissed it. Warm skin and that scent of her I had missed so long. I shut my eyes and made to pull her to me, but my arms closed on thin air. I opened my eyes. Nothing. Silence. Amy had gone. The pills had done their work and the hallucination was over.

With tears streaming down my face, I sat clasping my knees and rocking slowly backwards and forwards, sobbing in paroxysms of despair. I could hear a voice calling her name, neither knowing nor caring that it was mine.

How long I stayed like that I do not know, for a grey winter dawn found me on the floor, shivering in a tangle of duvet, light flex and the scattered detritus from my bedside table. I wanted to see her again, had to see her again. If this was madness, then so be it. I considered giving up my medication – but did I really have the courage? On the other hand, was this shadow land with its dancing demons really so much worse than the tedium of reality?

Chapter Five

Tired and gritty-eyed, I dragged myself into work. The images of the night world were burned into my mind, and even by daylight, in the land of the living, they haunted my imagination. Trying to distract myself from thinking about Amy, I picked up a copy of the morning's Lincoln Post and found my article.

Attempted Murder at Leckonby, ran the headline.

Police are treating a shooting and firebomb attack on a traveller encampment yesterday evening as attempted murder.

An unoccupied caravan was left a smouldering wreck on the edge of the disused airfield, soon to be the site of Lincolnshire's first eco-town. The emergency services were called to the scene but no injuries have been reported. According to police sources, their investigation is focussing on a possible drug-related feud between rival traveller gangs.

I hoped it was vague and low-key enough to keep Grimes happy. I understood my readers well enough to know that travellers shooting at each other over drug-dealing rights should dog-whistle just the right prejudices to stop any awkward questions being asked.

Later, acting on nothing better than a hunch, I phoned the landlord and went back to the Rose and Crown. When I got there I was afraid of what I might find, but none the less, I explained in more detail the story I was writing on the airfield, the new town and the tragic history of the men of 362 Squadron. He lent me a screwdriver and in a few moments I had unscrewed the framed photograph from the wall. Its absence left a vivid white rectangle. 'Don't worry,' I told him. 'I'll have it back to you tomorrow.' Turning it over, I saw to my satisfaction that the backing card was held in place by cheap metal clips – no need to cut it out of its mount.

Back in the office I took several scans of the photo at the highest possible resolution. I then spent nearly an hour poring over it with a magnifying glass, trying to find more clues about when and where it had been taken. In the background, I could just about make out a group of single-storey buildings which had probably been demolished years ago. On the back, I could just make out a list of names. L-R: Jones, McIntyre, Bailey, Skipper (I took this to mean Preston, who, according to the odd young man at *The Lags* meeting, was captain of the crew) Armstrong, Foster, self. Clearly, the photo had once been the property of the man on the extreme right. If the crew had indeed all perished in March 1944, the casualty records should put a name to the man who noted himself as "self".

I had just finished putting the photo back into its frame when my phone rang. It was Inspector Grimes. 'Liked your story in the paper,' he said. 'Nicely judged. Looks like I owe you an apology.'

This was a first. 'Really? Why's that?'

'That reference you gave me, how did you get it?' I reminded him about the eccentric young man in the pub and the cartridge case. 'And do you know what "RG 44 B7 VII" means?' he asked.

'Haven't a clue.' I replied.

'My Scene of Crime boys have. It means your cartridge was made at the Royal Ordnance Factory, Radway Green in Cheshire. It was loaded as an incendiary round – that's what the B7 bit means, apparently. But guess when it was made?'

'From RG 44, I'd say 1944.'

'Spot on,' said Grimes. 'Now guess what fired them.'

'No idea,' I lied. I had a very good idea but, just like the episode with the statue, the most logical answer was also the most impossibly absurd.

Grimes continued. 'From the firing pin marks on the cartridges and from the rounds they've recovered, forensics are sure that four automatic weapons were involved – '

'Brownings,' I said.

For the moment there was silence on the line before Grimes replied. 'How the hell did you know?' he asked.

'If I told you, they'd lock me up.'

'Try me.'

'You're not going to like this,' I said. 'But the place is coming back to life.'

'Don't talk in riddles, Bill, I haven't got all day.' Grimes the angry copper was back.

'Listen. It's very simple. Ever since my accident I've been having hallucinations. I'm perfectly sane and I know the difference between what's real and what isn't. But these aren't hallucinations, they're real. Something, someone, has woken up the past. RAF Leckonby is haunted. Somebody was test firing the guns mounted in the rear turret of a Lancaster. The gypsies' vans were parked in front of the old shooting butts.'

Another silence, longer this time. 'Bill, I'm not in the mood for leg-pulls. Pack it in.'

'I'm not pulling your leg. I didn't believe it either, but I do now. It all makes sense…' I started to explain what had happened but Grimes cut me off short.

'Bill, for Christ's sake, go and see a doctor.' He hung up.

That night, thoughts of Amy filled my head. Half dreading, half longing for another visit from her, sleep eluded me. So I resorted to the hated pills. Slipping through the gap between consciousness and oblivion, other uninvited guests stole into my mind. Some in battledress, others in bulky one-piece flying suits, they stood around the bed looking at me. One of them spoke.

'Was it for this?' he asked.

'For what?' I heard my disembodied voice reply.

'What you've done,' said another. They were all talking at once now, some speaking directly to me while others chatted animatedly among themselves. I strained to hear what they were saying but could only pick up the odd word.

A small, thickset man looked directly at me, I could see his battledress tunic was darker than the others' yet I couldn't make out his features. 'He doesn't get it. None of the bastards do.' The accent was broad Australian. 'None of you bloody understand that we didn't have a choice. We missed out. It wasn't worth it. I wish I'd never fucking bothered.'

An appalling feeling of dread came over me and I was aware of trying to wake up, anything to stop this nightmare. The pills had worked too well and my drugged mind had no control over my body, chemically coshed into a state of paralysis. 'Bothered doing what?' asked my borrowed voice once more.

'Fighting. Getting my stupid bloody self and all my crew killed just so you bastards could fuck things up. It was all supposed to be for something. I should've stayed home and got laid.'

'He's right you know.' Again, I could see the speaker, but his face refused to come into focus.

The Aussie voice continued. 'To think I came all this way to fight for you bloody drongos. And then what do you do once we've done our bit? Turn the country into a paradise for bludgers, spivs and boongs, that's what. Well, thanks for coming, Blue. Sorry you won't be going home, mate, but we've sent a telegram to your old mum to let her know you copped it in a good cause. Christ, what a prize mug I was.'

A muttered chorus of approval went up from the group of airmen. 'They're all as bad as Attlee now,' said one.

'So what was wrong with Attlee?' came the reply from the back of the group. An argument broke out and the figures swum in and out of focus as they all shouted at once. Their anger became a tangible force which turned itself on me, seeming to crush me under its weight. A roaring, hissing sound like a waterfall filled my ears and I couldn't breathe. I tried to call for help, but even my own voice remained beyond my mind's control. No sound came. I knew I was dying, drowning on dry land.

Somehow, lungs bursting, I clawed my way back up to the surface of consciousness. Agonisingly slowly, the nightmare faded until the last spectral outlines of my tormentors flickered and slowly vanished. I turned on the bedside lamp and lay, gasping lungfuls of delicious air, shivering and sweating with terror.

I rolled over and looked at the clock: one AM. This couldn't go on. The thought of facing monsters from the depths of my own mind every night was unbearable. My hand closed round the bottle of sleeping pills; it was still almost full. Washed down with a bottle of Scotch they would put a painless end to this torment. And after all, who would care, who would mourn my passing? Not self-pity, just reality. No. I put the bottle back down. There had to be another way.

After two nights of broken sleep I was in no state to go to work. I phoned in sick and then began the ritual battle to get an appointment with my GP. The receptionist was condescending and indifferent, but I finally managed to negotiate myself an appointment for 1030 that morning.

Eleven o'clock came and went and I began reading the same three year-old copy of *Country Life* for the fourth time. Finally, I was ushered in to the overheated consulting room of my GP, and at the sight of his tired, grey features my anger at being kept waiting drained away. He looked almost as bad as I felt. I recounted my experiences of the last two nights in detail and confessed that I felt my sanity was slipping away.

The GP gave what in another life may have started as a smile. 'No, you're not going mad, and given the cranial trauma you've suffered, I'm afraid it's likely to recur.' Cranial trauma, I noted. Never brain damage. Never, 'Well, the inside of your head's been scrambled, so what do you expect?' No, just cranial trauma. So that's all right then, I thought. To his credit, my GP knows his stuff, even if his bedside manner is non-existent, and he spent twenty minutes explaining that what I had suffered during the last two nights even had a name. Something he called 'Hypnagogic incubus hallucinations,' explained my visit from the embittered airmen. The roaring noise, together with the feeling of drowning was down to something he called 'Sleep

Paralysis', also a common feature of hypnagogia and triggered by a malfunction in a part of my brain called the amygdaloid complex. It even explained the sensation that I had held Amy's hand, he said. I took some comfort from the fact that I wasn't the only poor sod who had to put up with such things and left the surgery feeling very glad I had resisted the temptation to finish myself off with the sleeping pills.

As if to reflect my improved mood, the sun came out and the late November air lost its chill. I took out my mobile phone and called Inspector Grimes.

'Sorry for being a pain in the arse earlier,' I said when he answered.

'I've got used to it by now, Bill. What's up?'

'Nothing really. Just to say that I took your advice and went to the doc.'

'So what did he say?' His voice betrayed genuine concern.

'Says there's a lot of it about. Hypnagogic hallucinations, apparently.'

'Do-what hallucinations?'

'Hypnagogic. You don't even need a bash on the head to get them. Never know, you might be next,' I added. 'But I just rang to say sorry for all this haunting nonsense.'

'Don't worry about it, Bill. Glad you're feeling better.'

We spoke for another five minutes about nothing in particular before I hung up and made my way towards Lincoln High Street to buy a book. For the first time in I don't know how long, I felt almost at peace with the world. The winter sun felt warm on my back; my fears that I was going mad or worse still, had become the subject of paranormal activity I didn't even believe in, had faded; and I had ended the simmering row with Grimes. It had just turned noon and I felt hungry – even my long-departed appetite was back. I paused in front of the bookshop window, lost in thought and enjoying the normality. It was not to last.

My reverie was broken by a man's voice calling. 'Hey, Tommy, thought I'd find you here. What're you waiting for? They've been open five minutes.'

I took no notice, my attention already diverted by a series of green squares which were forming at the top of the bookshop window and then sliding down to form puddles on what I knew to be a dry pavement. If ever I needed a reminder of what was reality and what was a momentary reprieve, this was it. I screwed my eyes tight shut, willing the hallucination to go away and felt in my pocket for the pill bottle. Much closer this time, I heard the man's voice again. 'What's the matter, Tommy? Seen a ghost?' I heard him laugh and a hand clapped down on my shoulder. I opened my eyes and spun round. The Lincoln High Street I knew had gone. In its place was something more like a film set: people in drab, old-fashioned clothing; the younger men in uniform, the older ones in long overcoats and hats, many were smoking pipes. The women, like threadbare beetles, scuttled past clutching wicker shopping baskets. A scruffy Austin Ten in RAF blue wheezed by over the cobbles of a street I had only known as pavement. I made to speak, but stopped dead, my mouth hanging open. The bookshop and the jewellers next to it had gone. In their place was the façade of an old coaching inn. A sign over the entrance bore the name, 'Saracen's Head Hotel.'

I turned once more to face the owner of the voice but froze in disbelief on catching sight of his reflection in the hotel's window. Dressed in World War Two RAF battledress, a tall, slightly stooping blond figure, barely out of his teens, with a pilot's brevet over the left breast pocket and a Flying Officer's stripe on each epaulette, was chatting amiably to a slightly older, more solidly built Sergeant. I noticed the Sergeant's tunic sported the single-winged air gunner's brevet. As I stared in amazement at this bizarre cameo, I realised that I recognised the air gunner. It was me, but many years younger.

I'm not given to falling asleep standing up so this was clearly no dream. Half fascinated, half terrified, I followed the tall figure in front of me as he pushed open the doors to the hotel entrance. What little remained of my confidence to tell reality from hallucination ebbed by the second. This was obviously not happening, but never before had my misfiring brain succeeded in transforming everything around me, even down to the clothes I stood up in. The last time I had worn scratchy woollen battledress like this was in the cadet force at school. I felt the long-forgotten chafing of a hard, detachable collar, its brass stud pressing uncomfortably against my windpipe.

The hotel's interior was even shabbier than the street outside. The long, narrow entrance hall had once been lit by a vaulted skylight at second storey level, but it was now covered over with blackout material, faded grey by the sun, dusty and festooned with spiders' webs. Miss Havisham would have felt at home. On a table, its brass pot unpolished since peacetime, stood a lonely aspidistra, wilting and sickly from a diet of neglect and artificial light. Opposite the aspidistra was the reception desk and as we walked past her lair the receptionist treated me to a look that would have curdled milk. My companion obviously saw, or more likely, felt the waves of disapproval aimed at us for he came to an abrupt halt as if on the parade ground at Cranwell. 'Hat, Tommy, for Christ's sake take your hat off. We're indoors, you clot.'

'Oh, yes, sorry,' I mumbled, and removed the 'chip-bag' fore-and-aft forage cap I hadn't even noticed I was wearing. I'd owned a 'chip-bag' myself, but this one was cheap and badly made, the lining stained with a tidemark of what I took for hair oil. I looked a bit closer and saw the owner's details inked onto a grimy cotton label that had once been white: *Handley W A, 923041*.

To the right, a nicotine-stained illuminated arrow, its bulb flickering and buzzing like a dying firefly, pointed down to the saloon bar. The passage of countless feet had worn the carpet shiny. What had once been proud red Wilton was now the colour of beaten earth. At the top of the steps, a fug of tobacco smoke and beer fumes met us. To protect the carpet, the nose of each tread had been reinforced with canvas which had then been thickly painted with white emulsion – the last time I had seen anything like it was at a seaside boarding house in the sixties, as a small child on holiday with my parents. Although it was only a few minutes after midday, the small, airless space was packed with bodies, all in uniform, some wearing the darker blue of Australia, most of the men standing around in groups of seven – the standard component for a heavy bomber crew.

With a dozen *s'cuse me*s and *pardons*, we managed to make our way to a corner of the bar.

A voice called out to us. 'Bloody bad show, Skipper. Seven minutes late on target.' We were obviously among friends for five expectant faces grinned at us.

'It's that man again!' said my pilot companion, pointing at me. The others doubled up at what was clearly a hilarious joke, but which was entirely lost on me.

'Can I do you now, sir?' said one of them in a high falsetto, sending the others into fits of laughter once more.

While watching them dry their eyes and recover their breath, understanding slowly dawned. From somewhere in the still functioning part of my mind I remembered where the catch phrase came from: ITMA – *It's That Man Again*, and the star of the long-defunct radio show was called Tommy Handley. If the owner of the chip-bag hat shared the same surname, and clearly the hat seemed to be mine, then it explained why they were calling me Tommy. At least one part of this bizarre hallucination made sense.

'So where did you find him?' asked a small, weasel-faced Flight Sergeant who wore the purple and white striped medal ribbon of the DFM below his bomb aimer's brevet.

'Oh, not far off target,' replied the skipper, who had just lit a cigarette, shouting to make himself heard above the din of voices. 'Standing out in the street catching flies. Didn't even see me coming.'

'Well, he'd better see Jerry coming,' said the bomb aimer. 'Or we're all for the chop.'

'Chop, chop, chop,' chanted the others in unison, miming imaginary hatchets at me. I knew well enough what 'getting the chop' meant to a bomber crew, and the little pantomime caused an outbreak of laughter and good-natured barracking from the other aircrew in our corner of the bar.

'Well, it's a dry old do. Poor show, chaps,' said the skipper. 'How about five bob each in the kitty? That'll get us up to cruising altitude.'

I reached into my tunic for a wallet I hoped was there. To my relief, I found it and peered inside, looking for notes or coins, but all I found was my alter-ego's RAF identity card, an old cinema ticket and a creased photograph of a homely young woman in a pill-box hat. I dug around in my trouser pockets and came up with a handful of coins of a type I vaguely remembered from my childhood. I spread out my worldly wealth in a puddle of beer on the counter-top and tried to work out how much was there – if my calculations were correct, it came to three shillings and sixpence.

One of the crew peered over my shoulder at the heap of coins. 'Well, knock me down with a feather, Tommy's skint again. Whose turn is it to sub the mangy blighter this time?' he asked. More laughter.

'Don't worry, Tommy, me old china, you can add it to the slate,' said the bomb aimer, winking at me. 'If this war goes on much longer, with what you owe me, I'll buy meself a gold watch.' He slapped the money down on the bar and stood back while the navigator, a serious-looking officer, with a long, sad face, gathered up the coins and tried to attract the barmaid's attention. I noticed that when he finally managed to order, he was the only one of the group drinking barley water rather than beer. Apart from me, he was also the only one not smoking. The beer cost one shilling and twopence a pint.

'Well, bottoms-up, chaps,' said the skipper, raising his glass.

Although I knew this had to be a hallucination, how had I conjured the genie of the lamp into painting the canvas of my shadow world in such precise detail? I could smell the cigarettes and even feel the effect of the alcohol as I finished my first glass of beer. At the time it didn't taste that strong, but after only one mouthful of my second pint I began to feel giddy and unsteady on my feet. 'Sorry. Don't feel well,' I said, looking around for somewhere to sit. All the seats were taken but I managed to prop myself against the wall, slightly away from my newly adopted crew. The dizziness got worse and I could no longer see. The voices were still there, but indistinct now. Someone was shouting but I couldn't make out what he was saying. Then a bright light and a woman's voice too. Odd, very odd, the only woman in the place was the barmaid. Must have upset her. 'Ver' sorry,' I mumbled.

'There he is.' The woman's voice was closer now and even through my closed lids, the light was vivid. I opened my eyes. No bar, no bomber crews, just a windowless room with white walls, strip lighting and piles of cardboard boxes, one of which I was leaning against. Blinking in disbelief I saw that the woman whose voice I had heard was dressed in modern clothing and flanked by two uniformed policemen. I looked down and felt around my neck. The hard collar and battledress were gone, and in its place were the clothes I had put on that morning. However, in my right hand, I still held a half-full pint glass of beer.

'Put the glass down, sir. You are under arrest,' said the taller of the two policemen. 'Turn away from us and put your hands behind your back.' I did as I was told, felt handcuffs tighten around my wrists and a hand closing round my upper arm. They steered me towards the door, not the one I had come in by, but another, several feet away to the left. The steps with their white-painted reinforcements had gone, and in their place stood modern concrete and steel.

I had never been arrested before and so probably said and did all the wrong things. However, the mind is very adept at airbrushing out painful memories, so the details of what happened still remain a blur to this day.

The cell at the police station was functional, white and brightly lit, not unlike a smaller version of the storeroom where they had found me. In the corner opposite the aluminium shelf that served as a bed was a lavatory and a washbasin. How long I was in there I have no idea, it was probably no more than an hour but it felt like several days. Eventually, I heard the sound of the spy-hole cover being moved back, followed by the rattle of keys in the lock. I recognised my visitor at once – Inspector Grimes.

He stood in front of me, hands on hips, looking down at me with a mixture of exasperation and bewilderment. 'Why, Bill? What the hell do you think you were doing?' I expected angry copper Grimes, but his voice seemed to show genuine concern.

I put my head in my hands. 'Sorry. Had a hallucination, a really bad one. Nothing like I've ever had before. One minute I was standing in front of the bookshop, next I was back in the 1940s. Then your boys found me.'

'So how did you get through two locked doors into the storeroom? You scared the manager of the bookshop half to death, poor woman.'

I shook my head. 'I don't know,' I replied.

'Bill, I know you're not well, but you need to help me. The other side of that storeroom is a jeweller's shop. If I wanted to, I could make this look very bad for you.'

'I know. Listen, it was a hallucination. There was no bookshop, no jewellers, just a grotty old hotel. I walked through the front door, down the steps into a bar, someone bought me a beer and I had a funny turn. Then your boys arrested me. That's all I can remember.'

'Have they taken blood or urine samples?' Grimes asked.

'Both.'

'How much had you drunk?'

'A pint and a half at most.'

'Did you mix drink and pills?'

'No.'

'Well that's something at least,' he replied. 'I should be able to get you off with a caution, but for Christ's sake, go back to the doc and get some stronger pills. One minute you ring me up saying you're fine, and the next thing I know my boys have nicked the only safe cracker in the business who goes tooled up with a pint of flat bitter.'

Chapter Six

I suppose an analogy about moths and flames would be suitable, but as soon as the police released me I got in my car and drove out to Leckonby. The light was fading by the time I arrived but I reckoned I had at least half an hour. A walk would clear my head and let me do some thinking. I parked in my usual spot and set off around the perimeter track towards the bomb dump. I usually reckon to cover a mile every fifteen minutes and by the time my watch told me that it was time to turn back I had almost reached the shooting butts where the gypsy encampment had been. The burned-out remains of the caravan were still there, as were the heaps of rubbish left behind. The piles of cartridges had gone as had all evidence of the police presence, but I spent far longer than I had intended, poking about in bushes and in the shell of the old brick building that had once supported the giant sand banks into which the aircrafts' guns were fired.

By the time I turned to retrace my steps it was clear I wasn't going to make it to the car before night fell and I quickened my pace accordingly. As the sun set a chill pervaded the air and a thin layer of mist settled over the old airfield.

I was just passing the bomb dump, not five minutes from the car when I heard it. A low, rumbling growl, close at hand from somewhere just in front. I stopped, hairs bristling on the back of my neck. Whatever it was, it was between me and the safety of the car. I peered into the gloom, trying to see what had made the sound – guard dogs turned loose on the airfield to deter thieves and vandals seemed the most logical answer. I hoped that if I just kept on walking slowly, they would ignore me. I edged away from the perimeter track, trying to skirt round what I hoped was only a single dog and not a pack, but the growl came again, closer now and louder. A voice in my head told me what I feared to admit. Whatever was making that unearthly sound, it wasn't a dog. The growl came once more, but from behind. I spun round and saw a monstrous black shadow emerge from the mist towards me, as tall at the shoulder as a pony. This was no dog. Two red, glaring eyes fixed me and the creature moved closer, a vile, snarling coming from its jaws. I turned to run, but in the dark I didn't see the raised edge of the concrete slab and sprawled headlong, winding myself as I fell. I felt rather than heard the beast approaching and turned to face it.

'Snipe! Leave.' A man's voice, from where I couldn't see. The creature stopped at once, lowered its tail and turned away from me, disappearing into the darkness from which it had come. Too shocked to move, I lay where I was. Standing over me, his features just visible in the moonlight was Colonel Cavendish. He looked down at me with contempt. 'You don't listen, do you? This place isn't safe for you. And now it's too late. You've looked him in the eye.' Like the dog, he too seemed to have grown to outlandish proportions and now stood over seven feet tall. A vague smell of burning with a hint of sulphur seemed to surround him.

He stretched out a bony hand to help me to my feet. His grip was inhumanly strong and his flesh as cold as steel. I looked up into his features. His face wore the look of someone who had been mummified – waxy skin and lips pulled back over yellowing teeth in a death-mask's grin. Worst of all were his eyes. The sockets were empty yet it was clear he could see me. This had to be another hallucination. Nonetheless, I found myself compelled to respond to this nightmare product of my own damaged mind. Somehow I found my voice. 'What was that thing? Who have I looked in the eye?'

'A twelvemonth at most and then you must join the others,' he answered. This made no sense.

'What others?' I asked, emboldened now, still uneasy, but ready to play along with the hallucination.

'You will find out soon enough,' he said. 'Come, Snipe.' From somewhere uncomfortably close, I heard the creature rumble in reply. I turned instinctively towards it, fearing its return. When I turned back, Cavendish had gone, the mist had cleared and not far away I could see the moonlight reflecting from the roof of my car. From the spot where he had stood, I saw what at first I took to be rising mist, then my nostrils caught the burning smell again. Smoke and sulphur.

When I got into the car and made to put the key in the ignition, to my irritation I found my hands were shaking and it took me several tries before I could get the engine started and turn the car towards Leckonby village and the road home to Lincoln. As I drove, a little cussed demon on my shoulder taunted me for cowardice. The old airfield had somehow wormed its way into my subconscious which was now having a fine old time conjuring all manner of imaginary bogeymen into being. Well, I reasoned, they weren't real, and they weren't stopping me from finding out who was trying to frighten me away from coming back there. And what was all the nonsense about having to join the others within twelve months? Which others? No, I decided, it was a hallucination and I wasn't going to let anything put me off: if anything, it made me more determined to go back. How could I have been so stupid?

***

A few days later, Martin Watson, chairman of The Leckonby Action Group phoned me in the office. He sounded a far happier heron than the one I had met in the pub. I didn't follow the exact details, but from what I could gather, *The Lags'* lawyer had found a vital omission in the planning documentation and had successfully applied for an injunction to halt all building work at RAF Leckonby. A public enquiry would now have to be held.

Later that evening I drove to the airfield once more. It was already dark but this time I had a torch with me. It was a clear night and frosty grass crunched underfoot as I retraced the route I had taken during my previous visit. Stopping just short of the bomb dump, I turned on the torch and looked all around me. Out of devilment I called out to Cavendish and to Snipe but answer came there none. I had already taken two of my blue and white pills as a precaution against unwanted visits from whatever horrors the genie of my hallucinations might produce from his lamp. Satisfied that I was alone, I followed one of the overgrown runways, picking my way between the foundations of the chicken sheds that had been removed in preparation for the building work. I could see the control tower and the roofless shell of the operations block silhouetted against the sky and turned the torch off. If anyone was hanging around, waiting to frighten the credulous then I didn't want them to know

I was coming.

For the moment all seemed quiet. I followed the wall of the operations block as far as the bricked-up doorway opposite the control tower. There I waited, hoping to remain unseen. I'm not a patient man at the best of times, and standing in the freezing cold in the dark in the middle of a disused airfield lost its appeal after only a few minutes. I was about to leave my hiding place when I saw a light flickering through the glassless windows at the base of the control tower. Was this going to be a repeat of the episode with the Very flare? I wondered. Leaving the torch switched off and keeping to the shadows I crept towards the light. My question was soon answered. I had only covered half the distance when I heard a loud pop and a brilliant green ball of fire lit up the night sky. I watched it trace a graceful arc before bouncing on the concrete taxiway and going out, leaving my night vision temporarily ruined. I closed my eyes but the glowing image stayed fixed on my retina for several moments. When I opened them, my reverie was broken by a muffled bang and the sound of an engine. For an instant, my imagination ran riot and I thought it was the sound of a Lancaster starting up, but then I saw headlights approaching along the taxiway and prosaic reality in the form of a Land Rover drew to a halt outside the tower. I flicked on the torch so as not to alarm what I assumed was a security team. The door of the Land Rover slammed shut and a figure, rendered bulky by a thick anorak over several layers of clothes, appeared out of the darkness waving a torch beam ahead of him. I called to him and shone my torch to indicate my presence.

'Over here,' I called. 'I saw the flare too.'

He came closer, uncomfortably close, and shone the light in my face, blinding me for an instant. Putting my hand up to shield my eyes, I saw in the background another figure approaching.

'Who are you? What are you doing here?' asked the first man. I noticed as he lowered the torch that he had the logo of a security firm on his jacket.

'Bill Price from the Lincoln Post,' I replied. 'Some of the locals reckon Leckonby's haunted. I'm writing a piece on it.'

'Well you've no business here. This is private property –'

'He's doing no harm. Leave him be.' The second man had now joined us, standing slightly further away, making it difficult for me to see him properly. 'He didn't fire the flare. It came from the top of the tower. It's the signal to start engines.'

'I don't care what it is. Whoever did fire it must still be up there.'

'Oh, beyond all doubt. Pretty obvious I'd have thought.' It seemed a slightly odd reply but I made no comment.

'Well we can't spend all night gassing, I'm going up. I'll bet it's those bloody pikeys again.'

'I'll come with you,' I said, regretting the words as soon as I'd spoken them.

With the security guard leading the way I followed him up the irregular concrete steps. Of the second man there was no sign. I had expected him to join us but my mind was entirely focussed on not slipping and trying not to think about how high up we were.

We reached the balcony in front of the wrecked visual control room and our torches lit up the same picture I had seen before – piles of rubble, graffiti and broken window frames. 'There's nobody here,' I said.

'You sure you didn't fire that thing?' he asked, his tone making it clear he thought I had.

'No, I was fifty yards away, by the ops block.'

'Hmm. Well whoever it was must've run down those steps pretty bloody quickly.'

'Not me. I'm terrified of heights.'

'Very convenient.'

We turned to go back down. I swept the balcony with my torch, hoping to find another cartridge case, but without success. We descended the steps with me in the lead, gingerly feeling each tread for ice before putting any weight on it.

If I'd been expecting any thanks for accompanying the security guard I was to be disappointed. 'Right,' he said, once more standing uncomfortably close and towering over me. 'I'm not going to report you because I can't be arsed to do the paperwork. But if I find you on this site again I'll give you a fucking good kicking. And the same goes for the muppet who was with you. Got that?'

'Hold on,' I said. 'I thought he was with you.'

'Nah. On me own tonight. Short-staffed.'

'But if he wasn't with either of us, who was he?'

The security guard seemed unperturbed. 'Fuck knows. Whoever he was, he'll get a shoeing if I get dragged out for nothing again. Now fuck off and don't come back.'

Any disappointment I may have felt in not getting a look at the culprits this time was more than offset by the knowledge that I had at least worked out how they were operating. I'm a creature of habit, and always park my car at the same spot when I visit Leckonby, thus making it easy for anyone to know when I visit the airfield. Twice now they'd pulled the same stunt with a Very flare and twice they'd worked the *tertium quid* routine, first with the pale young man at *The Lags* meeting and now with the second security guard who clearly wasn't any such thing. I'd fallen for the same "I thought he was with you" trick twice now – mentally I kicked myself for being so gullible and promised that they wouldn't fool me again.

Chapter Seven

My resolve not to get caught out led me to ignore good advice and so began the long descent into the hell of my current predicament. Allow me to explain.

It took me several days and a heavy dose of my anti-hallucination medication to summon the courage to visit the bookshop in Lincoln again. I stood, hesitating in the doorway, looking out for the manager who had found me in their basement store room clutching a half-finished pint of bitter, but seeing no trace of her I decided it was safe to go in. I chose a book, paid for it and turned to leave, pleased with myself at overcoming my irrational fears, yet at the same time feeling guiltily pleased that the bookshop showed no signs of morphing into The Saracen's Head Hotel.

I suppose I must have been so preoccupied that I didn't see the man coming. We collided and I stumbled and fell, dropping my new book.

'I'm most awfully sorry,' he said, picking up my book and helping me to my feet. 'Are you hurt?' There is something irredeemably English about apologising for things that aren't your fault and his voice came straight from an old black and white film.

'No, not at all,' I said, brushing the dust from the knees of my trousers. 'It was my fault. Terribly sorry. Head in the clouds, I'm afraid.'

'How very prophetic,' he replied. An odd reply I thought.

'What do you mean…' my voice trailed away. We had met before. The collision was no accident. Angry now, I thrust my hands into my pockets and glared at him. 'Hang on a minute. I know you, don't I? We met at *The Lags* meeting in the Rose and Crown at Leckonby.'

He brushed the dark fringe away from his pale features and gave a half smile. 'Indeed we did.'

I couldn't believe they were trying it on again, and this time in broad daylight. I took a pace towards him. 'So tell me, what the fuck are you trying to achieve by pissing around with flares and playing games of hide and seek? Trying to frighten people? If you are, it's not working. Just give it up.'

If I had expected a reaction, I was disappointed. He smiled once more and I could swear I saw pity in his eyes. 'You have actually seen me plenty of times before,' he replied. 'I suppose you just didn't notice. People don't now.'

'Look, stop talking in riddles…' I realised I was shouting when a passer-by turned to look at me and hurried away. Others were making exaggerated detours round us. The row was attracting attention.

He put his hand on my arm, his touch gentle, almost feminine. 'Shush, not so loud. I'm trying to help you, Tommy.'

'My name's not Tommy. I'm Bill Price,' I shouted into his face. Then I realised. In a ghastly pantomime of déjà vu, over his shoulder I could see my reflection in the bookshop window. In the mirror world of Lincoln High Street, behind me was a bank, people walking and doing their best to avoid an angry, middle-aged man, all alone, hands on hips, and shouting to himself. Of the young man in front of me, solid flesh and bone, his hand still on my arm, there was no sign. My jaw fell open and I thought for a moment I was going to be sick.

'I think you had better come with me,' he said.

'If it's the storeroom of the bookshop again you can forget it.'

That gentle smile once more. 'No, Tommy, not the downstairs bar in the Snakepit. If you take my advice you'll steer well clear of that place.'

'Well that shouldn't be a problem,' I snapped back at him as we walked down the High Street together. Once more, passers-by stared and veered away from the madman shouting to himself.

'Let's go in here.' He nodded towards a coffee shop. 'And let me do the talking. You're beginning to attract attention.'

Inside we were met by a welcoming atmosphere of coffee smells and warmth. Mothers with pushchairs were clustered round tables, chattering and trying to keep their infants occupied. Nobody looked up. 'Afraid you'll have to pay for this one, Tommy. Oh, and don't bother buying anything for me.'

I paid for my coffee and found a corner table for two. Picking up a newspaper from the rack, I set it down on the table and sat facing the wall with my mysterious new friend opposite me. 'So how do you do it?' I growled, trying, like an amateur ventriloquist, to keep my lips from moving.

'Do what?'

'Muck about with my hallucinations like this. I can see you, but nobody else can.'

'Not so loud, Tommy. The lady behind you is staring. Bad show, Tommy. Bad show.'

'Just stop calling me Tommy.' The last word came out as 'tongy'.

'You'd better let me talk. If you listen and do as I

say there's still time. If you don't…. well, that's not even worth thinking about, even if you believed me. Which you probably won't.'

'Go on.'

He put his elbows on the table and fixed me with his gaze. 'You've got yourself mixed up in something you cannot understand and you're in danger of ending up like me. Just because I'm picky about who can see me and who can't doesn't mean I'm one of your hallucinations. Do you follow me?'

I shook my head.

'Keep away from Leckonby and you'll be all right. You saw what happened to the gypsies.'

I took out my mobile phone to give me an excuse to speak. I pretended to dial and put it to my ear. 'So are you saying you killed the one using the disc cutter and shot up the caravan?'

'No. Well, not personally, anyway.'

'So who did?'

He paused and for the first time since we had sat down, turned his pale blue gaze from mine. 'Let's just say there's a lot of anger about what's going on at Leckonby. The building, the new houses, all the upheaval. People are upset, bloody livid to be honest. It's not what they wanted, not what they expected you see.'

'Who? *The Lags*?'

The Mona Lisa smile again. 'No, not them. Some of the men you met in the Snakepit the other day. I saw you come in, by the way. I don't think you noticed me.'

'Hardly surprising, the place was packed…' I stopped myself. This was ridiculous. Was I really discussing drinking a pint in a bar conjured up by my own damaged mind with someone who claimed to have been there too? 'Are you trying to frighten me?'

'No. Well, not directly. You'd be frightened enough if you realised what you've got yourself caught up in. It's not too late though. Just take my advice. Keep away from RAF Leckonby.'

'And since you insist on calling me Tommy, what am I supposed to call you?' I asked.

For a moment he looked puzzled. 'I'd assumed you'd worked that out from the photo in the Rose and Crown.'

The penny dropped. Putting down my phone I took my notebook out from my inside pocket and thumbed through the pages. I found the list of names I had copied down. *L-R: Jones, McIntyre, Bailey, Skipper, Armstrong, Foster, self.* 'Of course. It was your photograph. But all it says is "self"... but hang on, that picture must've been taken in 1944.'

'December 1943 to be precise. I used to keep it in my log book.'

I did a swift calculation. 'Which makes you over ninety years old. Come off it.'

'Let's just say that some people stopped counting in March 1944. I'm not a hallucination, Tommy, this isn't something you control. If you see me again, it may be too late.' I tried to remonstrate with him but he got up, turned away and without another word, walked straight through the solid door of the coffee shop and out into the street. From their lack of reaction, none of the other customers saw him go.

I left my coffee and hurried outside but there was no sign of him. This time as I walked back to the bookshop, nobody stared, nobody accosted me – the normality was overpowering. I went in and browsed the military history section, half expecting someone to start calling me Tommy once more. Nothing. I bought another book and wandered home.

It didn't take long online to find the name and the fate of the pale young man. *Lancaster LL984, CD-F for Freddy, 362 Squadron RAF Leckonby, captain Wg Cdr Geoffrey Preston, failed to return from operations against Brunswick on the night of 29-30 March 1944 (crew on 25th operation of first tour).*

I read on. Among the crew was Flying Officer Keith Harrison (410434) aged twenty-one – my sometimes visible companion. Seven lives snuffed out, promise unfulfilled, seven sets of hopes and dreams extinguished without trace. But why Harrison and why me? What had brought us into this contact between real and unreal?

Real or imagined and in spite of his warnings, I was desperate to see him again and to find out more. I had to know.

Chapter Eight

At the public enquiry into the Leckonby development tempers frayed, the heron's feathers were ruffled and worse. Harsh words and even blows were exchanged. To the horror of the anti-development lobby, the Secretary of State supported the planning application, and despite a ruinously expensive appeal to the High Court the builders won their case and building work continued.

Despite the process of law having run its course, it was obvious to me that someone didn't accept the decision. Almost from the first day that the surveyors started measuring up and the diggers opened their first trenches, trouble began – sand and water tipped into fuel tanks, hydraulic lines cut, windscreens broken, and on one occasion, what looked worryingly like a bullet hole through a workmen's hut. On several mornings, the police were called but each time the culprits were long gone. Local residents reported having seen lights on the airfield. In the end, the developers moved all their machinery into a fenced compound near one of the old hangars and the night-time security patrols were reinforced.

For a few nights there was no more trouble, then it started again. One foggy December evening the security patrol received a phone call reporting lights and movement on the airfield. Grimes phoned and gave me the tip-off.

Rather than go back and risk getting the beating I'd been threatened with during my last visit, I tried a different tack. This time I got the story first-hand from one of the guards, and my intention was to turn it into an article for the Lincoln Post.

We met at a pub near the city centre and his hands were shaking as he recounted the tale. The way he told it, the lights seemed to be coming from the area around the old control tower and, if I followed his description correctly, there were also lights in what had been the operations block. He was one of two guards on shift that night and they set off from the security compound, padlocking the gate behind them before driving over to investigate.

He wasn't a particularly impressive specimen – early thirties, running to fat, with a shaven head and a tattoo of a spider on his neck. His clothes smelled like they could do with a wash. 'I'll be honest with you,' he said, slurping the pint of bitter I had just bought him. 'I wasn't happy. There should've been three of us on shift that night with one staying in the compound at all times. But one of the lads phoned in sick, asked us to cover for him and sign his timesheet to make it look like he'd been there all along. You know how it is?' I nodded and he continued. 'Anyway, the fog was so thick in places you could only see a few yards, and it wasn't till afterwards, like, that I wondered how anyone could've seen the lights to report them. We could only see them when we got right up close.'

'And there definitely were lights in the control tower?' I asked.

'Yeah, and in the big building next to it, you know, the one with no roof.'

'That used to be the operations block.' I decided against telling him about my experiences at the airfield.

'Well, whatever you call it, there was lights there

99

too. At first, we could see people moving about through the windows – quite a few of them, seven or eight at least.' He cracked his knuckles – I caught a glimpse of the word "HATE" tattooed over them. 'I don't mind a ruck now an' then, but, well, two against eight ain't my sort of odds, so I was all for getting back in the van and calling the Old Bill. That's when it happened…' His voice trailed away.

Looking up from my notes I saw his face had turned deathly pale. 'When what happened?' I asked.

As he took another drink I noticed beads of sweat standing out on his forehead. 'All the bloody lights went out, didn't they? I thought they'd seen us and were coming to have a go, so we jumped back in the van, started the engine and I turned so's the headlights were dead on the building – y'know, the operations block. We called the police, told 'em what we'd seen but they didn't believe a word. I know what I saw, I know what we both saw, but the bastards wouldn't believe us. Said we was making it up to cover for our mate dodging his shift.'

I spoke softly, trying to calm the fear I saw in his eyes. 'You still haven't told me what you saw.'

'There weren't seven or eight of them, nearer a hundred more like.' He must have read the disbelief on my face. 'If I never move off this spot, so help me, there were at least a hundred blokes, all sitting there in rows. Just staring up in the same direction, like they was watching a film or something.'

'So what did you do then?'

'What do you bloody think? We got the fuck out. Never driven so fast in all my born days.'

'But what about the lights?' I asked. 'Were they still

on?'

'No, and that's what's really weird. There were all these blokes, just sitting there in the pitch dark, looking at nothing.'

I made another couple of notes before asking my next question. 'And that's when you called the police?'

'Well, yes and no.'

'What do you mean?'

He finished his pint in a single gulp and wiped his mouth with the back of his hand. 'When we got back, we unlocked the gates, right? The padlock hadn't been touched, no holes in the fence – it's got razor wire on the top, so they couldn't have got in that way.'

'Who couldn't?'

'Whoever trashed the diggers. They'd all been torched.'

'And you reckon this had something to do with the people you saw in the ops block?'

'Must've done,' he replied, anger now replacing the earlier fear in his voice. 'Couldn't have been anybody else, could it?'

'The police don't seem to agree with you.'

'How do you know?' A group of drinkers at another table turned round at the sound of his raised voice.

'No need to shout,' I said motioning him to calm down. 'I'm a journalist, remember. I talk to the police all the time. It's what I do.'

'Yeah, right,' he said, cursing the police under his breath. 'The Old Bill reckoned we bunked off for the night and then made up the story about the lights and everything. That's why I got the bloody sack.'

This didn't make sense. I checked my notes once more. 'Hold on. Just now you said the police phoned to say someone had reported lights at the control tower.'

He shook his head and looked downcast. 'Someone's playing silly buggers. Fucking coppers *did* call us but now they're denying it. Bastards.'

The solution seemed pretty obvious to me. 'Maybe it wasn't the police who called. You were lured away so that someone could destroy the diggers. They probably had accomplices in the control tower and the ops block mucking around with torches and things to try and frighten you. You know, night-time, foggy, creepy old disused airfield – that's enough to make anyone nervous.'

'Doesn't explain all those blokes we saw. My mate saw them and all, don't forget.'

'No it doesn't, does it?' I got up to buy him another pint. Whoever was sabotaging the building works had gone to a lot of time and effort to cover their traces.

There was only one thing to do. After the warning I had received from the pale shade of Flying Officer Harrison, the thought of it was terrifying, but Leckonby drew me like a moth to a flame.

Work had restarted on the site and the developers were making up for lost time. Sections of taxiway and runway had been dug up for aggregate and the remaining hangars demolished. New roads and foundations had sprung up near the shooting butts where the travellers' caravan had been destroyed. Parking at my usual spot on the opposite side of the airfield, I put my torch and a spare set of batteries into my coat pocket, pulled on my boots and set off across the grass. Unseen, in the darkness of the woods bordering the perimeter track, a vixen screamed and I suppressed a nervous shiver, doing my best not to think of my encounter with

Colonel Cavendish and his familiar. Tonight I seemed to have the place to myself and so I pushed on along the perimeter track, past the control tower and the operations block into the overgrown complex of huts that had once formed RAF Leckonby's accommodation and administrative site.

The weather was mild for once and the wind had swung round to the south west with a promise of rain. A gust, stronger than the others brought the sound to my ears. At first I thought it must be coming from the village, but no, it was louder now, quite distinct and coming from the opposite direction – male voices singing tunelessly, accompanied by a piano. A stand of birch trees that had grown up around the old foundations blocked my line of sight and I forced my way through, cursing at the brambles that tore and snatched at my clothes. Finally, I managed to get clear and follow the sound. I was close now – banging, crashing, drunken voices and the tinny rattle of a piano coming from a series of Nissen huts linked together into the shape of a capital H, their dark outlines just visible against the light of the full moon. Light shone round the frame of a doorway. The noise was almost deafening – I would need to move quickly before it attracted the attention of the security guards. So, with my pulse racing and sweat trickling down my neck I opened it a crack and peered inside to find a small entrance lobby formed by blackout material blocking my view. I slipped in, shut the door behind me and pushed the curtains aside. The sight that met my eyes left me open-mouthed with amazement.

The party was in full swing. In an atmosphere of beer fumes and cigarette smoke that I could have cut into cubes, a group of thirty or so young men in RAF uniform was packed into the makeshift bar, dimly lit by a row of dirty bulbs under green metal shades. Nerves jangling, fearing a repeat of the episode at the Saracen's head, I turned to go. As I did so, a baby-faced individual whose battledress jacket bore the single thin stripe of a Pilot Officer, walked unsteadily towards me. 'Gotta have a piss,' he said to no one in particular and thumped his pint glass down on the table next to me, adding yet more beer slops to the puddle on its surface. Ignoring me completely, he pushed the blackout curtain aside, opened the door and stood on the top step to relieve himself. Shouts of, 'Put that bloody light out,' and, 'Don't you know there's a war on?' came from round the room and a tall, dark-haired officer walked past me, seemingly oblivious to the existence of a civilian in their midst, pushed the Pilot Officer down the steps and shut the door. As he came back into the bar, he noticed the almost full glass on the table and, as he reached for it his arm would have touched mine had I not jumped out of the way. Then it dawned. I could see them, but they couldn't see me. Fighting back the adrenalin urging me to run for my life, I forced myself to stay and watch.

Centre stage was held by an upright piano. Next to it, on a trestle table which seemed sure to collapse at any moment, swayed two men. The first, dressed in an off-white bathrobe wore a white bandana around his head on which was drawn a red Japanese rising sun. Arm in arm with him was a second, shorter figure in pantomime drag sporting rouged cheeks and a gash of red lipstick for a mouth. A call for silence went up.

'Gentlemen,' shouted the pianist once the sound of voices had dropped enough for him to be heard. 'For your delectation, entertainment – and for those of you

104

what weren't brought up proper, your education – the 362 Squadron Sod's Opera Company, fresh from their sell-out tour of Essen, Hamburg and Berlin, is proud to perform Gilbert and Sullivan's *The Moon and I*.' With a crash of chords for introduction, the pair of drunks on the table launched into the aria from *The Mikado*. To my surprise, they sang in tune and an appreciative, almost maudlin silence descended on the party. As the last notes faded away and the performers took a bow, for a moment that seemed to last a lifetime, nobody spoke, nobody moved. Then, as though in sudden realisation that they were supposed to be enjoying themselves, with a single voice they cheered the performers, whistled, stamped and shouted for more. To me, the silence had spoken far more loudly than the yells of beery masculinity.

'All right, you bastards, pipe down,' shouted the male half of the duet in a broad Aussie accent. 'What'll it be?'

'Blue Moon! Blue Moon!' they yelled.

'Now *there's* a surprise,' he shouted back with a grin. This time, as the pianist struck up the tune there was no reverential silence and the entire room, including the white-jacketed barman, took up the refrain.

Next was *It's only a Paper Moon*, followed by *Shine on, Harvest Moon*. Even I could see the theme. Edging around the corrugated iron walls which were running with condensation, I took advantage of a beer break for the singers and tried to make my way closer to the centre of the party. Gaining in confidence, I was only a few feet away from the piano when my blood froze. A hand gripped my arm and I heard a familiar voice. Spinning round, I came face to face with my companion from

Lincoln High Street. It was Harrison.

'You didn't get the message, did you, Tommy? I warned you to keep away,' he said, brushing the dark fringe away from his eyes.

'But what is this?'

'A party. What does it look like? And anyway, this is the officers' mess. You shouldn't be here. You're a Sergeant, remember, Tommy?'

I pulled my arm free of his grasp. I've never liked men who touch too much. 'Listen, I'm Bill Price, not Tommy Handley. And I'm not a Sergeant.'

'Bill Price? Not here you're not,' he replied. 'Listen, Tommy. Go home, stay away from here. There's still time.'

The noise started up again as the pianist began his next introduction. 'Why?' I asked.

'Because if you don't your life will be in danger.'

'Oh, come off it. What harm can you do me?'

My question seemed to perplex him and he hesitated for a moment, deep in thought. 'Harm you? Why would I do that? You really don't understand, do you?' he said.

'Clearly not.'

'I'll bet you don't even understand why we're having a party.'

'Something to do with the moon?' I ventured.

'Everything to do with the moon. It means we stay alive another week. No ops for the eight days either side of the full moon, Tommy. That's our kind of bombers' moon, the one that lets us sleep in our beds rather than burn to death over Berlin. If that's not worth a party, I don't know what is.'

'I understand that, but how does it affect me?'

He shook his head as though in despair at my

stupidity. 'If you keep away, it won't. You've still time,' he said.

'And if I don't I'm in danger?'

'Yes.'

'What kind of danger?'

'What kind of danger? All right, Tommy, if you really want to know, be at Leckonby Junction in time to meet the seven minutes past ten from Lincoln next Tuesday night. But don't say I didn't warn you. Once you start, there's no going back, nowhere to hide, no going LMF.'

If only I had listened. Instead, I thanked him, promised I would be there and edged past the choir clustered round the piano to the door. As soon as it slammed shut behind me, the noise stopped. Perhaps one of them had spotted me. Curious, I turned the handle and opened it again. This time the door was stiff and I had to force the rusty hinges. Inside, all was quiet so I turned on my torch. As I swept the beam around the interior, all I saw was old farm machinery covered by fertiliser sacks. What had once been a solidly-built Nissen hut was now open to the elements along half its length, all its window glass had gone and the far retaining wall had been demolished. I switched it off. Moonlight streamed into the building through the holes in its structure. A perfect night for a party.

Chapter Nine

Obsession, irrationality or simple curiosity? It doesn't really matter now, but once these hallucinations, phantoms or whatever they were no longer held any fear for me, my mind was made up. At just before ten on a clear, moonless Tuesday night I parked next to the old station buildings at Leckonby Junction. Seven minutes past ten came and went so I got out of the car and paced around to keep myself from dozing off. Five minutes was enough to leave me shivering and I climbed back into the car and started the engine to get the heater going. By twenty past nothing had happened and I was on the verge of going home. Then I saw it.

A pair of flickering lights in the lane and a dark shape approaching. I had seen it before, it was the single-decker bus that had nearly run me off the road during one of my earlier visits to the airfield. I got out of the car and walked round to what had been the station entrance, keeping in the shadows to avoid being seen, I waited and watched. The bus stopped, turned off its blacked-out headlights and the driver hooted the horn three times. Moments later I heard the sound of voices coming from the direction of the Hobbs Bank Drain which paralleled the railway line. Turning to look I saw a brief flash of light as a door opened and closed, then the dim glow-worm of an electric torch. This was odd – there was no building that I could recall on the other side of the dyke, just the overgrown foundations of what had once been a pub. Then came the sound of oars creaking in their rowlocks and the gentle splashing as the craft crossed the slowly flowing watercourse. Hearty goodbyes, and moments later, a cluster of glowing cigarette ends resolved itself into seven men in RAF battledress as they came into full view at the top of the dyke. They chatted amongst themselves, walked past without noticing me and climbed aboard the bus. I made to join them but hesitated. Harrison had told me to meet a train, so I waited.

At just after ten thirty I heard the unmistakable sound of a train approaching. Among clouds of steam and acrid-smelling smoke it wheezed to a halt. Then, slamming of doors and the sound of laughter and catcalls as about thirty or more men in uniform trooped down the steps, some unsteady on their feet. Harrison hadn't given me any further instructions and I wasn't even sure whether any of these new arrivals would be able to see me. I looked down. Just like the lunchtime visit to the Snakepit, I was once more in battledress and so, heart pounding, I strolled as nonchalantly as I could towards the bus and joined the scrum by the door. As I put one foot on the step I looked back to where my car was parked – it had gone. If this was a hallucination, it was impressively real.

'Come on, mate, get a move on,' a voice from close behind and a shove in the back sent me on my way.

'Ah, Tommy, there you are.' Seated a few rows from the front was the weasel-faced bomb aimer I had met in the Saracen's Head. He moved over and patted the seat next to him. 'Thought we'd lost you. So what were you doing slumming it at the Ferry Boat? You missed a hell of a show at The Royal and there was even a punch-up outside the Snakepit.'

'What was on at The Royal?'

'You forgotten already? *Jane* in *Hi Diddle-Diddle*.

It was great. You should've seen her chorus girls – lovely bits of stuff they were.'

'Maybe next time,' I replied, trying to stay non-committal.

He paused and looked at me sideways. 'Not going flak-happy, are we, Tommy?'

'No, just feeling a bit funny, that's all.' If only you knew the half, I thought.

'So you thought getting pissed in the Ferry Boat would make you feel better?' He was clearly trying to needle me but I made no reply.

The hubbub of voices grew louder as the last of the aircrew, some of them none too sober, filed on board. Some were forced to stand in the aisle, one of them falling over to a chorus of cat-calls as the bus set off.

Someone tapped me on the shoulder and I turned round. At once I recognised the boyish face of the Flying Officer pilot who was captain of the crew. 'Have you spent all evening in the Ferry Boat, Tommy?'

'No, skipper,' I replied. 'I needed some fresh air so I went out for a walk. Came out this way and decided to wait for the bus back.'

I could see the scepticism written all over his face. 'Hmmm. I'll believe you, thousands wouldn't. Next time we have a crew night out I'd like you to come along.'

'Yeah, Herman Goering's playing in *How big is my chopper?* at the Berlin Hippodrome,' said the bomb-aimer. 'Mustn't miss that, Tommy.' The laughter from the rest of the crew defused the tension and I felt grateful for the reprieve. My alter-ego clearly had a few problems.

Singing broke out from the back seats. 'Stop the bus

we want a wee-wee...' bellowed to the tune of *John Brown's Body*. The WAAF driver turned round and grinned. In only a few minutes we were at our destination and she braked to a halt outside the guardroom. An RAF corporal policeman stepped out from his picket post, flashed his torch over the vehicle's bonnet to read the serial number and then raised the red and white striped barrier to let us through.

First stop was the officers' mess. At first I didn't recognise the building where the moon period party had happened – no trees, no brambles, just concrete, groups of Nissen huts and the smell of coal smoke from dozens of chimneys. As the officers trooped off the bus the singing started again. 'Good night, ladies, good night, ladies...'

I felt a hand on my shoulder – a touch that lingered uncomfortably long. I looked up into the pale features of Fg Off Harrison. 'Don't say I didn't warn you, Tommy,' he said, but before I could reply he had moved off towards the door.

The last of the officers slid the door shut as he got off. 'Hold tight inside. Next stop Portsmouth and Southsea,' called the driver over her shoulder, treating her passengers to a grin and a theatrical wink.

'Do we have to get off at Fratton?' everyone shouted in return. The jollity continued all the way back to the NCOs' accommodation which was the next stop. I followed the four other NCO members of my crew through the blackout curtains and into the Nissen hut. Along each wall were seven beds and in the centre, a black, coal-burning stove. Although its iron surface was almost red hot, the heat did not seem to permeate any further than a few feet, leaving the rest of the room clammy and cold. On one side of each bed was a simple bedside locker and chair, and on the other, a wardrobe with the owner's name on the door, chalked onto a painted black rectangle. It dawned on me that given the life expectancy of Lancaster aircrew, any more permanent display of the current incumbent's existence would prove too time-consuming to change.

I suppose I should have been surprised to see 'Sgt Handley W A, 923041' in my handwriting on one of the wardrobes, but so real was the illusion that I took it for granted and sat down on what was evidently my bed. Someone, me again presumably, had folded the neat, hospital corners at the foot and folded down just the right amount of sheet so that the three parallel lines running down its centre aligned precisely with those on the rough, grey blanket.

I opened the wardrobe. A length of string had been attached to the back of the door with drawing pins and from it hung a pair of braces, a frayed black tie and a pair of socks, damp to the touch, one with a badly darned heel. On the hanging rail I found a greatcoat, an Irvin flying jacket, two collarless blue shirts, a peaked RAF cap, and a 'best blue' parade uniform. A series of shelves was taken up with the rest of my kit; two jumpers, haversack, gas mask, steel helmet, webbing, more socks, baggy grey-white underwear and a pair of pyjamas. In the bedside locker I found a sponge bag containing my washing and shaving kit. On the back of the locker was a wooden rail on which I discovered a towel which might once have been white. It too felt damp to the touch.

The door banged open. Slurred voices singing were accompanied by an icy draught as the door slammed shut once more and the blackout curtains were swept aside. Six unfamiliar faces, but they all seemed to know me, so I nodded, smiled and made what I hoped were the appropriate replies as they each went to their bed spaces. It seemed that our crew had one side of the room and the newcomers the other. The beds nearest the stove were all taken and those in the corners, furthest from its heat were temporarily vacant.

Changing into my pyjamas, I did as the others, pulled on my greatcoat and boots and set off with my wash bag and dishrag towel across the duckboards to the NCOs' ablutions. Apart from the lack of hot water they were no different to the ones I had used as a member of the cadet corps at school.

After washing as best as I could in cold water I made my way back to the hut. An easterly wind was chasing high clouds across the stars of a moonless sky and I gave an involuntary shiver at the thought of what tomorrow might bring for my companions. I also felt a pang of anxiety at how long this hallucination, if that's what it was, might last. When I opened the door I was assailed by a miasma of farts, cigarette smoke, coal fumes and the smell of unwashed bodies and feet. My first instinct was to return to the car, but then I remembered that the last time I looked it wasn't there. More worryingly, I had no idea what I had done with the keys. Face the stink or spend all night outside in a pair of pyjamas and a great coat? It wasn't much of a choice, but the heat from the pot-bellied stove won by a narrow margin.

The sheets felt grimy and damp so I pulled the covers as tight around me as I could and muffled my face to keep out the fug. A few minutes later the lights went out and a chorus of snoring began almost instantly.

Unused to communal living since the early days of my training, I lay awake, wondering when this was going to stop – after all, I had work tomorrow.

***

When at last I awoke, everything seemed normal. I felt for my watch which I always left on the bedside table to my right, but instead my hand bumped into something solid. This wasn't right. Light was filtering through a crack in the curtains, but it was coming from the wrong place. I sat up with a jolt but the familiar surroundings of my house in Lincoln had somehow been rearranged. A hallucination, that was it. I reached out once more, this time for my pill bottle, but again my hand hit the same unyielding surface. I ran my palm down it. Wood. Then it got worse. Voices. There was someone in the room with me. Burglars or another hallucination? I made to get out of bed but my legs swung into the same object that had taken the place of my bedside table. More voices and a rattling noise – my father topping up the Aga from the coal scuttle. No, that was madness, he'd been dead these last fifteen years. A door banged and then a few seconds later light flooded the room. I wasn't at home, but where was I? Then it hit me. I was still in the hut at RAF Leckonby. This was getting beyond a joke.

'Come on, Tommy, or you'll miss breakfast.' It was the bomb aimer. He wore a white roll-necked jumper under his battledress and in his hands he held two red fire buckets, each one full of coal. 'Give me a hand before someone misses this, will you?' He said.

Mute and uncomprehending I stood up, pulled on

the greatcoat which I had used as an additional blanket in the night and shuffled over to him, the Lino agonisingly cold on my bare feet. He handed me one of the buckets and I stood, rooted to the spot, not knowing what I was supposed to do. 'Come on, you daft sod,' he said. 'I've pinched a key for the fuel store. Put it in your locker and for Christ's sake don't tell anyone.'

'Oh, yes, of course. I mean no. Right,' I replied, doing as he asked.

After a tepid shower I got dressed, jammed my 'chip-bag' hat on and followed him to the sergeants' mess. Some of the layout on the domestic site was familiar to me from my earlier visits, but the two type-T and one type-B hangars dominated the skyline in a way that was entirely new. What I formerly knew as cracked concrete was pristine, in places edged by flower beds, and buildings I had only known as crumbling foundations or piles of bricks, were bustling with activity.

Just like the officers' mess, the sergeants' mess was formed by a group of Nissen huts in the form of a capital H. Even without the guidance of the bomb aimer, whom I'd managed to identify as Flt Sgt Claude Unwin, I would have found the dining room just by following the smell of stale fat and overcooked vegetables. We each picked up a formica tray, two plates and a tin mug. Greyish white bread, margarine, jam, porridge, fatty bacon and a strange yellow concoction that I assumed was dried egg, were the choices. None of it looked in any way appetising, but hunger got the better of me, and by washing it down with mouthfuls of hot, strong tea, I cleared my plate.

Unwin seemed happy to do most of the talking

which was a relief for me. I fetched another round of tea and refused his offer of a cigarette which seemed to surprise him. Slowly, as he chattered, I began to piece together a little more about our crew. The skipper, Flying Officer Charles Brownlow, sounded like a typically decent English public schoolboy – a bit wet behind the ears according to Unwin and far too keen on being liked by his crew than on imposing the discipline that just might keep them alive. Unwin was, it seemed, the only one to have completed an earlier tour of thirty operations – that explained the DFM. From his black mutterings and a nervous tic around his right eye, I could tell that his pessimism about surviving a second tour with a sprog pilot was deep-rooted. The navigator, presumably the mournful-looking, non-smoking teetotaller I had met in the Snakepit, had clearly impressed Unwin. 'Heard the nav leader say yesterday he's the best on the squadron,' he said. 'Blokes like you and me are ten a penny, mate, but it would be a bloody shame if old champagne Charlie Brownlow got someone like Prentice killed.'

I took a risk. 'You know, I've never really spoken to Prentice much. Any idea what he did in civvy street?'

'Our Arthur? Training to be an accountant he told me. Somewhere up north. Stoke I think.' So that put names to both officers in what was now my crew – pilot Charlie Brownlow and navigator Arthur Prentice. Unwin paused and looked at me through the cloud of smoke he'd just exhaled. 'Thing is, that's not what worries me.'

'What worries you?'

He ground out the cigarette butt into the left-over porridge in his bowl, never for one moment taking his

116

eyes off me.

'You do, Tommy. You're going to get us all killed. Now don't get me wrong, we're bound to get the chop. I mean, how long is it since a crew last finished a tour?'

'Six months?' I ventured.

'Bollocks it is,' he replied, lighting another cigarette. I detected a tremor in the nicotine stained fingers as he brought it greedily up to his mouth. 'Come off it, mate. Nearer nine. Nah, you've gone funny, changed. It's like talking to a fucking stranger these days. What beats me is where you find the money.'

'What money?'

'Exactly. When you're down the pub or in the mess with the lads you're always skint, yet you still manage to end up legless. I mean, look at last night. You could've come to the show at the Royal with the rest of us, had a quiet pint in the Snakepit and caught the last train home. But no, you'd sooner go drinking at the Ferry Boat with Nobby Clark and his mob.'

'I told you last night, I wasn't with Clark's crew. Ask them if you like.'

He waved me away. 'Nah, Tommy, not worth it, mate. I've seen it all before – one of the flight commanders on my first tour was on a bottle a day. Scotch, mind you, not brown ale. Can't say I blame you – I mean, we all have to deal with it somehow, don't we? But if you're getting tight every night we're not on ops, it's bound to slow you down. Stands to reason, don't it?'

'I suppose you're right,' I said, feigning contrition.

He leant towards me and I caught the sour odour of cigarettes on his breath. 'Listen, Tommy, mate, just stay off the pop for another few trips and we're done. Not much to ask, is it? I mean, if you doze off back there, that's six other blokes for the chop and seven poor mums for a telegram.'

So I was the crew's rear gunner. I made to reply but was cut short by the blaring of a tannoy announcement. 'Stan' by fer broadcast, stan' by fer broadcast. The followin' crews are to report to their flight offices. Ah say again, the followin' crews…' The metallic voice droned on. I counted seventeen captains' names, among them Flying Officer Brownlow's. We were on ops tonight. That settled it, the illusion had gone on long enough, I was already late for work and had no intention of waiting to see what the prospect of getting airborne in a Lancaster from this shadow world might bring.

I walked alongside Unwin as we made our way to the B Flight office, watching him carefully in my attempts not to let him see that I had no idea where we were going. I needn't have worried. We were part of a growing tide of blue uniforms all converging on the same destination which turned out to be a group of Maycrete huts, set between one of the type-T hangars and the taxiway. Inside the B Flight office a huddle of aircrew had already formed round the notice board. There it was in black and white, briefing times for captains and navigators 1600, all other personnel, 1730. That settled it. Making my excuses, I left Unwin chatting to another bomb aimer and made my way back towards our hut. On my way from the sergeants' mess I had spotted a bike propped up at the back of the station barber's shop, my one hope was that it would still be there. Luckily it was and, taking a furtive look round to make sure nobody was watching, I swung into the saddle and set off for the main gate and freedom.

Unfortunately, the geography of the fully intact domestic site bore little resemblance to the scatter of ruins and brambles that represented the RAF Leckonby I knew, and I took several wrong turns before finding the guardroom. Not wanting to draw attention to myself I dismounted and made to push the bike around the side of the red and white striped pole which barred the roadway.

Then disaster struck. My path was blocked by an RAF Police corporal. 'Oi, where do you think you're going, Sergeant?' he spat the word 'Sergeant' with an ironic sneer – the old sweat's contempt for aircrew with stripes on their shoulders that most regulars took ten years to achieve.

'Just nipping down to the village,' I said lamely.

'Nipping down to the village? Christ almighty, pull the other one, it's got bells on. Operations tonight, all personnel confined to camp. Didn't no one tell yer?'

'Oh, sorry, yes. Completely forgot. How silly of me.' Turning the bicycle around I pedalled off and as I looked back over my shoulder in the hope no one else had spotted my *faux pas*, saw the policeman staring after me in disbelief like a man who had just survived an encounter with an escaped lunatic. Time for plan B.

After cycling back across the domestic site with only a couple of wrong turnings I reached the access road that ran round the airfield outside the perimeter track but inside the fence. On one of the dispersal points on the opposite side of the runway an aircraft was running up and I hoped that anyone watching from the control tower would be looking in that direction rather than mine. None the less I felt extremely conspicuous and progress on the heavy old bike with its half flat tyres was agonisingly slow. Near the point where I usually leave my car I found what I was looking for, a hole in the fence. By the look of the path worn in the grass I wasn't the first to use it either. Once in the lane I pedalled as fast as I could towards Leckonby Junction and, I hoped, reality. But as I turned the last corner and the station came into view my heart sank. Instead of the ruined shell with its potholed car park I saw that the buildings were intact, with a thin column of smoke rising from the waiting room chimney. On the other side of the Hobbs Bank Drain was a building I had never seen before. An ornately painted sign above the door proclaimed it to be the Ferry Boat Inn. Parked at the side of the pub was a flat-bed lorry bearing the words "Bateman's Fine Ales" and emblazoned with the brewer's windmill trademark. A man dressed in a white apron, whom I took to be the landlord, was helping the drayman unload wooden casks which they then rolled down a ramp into the cellar. From the far bank protruded a small wooden jetty to which was moored a rowing boat, covered against the elements by a faded green tarpaulin. With no bridge in sight to either horizon, the boat was the only way to and from the pub from this side of the water. At a loss for what to do next I climbed up on to the dyke to get a better view of the landscape. Apart from the absence of high tension pylons it looked identical to the one I knew from the twenty-first century – a monotonous flatland of ploughed fields, criss-crossed by lines of reed and willow which marked the watercourses that drained into the river Witham. I was stuck. What the hell was I going to do now?

I picked the bike up and cycled back the way I'd come. A Lancaster was flying training circuits and I timed my ungainly dash along the access road to coincide with the aircraft turning cross-wind, in the hope that any watchful eyes would be trained in the opposite direction.

At last I replaced the bike from where I had taken it, hoping that it hadn't been missed and that the owner wouldn't notice the mud splatters from its brief journey off-road. Returning to the hut I nodded a greeting to the two other inhabitants. Both were strangers from the other crew and each sat hunched over his locker, pen in hand, clearly deep in concentration. I kicked off my boots and lay on the scratchy grey blanket with my hands behind my head, looking up at the corrugated metal above me and hoping for inspiration. With a sigh, one of the men stood up, folded the piece of notepaper and slid it into an envelope. On it he had written in large capitals, "To be opened in the event of my death." He opened the door of his wardrobe and propped it on the top shelf against a tin of brass polish. That was the point at which I realised the seriousness of my predicament. This shadow world, whatever its true nature, was solid, tangible and, worse still, I was part of it. It had food, drink, warmth, running water and bicycles and, presumably, the capacity to do me harm. Harrison's words came tumbling back into my head – that was it, Harrison, why hadn't I thought of it before? He obviously knew how to get me into this and clearly, since I had seen him several times in the present day, he must know the way out too. I had to find him.

Grabbing my hat and pulling on my boots I almost ran the short distance separating the hut from the sergeants' mess. It was as I had hoped – the full listing of all seventeen crews taking part in tonight's operation was pinned to the main notice board. At the top of the list was Wing Commander Preston's name and, flying as his navigator, with a takeoff time of 2003 in aircraft CD-A for Apple was Flying Officer Harrison, K. Now all I had to do was find him, so I hurried over to the operations block, a building I knew from my previous visits to be a roofless shell. Now, all was spotless, freshly painted and the interior gave off a strong smell of floor polish. The first door I came to was marked "Station Intelligence Officer". It had been left ajar and I just caught the end of a telephone conversation and the sound of the receiver being replaced in its cradle. Deep breath, here goes. I tapped on the door and the voice bade me enter. Behind a desk sat a Flight Lieutenant, his tunic devoid of brevet and medal ribbons. Overweight and bald, his shiny features looked as though they had been polished by the same person who had done the lino in the corridor. He looked up and I saluted. 'Yes, what is it?' he asked in a tone that suggested that my presence was already boring him.

'Sorry to bother you, sir, but I'm trying to find Flying Officer Harrison, the CO's navigator.'

He looked at me with undisguised scorn. 'How the bloody hell would I know where he is? I'm not clairvoyant you know.' He paused and then shouted, 'Margaret! Come in here will you.'

A slightly dumpy WAAF corporal appeared in the doorway. 'No need to shout, I'm only next door, Hector, I mean, sir,' she hastily corrected herself upon spotting me. 'Hullo, Tommy. You trying to borrow money again?'

'We haven't got to that yet, thank God,' said the Flight Lieutenant. He obviously considered me incapable of intelligent speech too because before I could open my mouth, he said, 'Says he's looking for the CO's nav. Any ideas?'

'Yes, sir,' she replied. 'A-Apple took off about half an hour ago. The CO's checking out a new pilot before sending him on tonight's op. They're not due to land until just before first briefing.'

This was cutting things incredibly tight. If I didn't get off this madman's roundabout, I could well end up airborne over Germany. As an excuse for not coming to work, I didn't think it was one my editor would swallow easily. I made my excuses, saluted once more and left. It was only a short walk along the front of the hangars to the flight offices. The B Flight crew room was blue with cigarette smoke. There I found Unwin, sprawled in an armchair reading a copy of *Tee Emm*, the RAF's flight safety magazine. The rest of the crew were present as well: the two officers, pilot Charlie Brownlow and navigator Arthur Prentice; Sgt Gilroy, the Australian mid-upper gunner; the sergeant wireless operator, a rather bovine youth whose name I had yet to catch; and finally, our flight engineer, Flt Sgt Arnold Greaves. At thirty-five, Greaves was the old man of the crew and had been a merchant seaman before joining the RAF. His claim to fame was that he had initiated the squadron into the rules of Uckers, a maritime form of Ludo, complete with its own arcane vocabulary, most of it profane. Along with three others he was hunched over the Uckers board and casting obscure spells on the dice to deliver him a six by shouting "chest!" at the top of his voice.

In the admin office next door a telephone rang and the room fell silent as the duty ops clerk answered. Thirty silent prayers for the magic words "operations cancelled, all crews stand down" went up. They remained unanswered. He stuck his head round the door and called out, 'S for sugar unserviceable. Air-test delayed one hour.' S-Sugar's pilot stood up, swore and announced that he was going back to the mess. His all-NCO crew followed him out of the door. Our crew had been allotted Z-Zebra with a takeoff time of 1200 for a mission recorded in the squadron authorisation sheets as "air test, navigation and general handling."

The hands of the crew-room clock seemed to have frozen. The effort of moving up the second half of the dial against the force of gravity seemed too much for them. I was expecting the pilot to call the crew together for briefing, but at twenty-five to twelve, he looked at his watch and announced, 'All right blokes, let's get cracking.' He led the way down another highly-polished corridor and through a door marked "Flying Clothing. Authorised Personnel Only". Holding back a little in order to watch the others I found my locker and followed Gilroy's lead in my choice of clothing. The bulky thermal suit made movement almost impossible. I knew that on operations rear gunners wore an electrically heated suit over several layers of warm underclothes and on top of that a waterproof flotation suit. Last came the issue of parachutes and we trooped out to the Bedford van waiting to take us out to the dispersal where Z-Zebra would be waiting for us. The driver followed the same route I had used as a shortcut to Leckonby junction and I craned my neck as we drove past, desperate for any hint of encroaching normality. All I saw was a thin tendril of smoke rising from behind the trees which hid the station from view.

Compared to the pristine Lancaster I had flown with

the BBMF, Z-Zebra was a sorry affair. Soot streaks from its exhausts stained the top surface of the wings and a series of metal patches, riveted into place along the fuselage and hurriedly brush-painted showed where damage had been repaired. Flak? Night fighters? I shuddered at the thought.

Brownlow, as captain, went to the ground engineers' hut to sign the Form 700, Z-Zebra's servicing record, while the rest of us clambered aboard. One thing remained unchanged – that unmistakable Lancaster smell – for a brief moment my anxiety left me and I felt at home. Having flown in the rear turret on a couple of occasions I was at least able to avoid making my inexperience too obvious. Using the lid of the Elsan chemical toilet as a footstep I climbed over the tailplane spar. Then I slotted my parachute pack into its stowage on the side of the fuselage and wriggled into the confines of the turret. Once I had slid the doors behind me closed, I fastened my lap belt and plugged into the intercom and the oxygen supply.

Over the background whine of the intercom I heard Brownlow checking the crew one by one and answered, 'Rear gunner ready, skip,' trying to sound as nonchalant as I could. The start-up sequence seemed to go smoothly and soon I felt the aircraft roll forward a few feet and then stop once more as the pilot checked the brakes before continuing down the taxiway to the holding point. Just before the runway threshold stood a caravan painted in a bold red and white checkerboard pattern and as we drew alongside it, pointing down the runway, the controller flashed us a steady green light.

'All clear above and behind,' I called over the intercom and felt the aircraft shake as Greaves the flight engineer advanced the throttles to zero boost. It's funny how sometimes the mind retains minute details of long ago events but then skips the big things. I had simply forgotten how deafeningly loud it is inside a Lancaster at anything above idling RPM – the earphones in my 1940s headset did next to nothing to blot out the bellow of the four Merlin engines. As Brownlow released the brakes and Greaves pushed the throttles forward to full power, I noticed from the windsock atop the runway caravan that we had quite a strong crosswind from the left, something that would exacerbate the Lanc's tendency to swing to port during the early phase of the takeoff run. From my backwards-facing eyrie I had a grandstand view of our skipper's late appreciation of our predicament. First, he applied about half right rudder, nowhere near enough and it was only when we were almost on the grass that he fed in full rudder and I felt a couple of grabs of differential brake. Next to me, touching distance away I saw the trailing edge of the elevator controls dip down and the aircraft's tail came up in response, unmasking the rudders and giving us just enough control authority to stay on the concrete. Moments later, with a rather agricultural heave, he pulled the bomber off the runway and we were airborne. Christ knows what'll happen when he tries that in the dark with a full bomb load, I thought, shuddering at the prospect that if I didn't find Flying Officer Harrison, my chances of getting back to reality were slim.

As we climbed away from Leckonby and turned onto a northerly heading I saw the unmistakeable shape of Lincoln cathedral towering over the flatlands surrounding the city. At first glance, the countryside looked no different from the one I had flown over so many times myself. Lincoln itself was certainly smaller, with far less of the sprawl than it has today. Then I stopped myself. Today. Which "today"? What if I was stuck here in December 1943? What if this "today" was reality and my twenty-first century life lay over seventy years out of reach? Doing my best to put such thoughts out of my mind I occupied myself by trying to find familiar landmarks. In the distance, to the south of the city I could see RAF Waddington. To the north lay Scampton, but the biggest shock was the sheer number of airfields that I had only seen before as ghostly outlines in farmers' fields – barely visible crop marks, pale as skeletons under the plough. I ticked off the familiar names as we headed north; Bardney, Fiskerton, Faldingworth, Hemswell and Ludford Magna, all of them busy, bombers parked on almost every dispersal point, others flying circuits. The other difference was the smoke, every building seemed to have a chimney, all of them streaming smoke, surrounding each town we passed with a sickly yellow halo.

As we turned right to cross the coast between Grimsby and Hull, I made my first attempts at turning the turret. To my surprise it was remarkably easy. The lightest pressure on the downward sloping control levers, configured much like a racing motorbike's handlebars, was enough to swing the turret from side to side, causing the cooling slots around the barrels to howl in the slipstream. As I did so I was aware that each swing of the turret into the airflow was causing the aircraft to yaw in response. Either the pilot was used to it or had a poor feel for the controls because at no time did he attempt to correct the movement.

Once safely over the sea, we settled into the cruise

at about 2,000 feet and Brownlow gave the order to test the guns. From behind me, I felt rather than heard the rattle of Gilroy firing a long burst from the mid-upper turret and so, releasing the safety catch, I tried to do the same. Silence: the armourers must have forgotten to cock the guns. Gilroy came on the intercom, 'You asleep already, Tommy, you dozy bastard?'

'Nah, just looking for something to shoot at. A seagull at three hundred yards maybe. By the way, I reckon you missed the planet just then,' I replied. This got a laugh from the rest of the crew and seemed to break the tension long enough for me to find the cocking handles, depress the guns and send a long squirt of tracer arcing down towards the grey surface of the North Sea. Even above the roar of the engines and the slipstream, the noise was deafening and the turret filled with the smell of cordite. In a few hours I could be doing this for real, I thought, and then with embarrassment realised that I had forgotten to turn on the turret's gyroscopic gunsight. A ham-fisted pilot and a clueless rear gunner were not good portents of survival for any crew.

The rest of the flight passed uneventfully and we returned to Leckonby, where Brownlow once again either didn't notice or simply misjudged the crosswind so that Z-Zebra arrived on the runway drifting to starboard at such a rate I feared it would break the undercarriage. Luckily it held, and after fishtailing to a halt we taxied back to the dispersal we had left just over an hour earlier. While we waited for Brownlow to sign the aircraft back in, I overheard Greaves the flight engineer discussing the fuel load with one of the groundcrew. 'Only 1650 gallons,' Greaves said. 'Can't be Berlin then. Thank fuck for that.' He jumped up onto the tailboard of the lorry and announced the good news to the rest of us. 'Not Berlin tonight, lads. That's enough fuel for Hanover, but my money's on Happy Valley.'

Gilroy made a thumbs-up sign. Happy Valley – the Ruhr – it showed me how much crews feared the Big City if a mission to one of the most heavily defended regions of the Reich could be seen as a relief. Buoyed by the relative good news, the mood in the lorry that came to take us back to the flight office was jovial to start with, but after we reached our destination and handed back our parachutes, a collective realisation that the next time would be for real, stilled the chatter as each man retreated within his shell.

The atmosphere of artificial normality resumed when we returned to the flight office. Greaves rounded up a foursome to play Uckers, others sat and read. Perhaps, like me they were pretending to read – anything to banish the reality that waited for the unlucky few in the skies over occupied Europe.

Half past three. Surely A-Apple should be back by now, but there was no sign. Then, at twenty to four I heard a Lancaster overhead – it had to be Preston and his crew. If they landed straight away I might just get a chance to grab Harrison before the four o'clock navigators' and captains' briefing. I pretended to stifle a yawn, stretched, got up and ambled to the door with what I hoped was the nonchalant air of a man in search of nothing more than a breath of fresh air. Outside, it was already starting to get dark and the western skyline was tinged with pink. However, A-Apple didn't land. I watched the aircraft do a flapless circuit and, as expected, the young pilot got way too tight downwind, overshot the runway centreline and went round again.

His second attempt was far better and the next circuit was done on three engines, with one prop feathered to simulate battle damage. This time, the execution was faultless and on the next approach A-Apple landed and taxied in. The same driver who had collected us from our dispersal delivered Preston's crew and, to my horror I only counted five men walking back towards the flying clothing section. One of the remaining two pulled off his flying helmet to display an unruly black mop of a fringe, handed his parachute pack and harness to one of the others and sprinted over to the operations block by the control tower. Harrison. The shorter, more burly figure trotting in his wake with a seat type parachute pack slung over his shoulder had to be Preston. My last chance had gone.

Disconsolate, I wandered back in. Gilroy looked up at me over the top of his newspaper. 'Been out for a swift pint, Tommy?' he asked.

I ignored the bait. 'No, just went out to stretch my legs. There's a lovely sunset out there, you ought to take a look.'

'Fuck the sunset. It's seeing tomorrow's sunrise that interests me,' he snarled back.

Once again the hands of the clock seemed to freeze as they inched desperately slowly towards the time for the general briefing. By twenty-five past five, seventeen crews, over a hundred men, were seated in rows behind trestle tables waiting, in a haze of blue cigarette and pipe smoke, for the curtains at the far end of the briefing room to be pulled away and the target revealed. Outside the doors, armed guards were posted. I wondered for a moment whether they were to keep intruders out or backsliders like me in. Harrison and the rest of the CO's crew were in the front row and there was no way I could get to him.

At exactly five thirty a voice from the back of the briefing room called us all to attention and over a hundred chairs scraped the highly polished floor as the Station Commander and his section leaders marched down the aisle between the rows of men. A tall man with a ruddy complexion and sporting the traditional 'wizard prang' RAF moustache, he strode up onto the low stage in front of the curtains and stood for a moment, regarding us intently, almost as though he knew there was an imposter in their midst. 'Gentlemen, please be seated. You may smoke.' He strode to the back of the stage and, with a theatrical flourish, pulled the draw-cord and the curtains parted. The route to the target and back was marked out in red ribbon, a series of straight lines and dog-legs reaching into the middle of Germany, beyond the Ruhr but at least 150 miles short of Berlin. A chorus of gasps, muttering, whistles and swearing went round the room. The Group Captain had heard worse before and continued, affecting not to notice. 'Your target for tonight, gentlemen, is Brunswick, the city of Prince Henry the Lion. Your objective is simple, to destroy the city's capacity to support the enemy's war effort. It is a target that Leckonby's squadrons have visited before – the Commander-in-Chief himself wants it made clear to all units taking part that if you do your job properly tonight, you won't have to go back. Hamburg no longer functions as a city, his orders are that you reduce Brunswick to a similar state. As you will hear shortly, it is an important manufacturing centre, a key hub of the Nazi railway system and also a garrison town for an SS Division. I will now hand you over to the station intelligence officer who will give you further details. Good luck, gentlemen, and God speed.'

The same plump, shiny Flight Lieutenant whom I had met earlier now took the floor. He moved to the lectern at the side of the stage and peered at us over a pair of half-moon glasses. 'Good evening, gentlemen. As the Station Commander has just told you, Brunswick, or *Braunschweig* to its inhabitants, is an important industrial centre. Population of 150,000, many of whom work in the armaments industry. On the aiming point map which you will see later, the town has a VW motor works that is a major producer of lorries for the German army. There is also a chemical works, railway repair and marshalling yards and an SS barrack complex. Just like Stettin and Konigsberg, the old town is comprised of closely packed wooden buildings which will burn well.

'Previous attacks have been made on this target but with varying success. Our old enemy, 'creepback' is why you are having to return to the target tonight. I cannot stress strongly enough how important it is to find and bomb the target markers. We don't want any 'fringe merchants' on *this* station.'

Gilroy leant across and whispered to me. 'Easy to say when you're safe and sound, sat on your fat arse behind a desk.'

The intelligence briefing continued – history of previous attacks, known flak positions, night fighter beacons, escape and evasion, conduct in the event of capture. With the exception of the sprog pilot's crew who all took copious notes, the others ignored what was to them nothing more than a warm-up act. Cynicism came early in a tour and hardened with each trip a crew

132

survived.

Next at the dais was the navigation leader, a boyish Flight Lieutenant who looked barely old enough to be allowed out after dark, let alone spend his nights over Germany. Solely by having survived 20 trips he was by default the senior navigator, four previous nav leaders having gone missing in as many weeks. He ran through an edited version of the navs' and captains' brief that he had delivered earlier. With the aid of a billiard cue he traced the route into the target. From the Lincolnshire coast the line continued towards Denmark before turning onto a southerly heading, passing between the two known hot-spots of Bremen and Hamburg on a heading that the planners clearly hoped would fool the German air defence commanders into thinking that Berlin was the target. Next it skirted round Munster and Fassberg before turning almost due south for the final run. The route home was more direct: a north-westerly leg to avoid the Ruhr, with a couple of dog-legs to avoid fighter beacons and known flak concentrations and then a straight line to a landfall at Southwold in Suffolk.

Heights, heading, turning points and timings accurate to the second were all fine in theory, but the crews knew that however good the plan, it would soon crumble in the face of reality. The other unspoken truth was that many crews deserted their assigned heights at the first hint of night fighter activity in order to seek sanctuary at higher altitude.

I saw Prentice, our navigator, lean towards Brownlow and heard him say in a stage whisper, 'I think Butch Harris is playing join the dots with flak concentrations tonight.'

The bombing leader then took his turn to brief us.

133

The use of 'window' to blind the enemy's radar was to start well before the enemy coast, an announcement that caused groans among the bomb aimers. It was their duty to throw the bundles of aluminised paper strips out of the flare chute at preset intervals – a tedious and much hated task. However, the grumbling stopped as the briefing moved on to the focus of tonight's mission. 'Gentlemen,' he said in a strong New Zealand accent, 'your aiming point is the island in the centre of the Altstadt on which St Blasius' Cathedral sits.' He walked over to an easel and pulled away the blanket covering it to reveal what looked like a piece of abstract art. 'If cloud cover prevents accurate visual marking, this is an estimation of what the H2S picture of the target will look like on your radar screens when approached on a southerly heading. Bombing height is 18,000 feet, stick spacing 30 yards with a load comprising one 4,000 high capacity, and a mix of 250 and 500 lb GP bombs – fusing nose instantaneous – plus incendiaries.' Unwin, seated next to me wrote this all down in a childish round hand, his tongue following each loop of the pencil.

The engineer leader gave his briefing next. Fuel loads, boost and mixture settings were all covered before he handed over to the signals leader who spoke about frequencies, broadcast winds and use of 'Fishpond', an additional screen of the H2S radar system which the wireless operator could use to detect enemy aircraft approaching from astern. What I knew and they didn't is that post-war analysis had shown that the Germans were capable of homing onto H2S transmissions.

Last of all came my specialisation – specialisation, now there was an irony – air gunnery. Even as a first-timer it was obvious to me that wasn't a lot the gunnery leader could say that he hadn't said during his previous briefings. Recently promoted into dead men's flying boots, he stood five feet tall at the most and spoke in a strong Cockney accent which at times I found hard to follow. 'Stay alert, and if you feel you're dozing off, take your 'wakey-wakey' pills. Don't assume everything twin engined is hostile – there are Mossies out there supporting us tonight, so if in doubt call a corkscrew, don't just blaze away at everything you see.'

The final act in this little drama was led by the met officer. He covered times of moonrise, moonset and sunrise – this last announcement was greeted by a cheer. He repeated the wind velocities along the route that he had given at the earlier briefing. All knew that these were estimates at best and that crews relying on forecast winds alone to navigate could well end up tens of miles off track by the time they reached the target area. For those lucky enough to make it back to Leckonby the following morning, light mist was forecast. Lastly, and almost as an afterthought, he mentioned the possibility of light to moderate icing during the climb and on the leg towards the Danish coast.

When the met forecaster had sat down, the squadron commander, Wg Cdr Preston, a man with the build and swagger of a rugby forward, walked purposefully into the centre of the stage, scanning the upturned faces, looking for what? I wondered. Fear? Yes, that was there in abundance but no one dared show it in front of their comrades. Disbelief in the cause? Very probably, but that depended on which cause Preston held most dearly. From what I had heard of the man, it was a DFC and better still a DSO to go with it, followed by rapid promotion. A pre-war regular, he had spent the first four years of hostilities at flying training establishments – this was his first operational tour. His narrow-set eyes flickered along our row, missed me out and settled somewhere in the vicinity of Brownlow, our pilot. Then, looking up towards the metal rafters of the briefing room as though searching for divine inspiration he started his briefing in a high, reedy voice that, to me anyway, completely detracted from the image he was trying to present. It was little more than a series of platitudes – a head prefect encouraging the first XV before the big match against a rival school – stay in the stream, stick to your briefed heights, keep out of the flak belts, no weaving and no shortcutting off target – the last two orders were greeted with an undercurrent of muttering and from just behind me I heard the word 'bollocks'. Preston must have heard too but chose to ignore it. As the homily came to its conclusion I permitted myself a look back over my shoulder to see rows of upturned faces, all looking in the same direction. Then it hit me. This, or a scene just like it, was exactly as described by the security guard I had met in the pub. How could he have known?

The room was called to attention and the station commander, the squadron CO and briefing officers left. A babble of voices broke out as crews clustered together to discuss what they had just heard. I tried to find Harrison in the scrum of bodies but he was nowhere to be seen. The rest of his crew, including Preston, were there but the one man who I hoped could save me from this madness had gone.

After the briefing, the melee coalesced into seven-man clumps and I joined the other NCOs in our crew for the short walk to the sergeants' mess for the traditional pre-flight meal of bacon and eggs. Someone made a joke about 'fattening us up for the kill.' It wasn't very funny and, in the circumstances almost certainly not original, but it provoked a ripple of forced laughter from the crews sharing our table.

Then it was merely a question of killing time. The condemned men had eaten a hearty meal and now all that remained was for fate to decide who lived and who died. Some went back to their huts and read or wrote last letters, others drifted down to the flight office and carried on reading, but eventually, after a wait that seemed to last forever, Brownlow called his crew together and we went through to the flying clothing section to get ready. By the time I had clambered into the seemingly endless layers of insulation both under and over the electrically-heated suit that both gunners in a Lancaster always wore, I was sweating and red-faced. Unfamiliar catches and fastenings left my fingers and thumbs raw and bleeding.

At last fully kitted, we collected flight rations and escape kits, life jackets, parachute harnesses and packs. As the seven of us shuffled out to the waiting truck, it seemed to me that we embodied the start of Wilfred Owen's poem *Dulce et Decorum est*, 'Bent double, like old beggars under sacks, knock-kneed, coughing like hags…' In an unconscious act of life imitating art, Gilroy lit a cigarette and at the first puff, proceeded to hack and splutter as though his last moment had come.

It was fully dark now and in the blackout all I could see was the outline of each waiting Lancaster we passed and the red firefly dots of the groundcrews' cigarettes. With a jolt, the truck came to a halt and the other crew sharing it with us climbed down. We exchanged shouts of good luck and they disappeared into the darkness. In the cold night air, the sweat had condensed and I could feel it running down my back. If that freezes while we're airborne I thought, it's going to be a long, uncomfortable trip.

All the crew, except the pilot who had gone to the dispersal hut to sign the Form 700, gathered around the rear door chatting about nothing in particular while we waited for him to come back. I found myself worrying that I wouldn't be able to squeeze into the cramped turret with all this extra clothing padding me out to twice my normal girth. More worrying still was the prospect that I seemed to be trapped in a world that wasn't mine and with no immediate hope of escape. Brownlow, our skipper returned. Why in God's name I considered him 'our' skipper was beyond me. It was as though I was slowly coming to accept my fate. No, I told myself, you mustn't give in, this isn't real, you are not going to bomb Brunswick tonight, you're going to get into your nice, warm, twenty-first century car and drive back to Lincoln. This isn't real, it can't be.

'Right-ho, chaps. All aboard.' Without seeing his face, the tone of forced nonchalance in Brownlow's voice was enough to tell me just how frightened he was. He turned away, heaved his seat-pack parachute onto his shoulder and led the way up the aluminium ladder. The irony of turning left at the aircraft door was not lost on me – no business class on this trip and it might not even be a return, I thought with a shudder.

My fears about getting into the turret were realised. Swaddled in what felt like a cross between a straight-jacket and a fat suit I could neither bend nor turn properly. First I sat on my lap belt and couldn't free it. Next I couldn't find the lead to plug in my electrically-heated undersuit.

Then came a sight familiar to me from my earlier visits to Leckonby: a single green Very flare arced into the night sky, bathing the dispersal and the trees behind it in its unearthly glare. I watched it bounce once and then splutter out. So enthralled was I with this spectacle that I dropped one of my gloves, and by the time I finally got plugged in to the intercom, two of the engines were already running. I paused long enough to get my breath and checked in. 'Rear gunner on.'

'Nice of you to show up, Tommy. Thought you'd nipped off for a pint,' said Brownlow.

The others all laughed and Unwin's voice came over the intercom from his mid-upper turret, 'Nah, lazy sod was asleep already. Past his bedtime.' More proof, not that I needed it, that my alter-ego was not well regarded by the rest of the crew. If only they knew the half of it, I thought.

All four engines were running now and I felt the turret twitch slightly as the hydraulic pressure rose. I swung it left and right and, following Unwin's lead, confirmed that all was serviceable. We then waited while Brownlow, assisted by Greaves, the flight engineer, sitting just to his right, carried out the post-start checks. The engine note rose and fell as they exercised the propeller constant speed controls, then another almost imperceptible drop in RPM as each of the two magnetos on the four engines were checked in turn, and then it was time to go. Inching forward, a quick dab of the brakes to check they were working and we turned onto the taxiway, waved on by our groundcrew who were standing outside the hut, the clouds of condensation from their breath lit by a glimmer of yellow brightness showing through the half open door. Just behind us, uncomfortably close it seemed to me, I could see another Lancaster following. Soon, all along the taxiway I could see a string of red and green lights marking the wingtips of the aircraft behind us. Had it not been so bizarre, the spectacle of the amber outer taxiway lights and the blue inners framing this procession of lumbering black giants, could have almost been described as beautiful. However, all I could think of was the prospect of what might happen to us if Brownlow mishandled the takeoff. With a full bomb load and nearly two thousand gallons of volatile fuel on board, the best we could hope for was a quick end.

As the queue of departing aircraft inched forward and we neared the runway threshold I saw a large crowd of well-wishers, all come to see us off. As the landing light from the aircraft ahead of us swept across the group I recognised the Station Commander waving and giving the thumbs up to each crew in turn. Slightly behind him and out of his line of sight, a young WAAF was waving what looked like a pair of bloomers.

Finally, our turn came. The earlier crosswind that caused Brownlow almost to leave the runway during our daytime takeoff had dropped, and the windsock hung limp and damp, wrapped around its pole. Still conditions, though, were potentially even more dangerous – with no headwind to help the wings generate lift, the takeoff run would be long, leaving us with no safety margin in the event of an engine failure. I could tell Brownlow was nervous too. As he started the turn onto the runway he grabbed at the brakes and instead of being a smooth curve, our turn onto the runway centreline was a series of lurches and heaves.

So this was it. Somehow I had assumed, deep down, that this madness would end, leaving me to return to my car a wiser and chastened man. Instead I felt the skipper release the brakes and heard the engines' roar increase to a deafening bellow as Z-Zebra accelerated agonisingly slowly down the runway. I managed a desultory wave to the crowd and closed my eyes, convinced we were never going to get airborne in the 4,000 feet of concrete available to us. Finally, after what seemed like hours, the tail of the aircraft rose. I risked a look back but distance was difficult to estimate because all I could see of the runway from my turret was two tapering rows of white lights converging to a point that looked a horribly long way off. Just when I had convinced myself we were going to die in a blazing fireball, Brownlow snatched the Lancaster off the ground and into a shallow climb. Almost instantaneously the white lights stopped and I saw the red end of runway lights flash past only a few tens of feet below me.

The calm monotone of Prentice's voice put me to shame. 'Airborne at 2016 and 15 seconds, skipper.'

With a thump that I felt rather than heard, the undercarriage came up and locked into place. I had no idea of our rate of climb, but we still seemed dangerously low and I tried to remember how high the Lincolnshire Wolds were. We had taken off from the easterly runway so somewhere not far ahead was, literally, our first hurdle and a very solid one at that.

As we got higher, the western skyline lightened and gave me another view of the pale reds and oranges of the sunset. All around us like a million fireflies I could see the navigation lights of other bombers – from Coningsby, Woodhall Spa, East Kirkby, Binbrook, Metheringham and from the airfields north of the Humber, the sky was alive with aircraft.

As we crossed the coast Brownlow switched off the navigation lights and only the occasional buffet of turbulence from another aircraft's slipstream told us that we were not entirely alone in the darkness. Shortly afterwards we entered cloud and the skipper called the crew to check our oxygen masks which told me we must be at around 12,000 feet in the climb. Already, the discomfort was intense. The electrically-heated suit was burning my lower legs but the small of my back was freezing cold and my fingertips were already starting to go numb.

The feeling of isolation was overpowering. Outside was a dark impenetrable soup of cloud and the roar of the four Merlins, set at maximum continuous power for the climb, numbed my senses. I checked my watch. We had only been airborne for just over half an hour but already it seemed like a lifetime. Then, a flash of light caught my eye, then another. I had seen this before – St Elmo's fire – I watched in fascination as bright purple, magma-like blobs formed on the top of my turret, ran forwards against the slipstream and disappeared out of view up the fuselage. To left and right, the aircraft's fins were tipped with halos of lime green. The others had seen it too. Gilroy's Aussie twang came over the intercom, 'Glow Gremlins, skipper.'

'Thanks, mid-upper,' replied Brownlow. 'We've got it up front too.'

Beautiful though it was, I remembered well that St

Elmo's fire meant we were either inside or uncomfortably close to cumulonimbus cloud. Aircraft and cu-nims, as they're known, don't mix. Another buffeting – slipstream? Possibly, but there it was again, more intense and longer-lasting this time. Then a stomach-churning sensation of weightlessness followed by a thump told me that my fears were justified. Another jolt threw me against the turret side. Turbulence is rarely strong enough to destroy an aircraft in flight although it can and does happen. That wasn't the main threat though. Cu-nims have other ways of killing aviators and that was my big fear – icing. To get a better view of the fins I turned the turret as far as I could to one side and craned my neck in an effort to check the leading edge of the vertical stabiliser for ice but it was too dark. However, my ears told me what my eyes feared to see – a sound like a stone hitting a tin shed, a single metallic clang. Then another, and then a volley of blows. It was ice, the airman's deadliest natural foe, forming on the propellers and then being flung off into the fuselage side. By now the turbulence had become so bad that the aircraft rolled and yawed like a skiff on the open sea. Bang, there it was again, bang, bang, bang – impacts right beside my head, regular now, bang, bang, bang.

I turned to look, my neck stiff and limbs aching. A malevolent giant seemed to be hammering on the Perspex just by my right ear. For a moment I felt like a spectator, looking in at myself from a distance, but then a blinding light brought me back to reality. I put my hand up to shield my eyes. Faces. Two of them peering intently at me from close to. This wasn't possible. Warm now, not cold, but my neck ached abominably. With horror I realised that the roar of the engines had stopped

– for a moment I couldn't work out why. Then it dawned on me. I was back in my car, the engine was still turning over and a policeman was banging on the driver's window while his colleague rocked the car in an effort to wake me. I opened the window.

'Thank Christ you're alive,' said the first one. 'We heard the engine running and thought it was someone trying to top themselves. Are you all right, sir?'

'Yes thanks,' I replied, my voice thick with sleep. 'I must've dozed off.'

He thrust his head through the open window, putting his face uncomfortably close to mine. 'Have you been drinking, sir?' he asked.

'No, not a drop.'

'Then do you mind telling us what you're doing, sir?' I noticed the word "sir" positively dripped with irony.

I showed him my press card. 'I know this is going to sound daft, but there've been rumours of hauntings at the airfield and here at the station, so I came to take a look. I left the heater on to keep warm and must've dozed off.'

They looked at one another in a way that suggested disappointment that they couldn't arrest me for anything, bade me a grudging goodnight and returned to their car. I waited until their headlights had faded from sight, turned off the engine, got out of the car and walked over to the station. It was as I remembered it – derelict. No smoke rose from the stump of what had once been a chimney stack. I checked the time – half past ten.

Not for the first time since my accident I seriously doubted my own sanity. What I had experienced was too

144

real to have been a dream. It was as though the hallucinations had breached yet another line of my defences and were now invading my sleeping world too. How could it have been so vivid? I wondered as I walked back to the car, rubbing the sleep from my eyes. I got in, started the engine and put on my seat belt. As I did so, I felt a sharp pain as though something was digging into my chest. Fumbling inside my shirt, my hand closed round the cause. Slung around my neck on a short loop of parachute cord were two hard, flat objects. I slipped the cord over my head and turned the interior light on to get a better look. What I held in my hand left me numb with disbelief. One was circular and brick red in colour, the other, lozenge-shaped and dark green – RAF identity discs. Both were stamped with the same details: *Handley W A, 923041, C of E.*

Chapter Ten

My mind was a jumble of tangled thoughts as I drove back to Lincoln that night. The worsening of my hallucinations was something the doctor had warned me might happen, but how did that explain the two very solid identity discs that now sat in my pocket? Hallucinations are not supposed to take solid form and yet another one just had. First the cat's paw, then a pint of bitter and now a set of identity discs.

When it came to opening the front door my hands were shaking so badly that I took several attempts to get the key in the lock. Once inside, I turned on all the lights, just like I used to when I was little. I hated the dark then, fearing the things that lurked unseen behind curtains, inside wardrobes and, horror of horrors, maybe under my bed. It was never any use the grown-ups telling me that monsters didn't exist – what if nobody had thought to tell the monsters? Then what?

But now the rules of the game had changed. The monsters inside my head had indeed taken physical form and together we were locked in a crazy lovers' embrace, clinging to each other like two drunks swaying across a dance floor. They were haunting me and I was haunting them. No, I shook my head and knocked back a glass of cold water from the tap, none of this was possible, but yet all the evidence in front of me shouted the opposite. Not only was it possible, it was horribly real. I had to find out more.

Sleep was out of the question. The need to understand what was happening to me was too great, so I switched on my PC and opened the web page of the

Commonwealth War Graves Commission. With trembling hands I typed the casualty search details: surname – Handley, service – RAF, date of death – between December 1943 and May 1945, service number – 923041, initials – W A.

Return.

An egg timer.

An eternity.

Then the result I was dreading, but knew deep down before I saw it:

Name: Handley, Walter Albert

Rank: Sergeant

Service Number: 923041

Date of death: 21 December 1944

Age: 22

Regiment/Service: Royal Air Force Volunteer Reserve, 362 Squadron

Cemetery/Memorial Name: Runnymede Memorial

Additional Information: son of Francis George and Winifred Grace Handley of Oxford Avenue, Wimbledon, SW20.

So Tommy and his crew hadn't survived long. I did a search for the other members of the crew. As expected, I found them. They had all died the same night and were also commemorated on the Runnymede Memorial to the missing: Brownlow, the crew's skipper; Prentice the navigator; Unwin the bomb aimer; Greaves, the flight engineer and old man of the crew. Then came two names I didn't know: Sergeants Thomas and Barker; one of whom was probably the wireless operator whose name I had never caught, but where was Gilroy? I did another search, widening the dates and found him straight away – Barry James Gilroy of Freemantle,

Western Australia, date of death, 19th December 1943, buried at Leckonby Parish Church. Tonight was the 18th and however hard I wanted that to be a coincidence, an unpleasant feeling that set the hairs bristling on the back of my neck, told me it wasn't.

Bleary-eyed from a lack of sleep and with my neck still aching from having dozed off in an awkward position in the car, I made my way into work the following morning and went through the motions of writing a piece on the opening of a new meat processing factory near Scunthorpe. The irony of forcing myself to complete such an eye-wateringly dull task after my experiences, if that is indeed what they were, of the previous night, weighed heavily upon me and I fretted and fussed to get the words onto the page, but with little success.

To take my mind off the news story I turned to the National Archives website and searched for the Operational Record Book for 362 Squadron, using the Lincoln Post's credit card to pay the small access fee.

During my time in the RAF, as a young Flight Lieutenant it had been my task to write the Squadron's monthly entry in the Operational Record Book, better known as 'the Form 540' or the 'ORB'.

The Royal Air Force is a creature of habit and the format of the ORB has remained almost unchanged over the years. During periods of active service, the ORB is made up of two documents: firstly, the Form 540, effectively the squadron diary which I had written each month; and secondly, the Form 541, the record of 'Work Carried Out' on each operation. During the intense period of operations from 1939 to 1945, the ORB was updated on a daily basis. Luckily for me, 362

Squadron's wartime scribes had been meticulous in their work and the results of every mission, together with the fate of each aircraft and its crew, were recorded.

I located the entry for the night of the 18th of December 1943 and, half afraid of what I might read, found confirmation that whatever had happened to me the previous evening, it could not have been a dream. As I read, I felt the goose-pimples spreading across my skin and my mouth went dry with fear.

'Place – Leckonby. Date – 18.12.43. Summary of Events – Weather fair after earlier showers clearing to the east. Operations were ordered, 16 aircraft taking part (1 u/s after start).' I scanned down the list of aircraft captains: *'W/C Preston (a/c A-Apple), S/L Bates...'* then I found the name I was looking for, *'F/O Brownlow (a/c Z-Zebra).'* I read on, a cold feeling of dread creeping along my spine. There it was, written over seventy years ago. All my worst fears – a detailed account of what I had experienced less than twenty-four hours previously.

'Aircraft ED302 (Z). Captain F/O Brownlow. Duty – Bombing Brunswick. Time Up 2016/Time Down 2357. Severe icing over N Sea caused loss of height. Bomb load jettisoned inert. Fuselage skin damaged by ice flung from propellers. Damage assessed as CAT A (light, repairable at unit).'

Reading further down the list it seemed that Z-Zebra wasn't the only aircraft to suffer from icing. D-Dog had ditched thirty miles from the Dutch coast. A later entry in the ORB showed that its crew had been rescued by a Canadian Navy corvette.

As I read on I saw that "Press-On" Preston, 362's squadron commander, was well named.

'Aircraft PA693 (A), Captain W/C Preston. Duty – Bombing Brunswick. Time up 2009/Time Down 0230. A/C encountered severe icing and was unable to maintain height. 4000 lb HC and 4x 250 lb GP bombs jettisoned over sea. Crew continued to target area using dead reckoning (10/10ths cloud with tops estimated at 30,000 feet). No target markers seen and H2S unserviceable, so remaining bomb load (250 lb and incendiaries) released on distance/time basis. Target photographs inconclusive.'

Whatever his crews thought of him, Preston was not lacking in courage. To carry on to the target knowing that other crews had turned back and the protection offered by safety in numbers had gone with them, took guts. By today's standards he would probably have been criticised for taking unnecessary risks, pressing on alone, bombing on distance and time meant that he had endangered a valuable aircraft and its crew all for the sake of dropping a few bombs, probably in open fields, miles from the intended target. What really drove him? I wondered. Was this what courage looked like? Was it ambition for medal ribbons and promotion? Or was it the more prosaic and most common reason for bravery – the fear of letting your comrades down? Whatever it was, only Preston and two other crews managed to deliver their bomb loads that night and the C-in-C's threat of having to return to Brunswick to finish the job would no doubt have been put into practice. What actually happened on the second visit to Prince Henry the Lion's city in late March 1944, I will come to shortly, but there is much more I need to tell you first.

***

Settling to anything resembling work was beyond me so I left the office on the pretext of following up a story, called the doctor on my mobile phone and was lucky enough to get an appointment later that afternoon.

I sat in the stuffy, overheated waiting room for over an hour past the time the receptionist had given me. When eventually I got into the doctor's consulting rooms, one look at his tired features told me that, on balance, his day had probably been worse than mine and my plans to deliver some well-chosen remarks about his time-keeping evaporated at once. He listened patiently while I told him how much worse my hallucinations had got and failed to show any surprise when I told him that solid objects from my hallucinations were still there after the visions had gone.

His answer to my last question was sympathetic. 'No, Mr Price,' he said. 'You're not going mad. I told you this could happen. The hallucinations are getting worse, that's all. They can be very realistic. Just try to concentrate on what's possible and what's not.'

'You mean the identity discs aren't real?' I took them out of my pocket and placed them on the desk in front of him. 'Here, take a look.'

He picked them up, turning the two pressed fibre discs over in his hands. 'No, they're real enough. But there's a far simpler explanation.'

'Go on.'

'They may date from 1943 as you say, but they didn't come from someone in one of your hallucinations or from some non-existent spirit world. You've simply forgotten where you got them and your subconscious has very thoughtfully filled in the gaps.'

His tired, bloodshot eyes were fixed on mine, watching carefully for a reaction. I looked away, embarrassed. 'Yes, that must be it…' I heard my voice trailing away. 'It's just that it was so… ' I hesitated.

'Real? That's exactly the problem, Mr Price. The kind of hallucinations you're having can be incredibly vivid.'

Who was fooling whom? However much I wanted to believe him, a nagging voice told me that everything I had seen at Leckonby, and even here in Lincoln, was real. Impossible, but real.

'So what's the answer?' I asked.

He tapped his pen on his prescription pad, never taking his eyes off me for a moment. A rare glimmer of winter sunlight through the dirty window panes showed up the dandruff on his cheap suit jacket. 'I can give you a referral.'

'To the funny farm?'

'That's not a term we use these days, Mr Price. You're not mad, nor are you mentally ill. However, I think you need further assessment – first neurological and then psychiatric.' I made to interrupt but he held up a hand to silence me. 'As I've just told you,' he continued. 'You're not mentally ill, but if we don't get you the right care – and I'm not talking about stronger pills – you could end up that way.'

I nodded my acquiescence. 'And then what?'

'It all depends what the specialists find. But you may have to face the possibility that it may not be a good idea for you to carry on working full time.' He looked down at my notes. 'You're fifty-six, Mr Price. I presume you have a Royal Air Force pension?'

'I do.'

'Well, with what you'll get in sickness and other benefits, you'll probably earn as much as you do now.'

'I'd hardly call it earning.'

The doctor tutted and waved an admonitory finger at me. I noticed it was stained yellow by nicotine. He said, 'There's no stigma involved in asking for what you're entitled to, Mr Price. I regularly see people far fitter and younger than you asking to be signed off so they can go 'on the sick' as they call it. Let me make a couple of phone calls, eh?'

I nodded once more, thanked him for his time and the repeat prescription, and left the surgery, pleased to be breathing fresh air again. However, the idea of giving up work somehow seemed immoral and as I walked up Steep Hill towards home, I felt ill at ease.

As soon as I got in, I phoned my editor and told him I was sick but would be in tomorrow. He made the right noises but I knew him well enough to detect the irritation in his voice. Derek Bennett was one of the old school, and unless you were dead or had recently lost one or more limbs, then he expected you to show up for work.

I settled down in front of my PC and tried to carry on with the research I was doing on the planning application procedure. Having lost their battle against the building of the housing estate on the airfield, *The Lags* had now turned to tilting at the turbines of the wind farm, and their futile struggle was back in the news. However hard I tried I just couldn't settle to the task and my mind wandered back to the previous night. I knew it wasn't a hallucination, so who was I trying to fool by telling my doctor about it?

A grey winter's afternoon merged imperceptibly

into darkness and I sat down in front of the TV, trying to force myself to watch the seasonal inanities that all channels were showing in the run-up to Christmas. By nine o' clock my head was nodding and so I decided to have an early night. For some reason I decided that a glass of whisky before turning in would be a good idea. One glass became three and then a fourth. Whether I fell asleep or passed out is debatable, but at least I managed to do so without any visits from whatever it was that was haunting my subconscious.

At just before midnight I awoke with a start. My mouth was dry and a thin band of pain had wrapped itself round my forehead in a way that only whisky can induce. Sleep was now far away and my mind inevitably drifted back to RAF Leckonby and the events of the previous evening. Screwing my eyes tight shut I tried to think of other things, but even through closed lids I was aware of a cascade of bright, coloured lights, not unlike the St Elmo's fire I had seen dancing on the fuselage of the Lancaster – I knew the symptoms well by now. A hallucination was on its way.

I got up and turned on the light. Clearly, sleep was out of the question for now so I decided to read more of 632 Squadron's Operational Record Book online. As I shuffled towards my desk, it seemed to be tilting at a funny angle and then slowly rocking back to lean the other way. I swallowed two blue and white capsules washed down with a tumbler of water, and by the time the log-in process was complete, the desk seemed to have stabilised.

Even more awake now and nerves jangling, I needed a drink. The tumbler I had drunk from earlier was engraved with the name and logo of a whisky distiller.

It's a drink I used to like, but I had found out the hard way that it didn't like me. However, to borrow Kipling's words, "*the burnt fool's bandaged finger goes wabbling back to the fire*," and I poured myself half a glassful, on the feeble pretext that it would help me get back to sleep. Once more, it did nothing of the sort. I took another, promising myself this would be my last and final glass. After all, the doctor had warned me not to mix drink with the pills he had prescribed. Still I didn't feel drowsy – far from it, I was buzzing. Self-delusion can be a powerful temptress and she guided my hand to the bottle again. Just one more.

I squinted at my PC screen, trying to bring it back into focus. I still couldn't read it properly and my head began to ache. Why weren't the pills working? A movement caught my eye and I started in fright. To my relief, it was just a hallucination, in the familiar form of the ginger cat that walked along the kitchen worktop. This time, instead of continuing and disappearing through the wall, the cat stopped, sat down and looked at me. I put down the whisky glass and slowly made my way towards him. As I got closer, he stood up and turned towards me. I reached a hand out to stroke him, but faster than I could react, a paw full of needles lashed out and tore the back of my hand. I swore, and jumping back, raised my bloodied hand to my mouth. The cat took one last disdainful look at me, sauntered across the worktop and disappeared through the wall.

Badly shaken, after washing my hand under the cold tap, I went to look for the box of plasters which I seemed to remember lived in one of my desk drawers. It was too dark to see properly so I flicked on the desk lamp. The bulb gave a loud pop and all the lights in the house went out. Bloody great, that was all I needed. Fumbling in the darkness I managed to find the right cupboard and my hand closed around the torch. I turned it on. Nothing. The batteries were as one with the Dodo. As my eyes grew more accustomed to the dark I could just make out the pale rectangle formed by the moonlight shining through the kitchen curtains. I didn't fancy navigating the stairs down to the cellar and the fuse box in the pitch dark, so I opened the curtains. What I saw made me recoil in horror.

What was left of the man's face was blistered and red. Below an empty left eye socket, his skin hung down in sheets. The rest of his head was covered with a tight-fitting leather helmet. I staggered back, hitting the kitchen table and tumbling, off balance, to the floor. When I had picked myself up, the apparition was standing no more than two feet in front of me. He was dressed in a bulky one-piece suit with what looked like a parachute harness over the top of it. The cloth was charred and I saw, as he turned to face me that he had no arm from the left elbow downwards, a small length of bone protruding from his torn flesh glistened white. A powerful stench of burning and decay filled the room.

In spite of his injuries, I realised with horror that I knew him. It was Gilroy, the Aussie mid-upper gunner. Through a charred, lopsided gash of a mouth he spoke to me. 'Oh, wide awake now, are we, Tommy? Bit bloody late, isn't it?'

I turned to run but tripped over a kitchen chair and sprawled across the tiles. He picked up my whisky glass, holding it to the light. 'Skipper told you about this, didn't he Tommy? Keep off the sauce and you'll stay awake, he said.' With that he smashed the glass to the floor and took a pace towards me. 'But no, you wouldn't bloody listen. Hope you're proud of yourself.'

I tried to crawl away but with muscles petrified into inaction, all I managed was a few feet towards the kitchen door. 'Leave me alone,' I whimpered. 'You've got the wrong man. My name's not Tommy…'

'You answer to it quick enough when it's someone else's round.'

This had to be a nightmare, but the pain that stabbed through my leg as I knelt on a piece of broken whisky glass told me otherwise. 'What do you want?'

'Want?' he replied. 'I want you to stay off the booze. Then maybe you won't fall asleep on the job and six other poor buggers won't end up like me.' Then, he turned away from me and walked through the wall not far from where the cat had made its exit moments before.

Half stumbling, half running, with tears coursing down my face, I launched myself down the cellar stairs, pushing the door open with my elbow. My hands scrabbled against the rough brickwork until, after what felt like a lifetime, they found the plastic casing of the fuse box. I pushed the master switch back up and was rewarded with a pool of light shining across the foot of the stairs.

I put my foot on the first step but my legs gave way from under me. No sooner had I managed to crawl to the top than the fear, combined with the stench from the apparition, overwhelmed me and I only just made it to the lavatory in time before being copiously sick.

The rest of my night was spent curled up in the foetal position on the bathroom floor, with my back hard up against the bolted door. At around three in the morning, merciful sleep found me at last, but at the slightest sound I snapped awake. By six thirty the pain from lying on the cold, hard tiles and the throbbing of the cuts in my knee and hand were too much to bear any longer and I forced myself to get up.

Outside it was still dark and the glare of the kitchen lights combined with the after-effects of last night's whisky to produce a bilious, griping ache that clamped my head like a vice. Cupping my hands to the pane, I risked a quick look out through the kitchen window into my small courtyard garden. All was as normal, and the only reminder of my visitor was a lingering smell of burning and putrefaction. I picked up the kitchen chair and swept up the pieces of broken whisky glass – just catching a hint of the high-octane spirit made me retch, a good reminder of why I had sworn off it in the first place.

The antiseptic stung as I slopped it onto my cuts, the pain distracting me momentarily from the horrible reality of what had happened during the night. Hallucinations do not, cannot physically harm people, but two of mine just had. I considered going back to the doctor. And then tell him what? That a cat that wasn't there had scratched my hand? That a burned and maimed airman had walked into my kitchen through a solid wall, stopping just long enough to call me "Tommy", warn me off the demon drink, smash a glass on the floor and then go out the same way he'd come in? That way lay a visit from the men in white coats and a lifetime wearing clothing that fastens at the back with straps.

Somehow, I made it into work. I had considered phoning in sick again but the need to get away from the house was stronger.

I was just about to open the doors into the lobby of the newspaper's offices when I heard someone calling my name. 'Bill. Hey, Bill. I need to talk to you.' The voice was familiar and I turned to look. What I saw, froze me in my tracks. It was Harrison, wearing his RAF battledress, a whistle attached to his collar and his chip-bag hat at a rakish angle. 'You look dreadful,' he said.

I made no reply. The fact that his appearance in 1940s uniform at ten to nine on a twenty-first century work day told me that nobody else on the bustling Lincoln street could see or hear him.

'Coffee,' I said and carried on past the Lincoln Post signs towards the café we had visited before.

Harrison quickened his pace to draw alongside me. 'Can't have been much fun the other night,' he said.

I grunted in reply. Already three-quarters certain of my own insanity I did not relish the thought of confirming it to everybody else by being seen to talk to myself in the street. When we arrived, I pushed the door open and didn't bother to hold it open for him. Harrison showed no concern and caught the handle in order to follow me. Once again, somebody who could not possibly be there was none the less solid flesh and bone. I ordered a coffee and sat facing the wall, with my strange companion opposite me.

'Gilroy's not happy,' he said. 'He'll be back.'

A wave of despair swept over me. 'So what do you suggest I do?'

'Come back to Leckonby.'

'And have the same thing happen to me as happened to Gilroy? You must be out of your mind.'

'Let me finish. I can help you.'

159

I snorted. 'How? Tommy Handley and the rest of Brownlow's crew die on the night of the 21st of December. That kind of help I can live without.'

He shrugged and looked down at the table, fiddling with the corner of a paper napkin. 'Come back as Bill Price or take your chances with Gilroy. How well do you think you'll cope with a couple more nights like the last one? I don't need to tell you, do I? That way madness lies.'

'And this is sane, I suppose?'

'Funnily enough, it is,' he replied. 'I warned you to stay away but you wouldn't listen. What you've started, you'll have to finish. I can help you.'

I scoffed. 'So you keep saying.'

He wagged a finger at me. 'If you don't take my advice, Gilroy will take you somewhere that's no place for the living. Remember your little encounter with Colonel Cavendish and that creature of his?'

'All too bloody well,' I replied with a shudder.

Harrison's expression was grave. In hindsight I would have said he looked frightened. 'Well, you'll be seeing a lot more of them if you don't take my advice.'

I felt the goose pimples rising on my arms and a feeling of dread, far deeper than I can describe, came over me. 'So what do I have to do?'

'Meet me at the Ferryboat Inn at seven thirty tomorrow evening.'

'Then what? How do I know I won't run into Gilroy and Cavendish? And anyway, the pub's not there any more.'

He shook his head and then looked me in the eye. 'You'll just have to trust me, Bill. The alternative doesn't bear thinking about. You're haunting a group of people in the winter of 1943. Some of them are haunting you now. There's only one way to end it.'

My mouth opened and closed like a goldfish, but no words came out. Eventually I found my voice. 'But, but… how do I know I can trust you?'

'You don't, but believe me, if you don't the alternative will be far worse. I'll see you tomorrow evening.' With that, he got up and instead of opening the door, walked out through the wall next to the counter and disappeared.

So it had come to this. I put my head in my hands and stared down into the dregs at the bottom of my coffee cup. My last toehold on the rational world, all my smug assurance that such things were impossible, had finally crumbled. All that remained was the unthinkable.

I was late for work and, as I hurried back along the crowded pavement, I had already resigned myself to the prospect of facing Derek Bennett's sarcasm. My hopes of sneaking to my desk unobserved were dashed and I had to endure the public humiliation of explaining myself to him in front of the rest of the office. 'New medication,' I mumbled, hoping no one else would hear. 'Leaves me feeling spaced out half the time. Not sleeping well. The doc told me it might happen.'

Instead of ranting at me as he usually did, Bennett looked at me with what might, in a bad light, have passed for compassion. 'Come into my office, Bill. We need to talk.'

He cleared a space for me in an office that was only distinguishable from a council refuse tip by the absence of seagulls, and offered me a seat. 'Look, Bill,' he said. 'I know you've been having a rough time of late.'

Here it comes, I thought. Thirty seconds' of feigned

concern for my wellbeing and then a P45. However, Bennett hadn't lost his powers to surprise. My cynicism was misplaced. He continued. 'You do realise the quack would probably sign you off as unfit for work if you asked?'

I nodded. 'My GP said exactly that. He wants me to see a neurologist and a shrink. The hallucinations are getting worse. Even the pills can't stop them.' I wondered just to whom I was lying when I described what was happening to me as hallucinations – just Bennett or to myself too?

'So why don't you take his advice, old son?' The pug features crinkled into a smile that reached all the way up to his eyes.

I paused, trying to find the right words. 'Because, odd as it may seem, I actually enjoy this job. Swapping it for a life of daytime TV and living off benefits doesn't really appeal.'

'How would you feel about going part-time? I'd have to pay you less, of course,' he added.

I nodded. 'That might work.'

We spent the next half hour haggling over my new hourly rate and the key features of the contract he said I'd have to sign, but in the end we came to an agreement that suited both sides. In the interests of his not declaring me insane on the spot, I thought it best not to mention that there was an outside chance I might not be alive if I didn't survive my next rendezvous with the past.

At lunchtime, I risked a visit to the bookshop that now occupies the site of the old Saracen's Head Hotel – infamous to me as "the Snakepit" and my embarrassing episode with the manager. Today, the past seemed content to leave me alone and I managed to buy a

1:25,000 scale Ordnance Survey map of the area around Leckonby without any mishaps. Where I was going tomorrow evening, my car's GPS would not be of any help. As I walked back to the office, the streets of Lincoln were busy with people doing their last minute Christmas shopping – some clearly hating every minute of it, others smiling and happy. Everywhere, the shop windows were bright with Christmas decorations. Normally, at this time of year I can suspend my natural cynicism and go along with the tide of sparkly tat and 1970s Christmas chart-toppers blasting from every shop doorway. Now, I had other things on my mind and I couldn't get into the mood – however implausible the Christmas story might be, I was faced with something even more unbelievable but none the less real. I was used to Christmases on my own by now, but the gloom and foreboding I felt surpassed anything I had ever felt since that first Christmas without Amy and Julia.

Back in the office, I spread the map out on my desk. The disused airfield at Leckonby and its runways were marked in dashed lines. Even the ruined station buildings of Leckonby Junction were there alongside the dotted path of the disused railway line. However, when I looked for any signs of a building on the other side of the Hobbs Bank Drain, all I found was a line of dashes indicating a farm track running parallel to the dyke and stopping some 200 yards short of where I knew the Ferryboat Inn used to stand. This was going to take some finding.

It wasn't until later that afternoon that I realised that in my haste and confusion I had failed to answer two important questions.

The fate of Sergeant Gilroy was my first concern. I

went to the National Archives website and found 362 Squadron's Operational Record Book, paging forward to the entry for the 19th of December 1943. Fourteen aircraft had set out on operations that night. The report on the one I was looking for was blunt and brutally short:

Aircraft L7585 (F). Captain F/O Brownlow. Duty – Bombing Frankfurt-am-Main. Time Up 2143/Time Down 0312. Target markers clearly seen to west of aiming point. Target photo shows good results. A/C suffered light flak damage in starboard mainplane over target, holing No. 3 tank. Later attacked by night fighter near Coblenz. Sgt Gilroy RAAF killed by enemy action. Damage to port inner engine and fuselage. Enemy A/C driven off by rear gunner. Fire in region of bomb bay extinguished by wireless op and rear gunner who both put up a good show.

So did Tommy Handley miss the approaching night fighter, or did it sneak up on F-Freddie from below, using the gunners' blind spot? Given what I knew about German tactics and weapons of the time, the latter seemed far more likely and Tommy seemed to have done his best. If only I could tell Gilroy.

Harrison had told me that if I came back to Leckonby again it would be as Bill Price. My next concern was to discover what the winter of 1943-44 held in store for my namesake. I logged on to the Commonwealth War Graves Commission site and entered the search details. The results that came back froze me to the spot in horror.

Name: Price, William John
Rank: Pilot Officer

164

Service Number: 135487
Date of death: 29 March 1944
Age: 24
Regiment/Service: Royal Air Force Volunteer Reserve, 362 Squadron
Cemetery/Memorial Name: All Saints Church, Leckonby, Lincs
Additional Information: son of Edward John and Margaret Alicia Price of London N8.

My late parents were indeed Ned, as he'd always been called, and Maggie Price. They used to tell people we lived in Highgate, but in reality, our part of N8 was bang in the middle of Hornsey. I took a deep breath and gripped the edge of the desk so that none of the other staff in the office would see my hands shaking. When I had calmed down a little, I tabbed back to the National Archives site and consulted the 362 Sqn Operational Record Book for 22 December 1943:

"Posted in from No. 1 Lancaster Finishing School, P/O W J Price, 135487."

Today was the 21ˢᵗ of December.

***

I left the office early and reached the village of Leckonby just before sunset. The sky had that winter hue of clear, deep blue, fading to pink on the western horizon. The air was crisp and cold. Leaving the car in the Rose and Crown's car park I crossed the road towards the memorial statue. The mark on the bronze airman's leg left by the disc cutter was still visible, but the bare metal of the once bright scar had oxidised to almost the same matt colour as the rest of the figure. As I walked past, my feet sinking ankle deep into a carpet of fallen leaves from the horse chestnuts in front of the church, a movement caught my eye. The statue had turned round and was looking at me. No longer was the airman's right arm held up to his eyes, shielding them from the rising sun – it was on his hip and his torso had turned through almost a half circle, now facing me, dead bronze eyes staring down.

Terrified, I turned to run but lost my footing on the wet leaves and fell heavily onto my side, winding myself. An earthy smell of wet leaves filled my nostrils as I twisted painfully over onto my front and hauled myself to my feet, hyperventilating with panic. Dreading what might meet my eyes, I risked a glance over my shoulder to see if the thing was following me. Instead, all I saw was the statue's back, lit by the setting sun, immobile as statues should be and with one arm held up in front of its face. As I rose unsteadily to my feet, bent over with hands on my knees, gasping for breath, all I could think of was flight. Get back in the car I told myself, get the hell out of here and forget all about this whole lunatic enterprise. But then, with a jolt of fear I remembered Gilroy, and what Harrison had said might befall me if I missed my rendezvous at the Ferryboat Inn.

Nerves still jangling and casting anxious glances over my shoulder, I hurried through the lychgate and continued into the churchyard. There I soon found the military section with its rows of pristine white Commonwealth War Graves Commission headstones. Under the canopy of bare branches I could barely make out the inscriptions and had to use my torch to find what

166

I was looking for.

My worst fears were realised and the cold evening air caught in my throat. Carved into the white limestone below the Royal Air Force crest of an eagle and crown I read the engraving, "135487, Pilot Officer William Price, Pilot, Royal Air Force, 29th March 1944, Age 24." Below the formal inscription was the poignant Latin text, "*Fugo, non fugio*." I fly, I do not flee.

'I had hoped you wouldn't come here.'

I almost jumped out of my skin with shock. The statue? No... instead, standing next to me I saw the slim form of Harrison, dressed in the same long tweed coat he had worn when we had first met at *The Lags*' meeting. How had he got there without my noticing? 'I wish you wouldn't keep creeping up on me,' I said, still gasping for breath.

'It's a good job I was here,' he replied, nodding towards the statue on its plinth. He looked me up and down. Leaves and mud clung to the arm of my coat and I brushed them away with what I hoped was a nonchalant flick. 'Looks like you had a bit of a fright,' he said.

'A bit jumpy, that's all. You know full well I see things that aren't there.' My words rang hollow in my ears.

'Yes of course, Bill,' he said, ignoring my bluster and turning his attention to the inscription. 'Can't be easy seeing your own grave. Hope you're not going to tell me it's not real.'

'No. Bill Price is a common enough name. And anyway, whose body is down there? It can't be mine. I wasn't even born in 1944.'

He continued looking at the headstone rather than at

me. 'You're a stubborn man, Bill. When we're alive we think we understand things like time. Don't you see the pattern yet?'

My patience snapped. 'Oh, so you're telling me I'm already dead, are you?'

'Not at all. I'm trying to tell you that your understanding of time is all wrong and that's why the living can haunt the dead. That's why you were able to come for a pint in the Snakepit, to fly on ops and to get on the wrong side of Gilroy. That's why I'm talking to you now and why you're not lying in the grass behind the statue with your neck broken. I'm trying to help you, Bill. Stop being so stubborn and don't ask questions if you don't like the answers.'

'And if I do as you say? If tomorrow evening I come to a pub that isn't even there, then what? Do I die in March 1944? What happens to my wife and daughter, all the things I've done in this life, all the people I've met?'

'None of that changes, Bill. You don't understand now. But in time you will.'

This was all too much for me. The adrenalin surge from my scare with the statue now crashed, leaving me shaky and tearful. I dropped to the ground, babbling incoherently, feeling the cold dew soaking into the knees of my trousers.

'Are you all right?' The voice came from close to, but it wasn't Harrison's. I looked up to see the outline of a shorter, older man, the last rays of the setting sun lighting his balding pate and reflecting off the clerical collar at his throat. 'I heard a voice and saw someone flashing a torch,' he said. 'We've been robbed twice in the last year, you see.'

168

Embarrassed, I stood up. 'Don't worry, I'm not a burglar. I was… I was…'

He put a consoling hand on my muddy sleeve. 'You don't need to explain. Talking to a loved one who's departed is perfectly normal. They hear us, just as the Good Lord hears us, and they're close all the time.'

Too bloody close by half, I thought, but made no reply. I looked around for Harrison, but he had disappeared as suddenly as he had arrived at my side.

'I'll, er, leave you be then,' said the clergyman. 'Sorry to have disturbed you.'

'And sorry to have given you a fright. I promise not to steal the lead off the roof,' I replied, trying to draw a veil of humour over my embarrassment.

He turned back and said almost imploringly, 'Look, why don't you come in and have a cup of tea?'

I accepted and, as I turned to follow him, for a reason that I still cannot explain, I looked back towards the statue. It was still immobile on its plinth, but what troubled me most were the footprints in the wet grass. From where I had left the footpath by the churchyard lychgate there was only one set: mine. Harrison had left no trace of his presence.

My host introduced himself as the Reverend Paul Davis, vicar of All Saints, and led me through a side door into a modern, brick-built extension tacked onto the nave of the old church. In the light I got a better look at him – mid-forties, wisps of grey hair straggling round a shiny bald head, crooked teeth, a threadbare tweed jacket. Everything about him was suffused with that relentless forced jollity that I have always associated with C of E vicars.

Inside was a joyful clutter of decorations, balloons

and two decorated Christmas trees, each with a pile of gaily wrapped presents underneath. 'Children's carol service tomorrow,' he said. 'Huge fun, but lots of work. Worth it of course when you see all their happy little faces.' The Reverend Davis bustled about clattering cups and plates in the kitchen and soon returned with a tray of tea and biscuits which he set down on a low table between us.

'Are you doing all this on your own?' I asked.

'Oh my word, no,' he replied. 'Some of my parishioners are coming round at six thirty to give me a hand, but I thought I'd make a start.'

I noticed the wedding ring on his left hand. 'Mrs Davis not on duty tonight?'

'Afraid not,' he said, and at once from his tone I realised I had made a gaffe. 'Sadly, Mrs Davis decided a while ago that life as a rural parson's wife wasn't for her. So, no.'

'I'm sorry.'

'Please don't be. These things happen. Anyway, what about you? I take it you were visiting the grave of a family member. Grandfather in the RAF?'

'Yes, that's right,' I lied. 'My namesake, Bill Price...' I stopped. No. This was bloody silly. 'Actually, that's not strictly true. My wife and daughter were killed in a car accident several years ago. I survived the crash, but with what the doctors call cranial trauma. And now I have hallucinations. I see things that aren't there. That's why I came here today.'

He frowned and I thought I caught the same look of fear I had seen on Harrison's face earlier that day in the café. 'I don't wish to intrude,' he said. 'But would you be willing to tell me what sort of things you see?'

170

I started with the harmless ones – the cat walking along the worktop and out through the wall, the flying teacups, the splashes of colour. 'That's about it, really,' I said.

His eyes bored into mine as though they could see right through my untruths. 'It's not though, is it, Bill? What else have you seen? What did you see that brought you here?'

I took a deep breath. 'OK, but please don't think I'm a madman. I see people who are dead. Buildings on the old airfield that were demolished years ago. Lancaster bombers and their crews. A few weeks back, I drank beer with some of them in a pub that closed in the 1950s. Then there's the man I was with just now in the churchyard.'

'But I saw you quite clearly. You were alone.'

'No I wasn't. I was talking to a man named Harrison and he's solid flesh and bone. The one minor problem I have with him is that he died in 1944.' What I saw in the vicar's eyes was not the sceptical pity for yet another social misfit pouring out his deranged ramblings to anyone who would listen. No, once more, it was a look I had come to associate with Leckonby – fear.

'You say you've been onto the old airfield. Who else did you see?' His lower lip trembled as he awaited my reply.

I decided to sound him out. 'A man and his dog. Well, when I say dog, I…'

His face fell. 'Cavendish,' he said.

'So you've met him too?' I asked. He nodded. 'And that creature of his? Whatever it is, it's not a dog.'

Davis finished his tea and replaced the mug unsteadily on the tray. He got to his feet. 'By day it's a black Labrador,' he said. 'By night, they say… well, come with me and I'll show you something.' Davis led me into the church. After the bright lights and decorations in the hall, the nave was gloomy, with the altar and side chapels in near darkness. I hoped it was the cold damp air that made me shiver, rather than anything else. Reaching the transept, he turned left and led me to a stout wooden double door set in a Gothic arch. 'Have you still got that torch with you?' he asked.

'Yes.' I handed it to him.

With a clang that reverberated round the church, he drew back the bolts and swung the doors open. Then he turned on the light in the north porch and shone the torch on the right hand door, just below the lock plate. 'What do you see?'

I shrugged. 'I'd say someone hacked at the door with an axe and then tried to set fire to it. Those look like scorch marks. The damage doesn't look recent though.'

'Apparently, it was done by that creature of his,' said Davis.

'You're kidding?' I said, aghast.

'No, I'm deadly serious. It happened in 1745 according to the parish records.' I noticed his hands were shaking as he spoke. 'Tell me, Bill. Have you seen it? I mean close to. Have you looked it in the eye?'

I shuddered at the thought. 'Yes. Horrible, bright red burning eyes. I'm sure it was a hallucination, but then Cavendish helped me up. I felt his hand.' The memories came flooding back. 'He looked terrible – like a corpse. And then there was this horrible burning smell.'

Davis stood rooted to the spot, staring out into the darkness of the churchyard. 'Brimstone they used to call it. And as for that creature, if you saw its eyes, then God alone can help you. According to the legend you have twelve months at most to live.'

I rolled my eyes and said, 'Not you as well? Cavendish… my hallucination or whatever it was said the same thing. What is this nonsense?'

'Black Shuck.'

'Black what?' I was clearly dealing with a madman.

'According to the legend, Black Shuck – and yes, I thought it was just a silly fairy story too – is a spectral dog, a hell-hound if you like. Not only is it rumoured to have killed people, but as I just told you, anyone who has looked it in the eye has less than twelve months to live.'

'And you believe this tripe?'

'I believe in evil, if that's what you mean,' he replied.

'And you're telling me that evil can take physical form?'

'Yes. I didn't used to, but I now think it can.' Hurriedly bolting the door against the night and its terrors, he turned to face me once more. 'I fear it's starting again.'

'What is?' I asked, wondering whether Davis hadn't at some time received an even bigger bang on the head than I had.

At first he made no answer, but as we walked back down the nave towards the west door he asked. 'Have you noticed something about Leckonby? The names I mean.'

'I'd always thought that place names ending in "–by" were Viking settlements.'

Davis stopped and turned to face me. Despite the cold in the unheated church, beads of sweat stood out on

173

his forehead. 'They are. I was talking about all the "Hobbs". This very church stands in Hobbs Lane. The Cavendishes lived for generations at Hobbs End Hall. The river by the old railway station is called the Hobbs Bank Drain. Everywhere you go, you find the same name.' He shone the torch into a niche above the west door. 'Do you know what that is?'

I squinted into the darkness. In the niche a carved stone goblin stood on one cloven-footed leg, the other was raised, folded across its knee. Its head was crowned with horns and a leering, toothy smile glared down at us. 'Looks like the Lincoln Imp. Same as the one they've got in the cathedral.'

'It is. Only here, it's called the Leckonby Hobb. Hobb is the old English word for The Devil, of course.' He turned off the torch and handed it back to me.

I put it into my coat pocket. 'Fairy stories to frighten the children,' I said, trying to convince myself and failing.

'How you can say that after what you've seen amazes me,' said Davis, shaking his head. 'You asked what I meant about things starting again. Do you really doubt the evidence of your own eyes?'

I shook my head. 'I don't want any of this to be real. It's too horrible to contemplate.'

Davis tried to force a smile. 'My wife felt the same. But she saw too many things happen here that were just not possible. Little by little, she lost her Christian faith and then one day she gave me an ultimatum. Either I give up the job here at Leckonby or she would leave.'

I saw tears glistening in his eyes. 'But you felt it was your duty to stay and try to stop it?' I asked.

He nodded. 'Yes. I'm doing my best.'

'Not working, is it?'

He looked down at his feet. 'Not yet, I admit. However, I still have faith in the Lord.'

A conversation about the existence of God was the last thing I needed, so I changed the subject. 'The memorial statue outside the church, the bronze airman –'

'Not you too,' he said before I'd had chance to finish. 'That statue was the final straw that caused my wife to leave.'

'Pretty weighty old straw.'

'You wouldn't joke if you'd seen what she saw.'

'Don't tell me, it killed the gypsy.'

'Come,' he said, leading me by the arm back towards the warmth and light of the hall. 'The House of God is no place to discuss such matters.'

We sat back down, facing each other once more across the biscuit crumbs and empty tea cups. Davis continued. 'Madeleine hadn't been sleeping well and that night she heard a noise. You see, the vicarage is on the other side of the road, just along from the pub. Anyway, she got up to get a drink of water from the bathroom and that's when she saw it.'

'Saw what?'

He coughed and tugged at his ecclesiastical collar as though it was too tight. 'She heard the noise again, looked out of the landing window and saw that the statue had gone. She thought someone had stolen it and was about to call the police when she saw something that – well, there's no other way of putting it – simply isn't possible. She swears on the Holy Bible that the statue came walking up the road and climbed back onto its plinth.'

The cold feeling of dread I had felt earlier in the church overwhelmed me again and I tripped and stammered over my words. 'Tha- that ties up with what the other gypsy said.'

'I know,' he replied, avoiding my gaze. 'But it's not possible, is it?'

'No, it's not. Nor is what I saw just now.' The words tumbled out as I told him about the statue turning to stare at me and the sensation of brooding malevolence that I had felt from it. 'So what's causing all this?' I asked.

He furrowed his brow and shook his head. 'Blessed if I know. I've spent hours in prayer, but the Good Lord hasn't seen fit to tell me yet.'

I thought back to the group of dead airmen crowded round my bed. 'Do you think that building a new town on the airfield may've disturbed something?'

He thought for a moment. 'It's possible. If it *is* something to do with the airfield, there is someone who might know more. One of my parishioners served there during the war. She's in her nineties now and nearly blind, but her mind is still sharp as a tack.'

'Where would I find her?'

'The old peoples' home – Hobbs End Hall. Her name's Miss Elizabeth Clark, and don't forget the "Miss" or you'll be in trouble,' he said with a smile.

With a feeling that I had already divulged far more than I'd ever intended, I thanked the Reverend Davis for his time and promised to let him know if I found anything of interest to him. He stood, framed in the lighted doorway, watching me as I followed the path down to the lychgate. I heard the door close and permitted myself a nervous glance up at the statue as I hurried past it. This time, there was no feeling of menace – all I saw was an inert, harmless bronze figure, keeping its lonely vigil and watching the eastern horizon.

I crossed the road and followed the pavement that led the few yards towards the Rose and Crown's car park. That's when I heard it. At first I thought it was a bird fluttering in the hedge next to me, but then I realised the sound was more regular – it was the rhythmic crackle of animal paws over fallen leaves, keeping pace with me on the other side of the hedge. I stopped and turned towards the sound. As I did so I felt rather than heard a low rumbling growl. Two piercing red eyes stared at me through the tangle of branches and, not far away I heard a man's voice laughing. In terror, I sprinted back towards the car, activated the remote control as I ran and tumbled though the door, slamming it shut behind me. Then I turned round, kneeling on the seat to make sure nothing had got in with me – I knew nothing was there but after what I had seen I no longer trusted my own mind. Somehow I managed to get the car started and slammed it into gear before setting off, wheels spinning and swerving, way too fast, into Hobbs Lane in the direction of Lincoln and home.

Chapter Eleven

Not for the first time, I seriously contemplated suicide. For several hours, I sat at my kitchen table looking at the unopened bottle of Scotch and the three new packets of sleeping pills next to it. By the time the clock showed midnight, some of the horror had subsided and, by executing a strenuous logical back flip, I finally convinced myself that taking an overdose could wait until I felt less tired.

Then I thought about what Harrison had said and I weighed my options – an ignominious suicide in the present day or the chance to know what it was like to live as Bomber Command aircrew, knowing that until the 29th of March 1944, no harm could befall me. It was an easy decision to make.

I forgot to switch off my alarm and the following morning I had already showered, had breakfast and was about to leave the house when I remembered that I was signed off until after the holidays. With no work to occupy me, I tried to prepare myself for what I hoped would be a non-eventful evening by a cold, damp riverbank. I tried without success to banish the thought of what might be waiting for me out there in the darkness.

Spreading out the 1:25,000 scale map on my dining table, I sought distraction by trying to memorise the route to the spot where the Ferryboat Inn had once stood. Map reading at night meant using a torch and the last thing I wanted was to draw attention to myself. I didn't fancy trying to explain to an angry farmer that the reason I was trespassing on his land in the dark was because I was looking for a pub that no longer exists.

With no work to keep me busy I decided to kill the hours that hung between me and my rendezvous with the unknown by following up on the vicar's advice to contact Miss Elizabeth Clark. I phoned the old people's home at Hobbs End Hall, explained that I was a journalist and asked if she would be willing to speak to me about her experiences at RAF Leckonby during the war. About thirty minutes later my phone rang and one of the staff, speaking in a heavy Eastern European accent, surprised me by confirming that Miss Clark would be delighted to meet and would I come for tea at half past three.

The sign by the roadside as well as the front of Hobbs End Hall was festooned with coloured lights and inside the overheated entrance stood a Christmas tree. The receptionist showed me into a room, separated from the residents' lounge by a sliding door. Seated at the table, hands folded in her lap, was an elderly woman, her skin was stretched like delicate parchment across what in youth must have been cheekbones to die for. She sat ramrod straight, despite her years, pale blue, filmy eyes flickering left and right as she tried to bring her visitors into focus.

'Mr Price is here, Miss Clark,' said the receptionist.

'No need to shout, dear. I'm not deaf you know.' She paused and added with a laugh. 'Well, only a little.' The smile was infectious. From the Reverend Davis' description of her, I had been expecting a battleaxe, not someone like this. The receptionist left and I introduced myself to my host. Her handshake was firm and I saw the pale eyes trying to find mine. I offered her my business card which she politely declined. 'Not much

179

use to me, I'm afraid. Nearly blind you see. Terrible nuisance not being able to read.'

I poured the tea and sat down opposite her. 'It's very good of you to see me at such short notice,' I said. 'I'm doing a series of articles on the history of RAF Leckonby during the war.'

'Yes, so they told me. And now they're going to build houses all over it. Doesn't seem right somehow, but I suppose people must have somewhere to live, poor things.' She paused. 'It was all so long ago but it still seems such an awful waste.'

'I don't follow you.'

'The war. All those young lives. It had to be done of course, but so many didn't come back. So sad.' She stopped again and the pale blue eyes seemed to stare back into a vanished past.'

'You were an air traffic controller. Is that right?' I asked.

'Yes, I think that's what they call it now. Back then I was a signals officer, I worked in the watch office.'

'And nobody's asked you about what you did? You know, journalists, writers, busybodies like me?'

That smile again. 'Oh, yes. Some silly beggar wanted to write a book about me. Sent him packing all right.'

'Well then I'm honoured that you decided to change your mind,' I replied.

She thought for a moment. 'It wasn't really a matter of changing my mind. It was your name you see. I knew a young man called Bill Price during the war. He was killed in March 1944. His aircraft developed a fault after takeoff and crashed back on the airfield when he tried to land.' Tears welled up in her eyes as she spoke. 'Bill and

180

I were very fond of one another. I was on duty in the watch office and I saw him die along with all his crew that night. That's why I don't like talking about the war.'

'I'm sorry,' I stammered. 'If it's distressing for you, I'll leave.'

'No, please don't,' she said, putting her hand on my arm. 'I'm old now and not likely to be around very long. If people read about those boys, then they won't be entirely forgotten. I think that's important, don't you?'

'I do,' I replied, trying to hide the fear in my voice.

'There is one other thing,' she said and then paused. 'No, it's silly of me to even mention it...'

'Go on,' I replied.

'Well, the uncanny thing is that although I can't see you properly, you sound so like the Bill Price I used to know. It really is quite a coincidence.' She paused again. 'Or perhaps I'm going crackers,' she said with a laugh, trying to hide the tears that had once more formed in her eyes.

We spoke for over an hour. With Miss Clark's permission I recorded the conversation, taking frequent notes to remind me to research some of the topics she covered. She had just got to the period when Wing Commander 'Press-on' Preston took over as commanding officer – a man she described as "a colossal shit" – when a nurse reappeared to chivvy me out before I tired Miss Clark too much. I stood up to leave. As Miss Clark took my hand, she said quietly, 'You will be careful, won't you?'

'Yes, of course,' I replied without thinking and it was only after I was on my way out of the building that the incongruity of her words struck me.

It was too early to set out for my rendezvous with Harrison, so I decided to take another look at the airfield. The route to my usual parking spot was blocked by 'road closed' signs so I got out and walked the last few hundred yards only to find my way barred once more. A high, chain-link fence now surrounded the site where signs in English and Polish warned the public to keep out. Under the yellow security lights, I could see roads laid out across what once had been grass, and the walls of the first houses stood in neat rows. The control tower had been demolished too. I turned away, saddened by the sight.

I drove back to Lincoln, a sense of foreboding hanging over me. To provide some welcome distraction I decided to play back the recording of my conversation with Miss Clark. I pulled over and plugged the recorder into the car's MP3 socket as I'd done a hundred times before, but what happened when I hit 'play' left me numb with disbelief. At first I thought I'd left it on 'record' at some point because, instead of hearing Miss Clark's clipped tones, what I heard was a muffled conversation between a man and a woman with a third male voice butting in. I picked it up, checked that I was at the start of the recording and tried again. Once more I heard the same voices and, cursing my own stupidity at losing Miss Clark's priceless reminiscences, was about to turn it off when I paused. What I heard simply wasn't possible. It went something like this.

First, I heard a man's voice saying, 'O-Orange airborne at 2107.'

In reply, a young woman repeated, 'O-Orange, Pilot Officer Price, 2107. I could make out a faint tapping and scratching, presumably the sound of her chalking the details onto a blackboard. Then came a pause followed by what sounded uncannily like aircraft engine noise. The man spoke again. 'B for Beer airborne at 2108.'

The recital of aircraft and their takeoff times continued, punctuated here and there by radio transmissions from an aircraft that seemed to be having engine problems. I listened for about five more minutes. Further aircraft were announced as airborne and I was about to turn off the recording when I heard something that made me pause. Z-Zebra had just taken off, the female voice began to repeat the details when a burst of static cut her off and an airman's voice, tinny and muffled as though from far away, broke through. It was the aircraft with the engine problems again. 'Starfish, this is O-Orange calling. Request immediate landing. We've lost the port outer...' then another burst of static. 'Starfish, we can't maintain height.' The rest was too indistinct to make out but the exchanges between the pilot and the controllers in the watch office became more urgent over the next few minutes until finally a man's voice said, 'Oh my Christ, no,' followed by a woman's screaming. Then silence. I turned the recorder off. With what I might have to face in a few hours, this was the last thing I needed.

***

With no idea of how long I might be away, I returned to Leckonby by taxi. It was outrageously expensive and the driver seemed convinced he had a madman aboard when I insisted on being dropped off in the dark on a deserted lane a mile outside the village. I waited until the taxi's lights were out of view, climbed over a five bar gate and walked the short distance across the fields to the dyke beside the Hobbs Bank Drain. There was no moon, and mist was rising by the time I reached the dyke. All I had to do now was turn left and follow it until I reached what I knew to be a patch of nettles on the opposite bank to the old station. The first few hundred yards were easy going with a clearly-defined path running along the top of the dyke. However, as I pressed on it became more overgrown until a painful encounter with a patch of brambles sent me sliding back down the bank and into the field.

That's when I saw it. Almost as tall at the shoulder as a man, the creature was jet black and so close I could hear its breathing. Not daring to take my eyes off it for a second I attempted to back away but it moved soundlessly towards me. I tried to call for help but no sound came. So this is how it ends. Please, God, no, anything but this.

Harrison had warned me that Cavendish would take me and now his abominable familiar was right in front of me. This time there would be no escape.

To my right a movement caught my eye – half expecting to see Cavendish I was appalled to see the outline of another animal form in the mist. There were two of them. This wasn't possible. I turned to run but a deafening bellow from close behind froze me to the spot. Then another to my right. Slowly the reality dawned on me and I fumbled in my coat pocket for my torch. I flicked it on and shone it at the shape in front of me. A jet black calf. Another bellow from close at hand and the harmless creature trotted past me to its mother. For the first time in my life I wanted to kiss a farm animal.

After I had recovered from the shock I continued on my way, sometimes on top of the dyke, but more often down in the field where the low-lying mist had reduced visibility to only a few yards. Within minutes it was so dense that I quickly lost track of how far I'd come, and after an hour of tacking up and down the bank to avoid brambles, nettles and barbed wire fences I was hopelessly lost. As I expected, there was no sign of the Ferryboat Inn and was inwardly cursing myself for once again being so credulous when I saw a brief glimmer of light ahead. As soon as it had appeared, it went out again so I moved into the cover of a clump of gorse bushes and waited.

After what seemed an eternity but was probably only a few minutes I saw it again. This time, I realised that it was close to. What I'd seen was the light from a door being opened. The silhouette of a man filled the doorway for a moment and I caught the sound of his voice as he turned to speak to someone inside the building. A feeling of dread in the pit of my stomach replaced my earlier complacency – no butterflies, these were jet black ravens. The door banged shut and as I inched forwards I could just make out the form of a two-storey building surrounded by a wooden picket fence. The hinges creaked in protest as I pushed open the gate. I shone my torch on the wall. On a wooden sign, faded and cracked by the elements, I could just read the words, "The Ferryboat Inn – Bateman's Fine Ales."

'Put that bloody light out!' a voice shouted from close by. I turned and saw a tall, spare-boned man in his mid-fifties, hands on hips and staring at me like I was something the cat had dragged in. He wore a collarless shirt covered by a grubby white apron. I recognised him

185

as the man I'd seen rolling barrels down to the cellar – the pub landlord. He greeted me with, 'Come in or we'll catch our bloody deaths of cold out here.' He opened the door and I followed him along the corridor towards a rising hubbub of beery voices. From his lack of surprise at seeing me I assumed I was expected, but then he turned through an open door to the left which led behind the bar. I stopped, confused and uncertain what to do next so I peered round the doorway to get a better view. Then the door leading into the bar itself opened and I saw a familiar figure. Harrison.

'Pilot Officer Price, I presume?' he said, offering me his hand. I shook it and, as I did so, saw that once more I was clad in RAF battledress. 'Wait here, I'll be back in a second,' he said. Moments later he reappeared with the landlord who led the way back down the corridor, pausing only to take his coat from a peg by the door. I followed them round the side of the building and onto the planks of a low, wooden jetty that stuck out into the black waters of the Hobbs Bank Drain. At the end was moored the rowing boat I had seen before. While the landlord removed the tarpaulin, Harrison took me aside. 'You do of course realise you can go back any time you like. Just go out of the pub using the same door you came through and keep on walking. It won't make any difference of course, but you can come and go as you please.'

'What do you mean, "it won't make any difference"?' I asked.

'I mean, it won't make any difference to what happens, that's all.'

This was infuriating. Agitated, I tried to press him further but he refused to answer. The conversation was cut short by a voice from the darkness calling out, 'Do you want me to row you across or not? I haven't got all night.'

The landlord got in first and gave me a hand down. Harrison followed and joined me, sitting in the stern. At our feet was an RAF holdall. He nodded to it and said, 'Yours, of course.'

The landlord undid the painter, set the oars and pushed off. The rowlocks groaned and complained as he rowed through the mist towards the far bank which loomed black and forbidding above us. With a final sweep of the oars, he brought us alongside a flight of concrete steps and held the boat steady as we climbed out. 'Don't forget to pay the ferryman, Bill,' said Harrison. Fearing a repeat of the penniless Tommy Handley's embarrassment in the Snakepit I rummaged in my pocket and, to my relief, came up with a handful of heavy coins, some of which I thrust into a calloused hand.

The landlord glanced down at the money. I caught a note of surprise in his voice. 'Much obliged, young man. No doubt we'll see each other again.'

'Come on,' said Harrison, before I had time to reply. 'I've borrowed the CO's car. Better get it back before he misses it.'

The station buildings of Leckonby Junction were in darkness and only a think sliver of light escaping round the edge of the black-out curtains gave any hint of human activity. Outside the station stood an Austin saloon painted RAF blue and bearing a roundel and white serial numbers on the doors. I put the holdall in the back and got into the passenger seat next to Harrison. He turned on the ignition, pulled the self-starter and the car wheezed into life. The route was familiar to me now and the RAF Policeman at the main gate raised the red and white barrier to let us through and treated us to a crisp salute. Harrison chuckled. 'Must've thought it was the old man himself driving.'

He left the car outside the officers' mess and led me through the door. Inside, the building carried a strange aroma that I remembered from my school days – a mixture of floor polish and boiled cabbage. I followed him down a corridor and saw that the Nissen hut we were in had been divided into two-man rooms. Harrison stopped, checked the number on the door and stood back to await my reaction. 'There you are,' he said. 'All the comforts of home.'

I took in my new surroundings. Two beds with grey blankets folded into hospital corners, two standard issue wardrobes and a sink; apart from a threadbare rug by each bed, that was it. I noticed that one of the wardrobe had a piece of string across its door, held in place by two red wax seals. I knew what this meant, but felt compelled to take a closer look. Threaded onto the string was a luggage label bearing the words, "P/O Chapman, missing 18/12/43. Effects officer F/L Carter." 'Poor sod got the chop on his first op,' said Harrison in a tone that suggested oriental levels of fatalism. 'Don't think he'd even unpacked properly. Still, means you'll have the room to yourself for a bit.'

We were too late for dinner but I accepted Harrison's suggestion of a drink. In the ante room I flopped into a scruffy but comfortable leather armchair while Harrison rang the bell for the mess steward. Moments later she appeared. There was something familiar about her but before I even had time to think, she screamed, dropped her tray and ran back out, sobbing and howling. I looked to Harrison for an explanation but he just gave one of his diffident shrugs. 'To be expected, I'm afraid,' he said.

He was starting to annoy me. 'What do you mean?' I asked.

Before he had chance to explain, the Mess Manager appeared with the tear-stained steward in tow. 'It's Tommy. I told you he wasn't dead,' she cried, running towards me and flinging her arms around my neck.

The mess manager's jaw fell open and he too went white. 'My God, I see what you mean,' he said, gawping at me as though I was a two-headed monster from a freak show. Harrison gently removed the young woman who by now had drenched me with tears and kisses.

The mess manager composed himself at last. 'I'm sorry about that, sir,' he said. 'LACW Morris is a little overwrought, but you do bear an uncanny resemblance to Sergeant Handley. He went missing last night. LACW Morris and Sergeant Handley were, um, close friends.'

I now remembered where I had seen her before. It was the same young woman whose photo I had found in 'Tommy' Handley's wallet during my escapade in the Saracen's Head bar.

'That's all right,' I said, smiling at her. 'I'm sorry if I gave you a fright. And I'm sorry to hear that Sergeant Handley and his crew are missing.'

Chapter Twelve

It was still dark when I awoke. For a moment I thought I was back at home in Lincoln, but then I remembered. I turned on the bedside light and swung myself into a sitting position. As I did so it was obvious something had changed. Limbs that usually took several minutes to get going and a right knee that didn't want to bend suddenly felt light and supple. I felt ridiculously fit and well. I'd forgotten what it was like – I was twenty-four again and it felt wonderful.

After a breakfast of fatty bacon and congealed dried egg, the morning was taken up with the administrative trivia of getting my 'arrival chit' signed by just about every section at RAF Leckonby. Once more it turned out to be a procedure that had been handed down intact to my time in the RAF.

Having got the requisite numbers of stamps and signatures on the blue cardboard chit, I was then sent for an interview with the squadron commander, the squeaky-voiced *Press-on* Preston. I knew that Bomber Command normally sent entire crews to its squadrons so I was curious to know how I came to be "a spare bod" and to find out what had happened to the rest of my crew.

Preston called me into his office. I stopped, stood to attention and saluted. His eyes came out on stalks and his mouth opened and closed like a goldfish. This was getting tedious. For a moment, Preston seemed to be struck dumb. When at last he did find his voice, he could barely speak for coughing and spluttering. 'Christ, you gave me a fright,' he said, dabbing at his brow with a handkerchief.

I feigned surprise. 'I'm sorry, sir, I'm not with you.'

'Thought I'd seen a ghost. You look just like young Brownlow's rear gunner, Sergeant Handley. Poor buggers got the chop the night before last. Direct hit from an 88mm flak shell over the Dutch coast. Still, at least they can't have known much about it.'

After he'd got over his shock, Preston invited me to sit down and started chatting about my training on the Lancaster, alluding to a 'regrettable and entirely avoidable accident,' so I could only assume that my entire crew had been killed while flying with someone else, presumably during our last few days on our Lancaster training course at the Heavy Conversion Unit. After a tedious and rambling homily about God, duty and The Empire, he handed me back to Harrison who led me down to the B-Flight office. On the way he filled in the details about the fate of my former crew.

'It was the CO of the HCU,' he explained. 'You were off sick with Delhi belly and he pinched your crew for a fighter affiliation trip against a squadron of Hurricanes. Thought he'd show those fighter boys how a Lanc could be flown. Silly sod overdid it and ended up colliding with one of the Hurricanes. No survivors and two perfectly serviceable aircraft destroyed.'

'So I'm the bastard stepchild,' I replied.

'You could put it that way.'

'But what happened to the skipper of the crew I'm joining here?'

'LMF,' replied Harrison with the same air of indifference I'd heard him use the previous evening. 'Lack of Moral Fibre. Did two trips, and on the second they had a dicey time with searchlights and flak near

191

Cologne. Ordered his bomb aimer to drop way short of the target. Then, he nearly wrote the aircraft off on landing and went straight to see old Press-On to tell him he didn't want to be a Lanc captain after all. He was off the station within the hour.'

'So where is he now?'

'RAF Norton in Sheffield I believe,' said Harrison, studying his fingernails. 'It's where they send the LMF types to sew mail bags before packing them off to join the infantry as privates. Bloody good riddance if you ask me. Oh, and by the way, don't be surprised if everyone else thinks you're 'Tommy' Handley come back to life.' Then he paused. 'Which in a way, I suppose you are,' he said.

At the B Flight Office, Harrison introduced me to my Flight Commander, Squadron Leader Mc Evoy, a dark and brooding Ulsterman, well over six feet tall. The DFC ribbon on his chest and the nervous tic in his right eye told me he was on his second tour of ops. He too did a double-take and told me I was the spitting image of 'Tommy' Handley. Once he'd recovered from the shock, his words of welcome were perfunctory and gave me the strong message that he did not expect our acquaintance to be a long one.

Next came the moment I was dreading – an introduction to the six other members of my crew. What I knew and they didn't was that all of them would die on the night of the 29th of March. They had just over three months left to live.

Five of them were NCOs, the only officer was the navigator, a small, prematurely balding Pilot Officer called Hudson. He spoke quietly but with a strong West Midlands accent. 'I hope you don't mind my saying…'

I finished the sentence for him. 'Yes, I know. I'm the ghost of Sergeant Handley come back to haunt you.' If only you poor sods knew the half of it, I thought.

'Well anyway, I hope you're going to look after us,' he said, offering me a limp, sweaty hand to shake.

'I'll do my best,' I replied. It was a response as feeble as his handshake, but all I could manage faced with six condemned and frightened men.

Next came Sergeant Boyle, the flight engineer, who looked barely out of his teens and sported a pencil moustache which made him look like a caricature spiv. He proudly told me that he'd been a motor mechanic in Southend – "Sarf'end" he pronounced it – before the war and followed this unasked-for information with what I'm sure he thought was a gem of advice. 'Don't take no notice of them miserable bastards, skipper. We'll be all right with you, I can feel it in my bones. An' when I gets one of my feelings, I'm never wrong.' Hudson glowered at him. Clearly no love lost between those two.

'Well that's good to know,' I replied. 'Any feelings about who's going to win the 1:30 at Sandown?' This at least got a laugh from the others. I caught a look of annoyance in Boyle's eye – clearly one of the many who enjoy dishing out the mickey-taking but can't take it themselves. A big mouth and a thin skin. Not a combination I'd have chosen for one of my crew.

Tall and gangling, with a mop of unruly blond hair, Sergeant Peters, the bomb aimer, was next in line. He had the thousand-yard stare of a man whose reserves of courage were already spent, but with another twenty-eight operations to go before the end of his tour. A man of few words, it took me several minutes of cajoling even to get him to tell me that he came from Huddersfield and had been an accounts clerk before signing up.

My next introduction was to Sgt Wells, the wireless operator. He had the taut features and darting eyes of a man who saw danger lurking in every shadow. His white face was heavily freckled and topped with a badly-cut shock of ginger hair. Home for Wells was Plymouth and he spoke with a soft west-country burr. He too seemed ill at ease in my company, and appeared to share the others' unspoken anxiety that I would probably get them all killed.

Last came the two air gunners. Rear gunner Sgt 'Charlie' Chester was a stocky Londoner with a crooked and well-worn face that spoke of his early career as a fairground boxer. He was the only one so far to treat me to a firm handshake and to look me in the eye when he spoke. Like Boyle he was already happy to address me as "Skipper" but without the flight engineer's over-familiarity. Sgt Grey, the mid-upper gunner was a whippet-like Glaswegian, barely five feet tall and who looked as though he should have been still at school. Like Peters, the bomb aimer, he was a man for whom conversation with me seemed an ordeal. I remember clutching the naïve hope that he was harbouring his reserves of enthusiasm for when we got airborne.

We stood looking at one another while an embarrassed silence fell. Nature abhors a conversational vacuum and I felt that awful compulsion to fill the void, even though I knew I was about to say something stupid. Rescue came in the unlikely form of Mc Evoy who put his head round the door. Clearly, he'd already forgotten my name because I saw him consult a printed sheet of paper before he spoke. 'Price, grab your flying kit, the CO's going to check you out. Airborne in forty-five minutes,' he said. And then added, almost as a casual afterthought. 'Your crew's on ops tonight, briefing at six.'

Boyle, the cocky flight engineer, forced a smile and said to no one in particular, 'One more trip off the list. Then it'll only be twenty-seven to go.'

Nobody replied. With the exception of Sgt 'Charlie' Chester, the others' features wore expressions of dread.

My check ride with *Press-On* Preston went surprisingly well, my fears that I would have forgotten how to fly a Lancaster were dispelled from the moment we started the first engine – it was like I had never been away and the confidence of youth came flooding back. After just over an hour airborne he pronounced me fit to take a crew on ops and we landed back at Leckonby.

Just before the main briefing I gathered my reluctant crew together to brief them on what I expected of them; no unnecessary chatter on the intercom, keep a sharp lookout for night fighters from takeoff to landing – no slacking and thinking we were home and dry once we'd left enemy airspace – full concentration from start-up to shut-down. They listened to me in silence, I suppose they had heard it all before and were just going through the motions of paying attention. 'Any questions?' I asked. Silence and avoidance of eye-contact was my only reply. I was certainly going to have to find another way of bonding with this sullen gaggle, the only question was how?

The briefing followed an identical format to the one I had attended before. The nav leader and air-gunnery leaders were unfamiliar to me – it didn't take a huge leap of imagination to work out what must have happened to their predecessors. I knew from my research prior to setting out for Leckonby that 362 Squadron had lost eight aircraft so far in December 1943, four of them on the night of 16th-17th during a raid on Berlin. Tragically, three of the crews who died did so on British soil when low cloud and fog had closed every airfield in Eastern England. Two aircraft crashed when trying to land at RAF Downham Market and another was destroyed when it ploughed into woodland just short of the runway at Graveley.

In a blue fug of cigarette and pipe smoke, bantering and noisy we shuffled along to take our place behind the long rows of trestle tables in the briefing room.

The shiny-faced intelligence officer was still there, as of course was *Press-On* Preston. The station commander strode up onto the rostrum and with a theatrical sweep of his arm, pulled aside the curtain. 'Gentlemen, your target for tonight,' he said, 'is Dusseldorf.'

A collective sigh of relief went round the briefing room. Although sandwiched between the hotspots of the Ruhr valley to the north and Cologne to the south, and well defended by flak and night-fighters, at least Dusseldorf would mean a short trip compared to the previous night's long slog to Frankfurt. 'Thank fuck it's not Berlin,' said a voice close at hand, speaking aloud the thoughts of every man on ops that night.

As the briefing continued, an unfamiliar face caught my eye. The wireless and signals briefing was given by a WAAF Section Officer. Even the coarse fabric of her badly-cut wartime uniform could not disguise the grace with which she carried herself, nor did the severe perm

196

inflicted on her light brown hair detract from the beauty of her face. An unwise Sergeant pilot sitting somewhere behind me gave a wolf-whistle as she walked up the steps to the lectern, but the ripple of laughter this caused was instantly stifled as a pair of china-blue eyes fixed the culprit with a glare that left him red-faced with shame. 'She's pretty,' I said to Hudson, my new navigator who was sitting next to me.

'Many are called but few are chosen,' he replied, enigmatically. 'None so far, anyway.'

After the briefing, the navigators went into a huddle to make their final calculations based on the latest forecast wind and the rest of us trooped off to our respective messes for the pre-flight meal. Then came the now familiar routine of changing into flying kit before collecting our parachutes and escape kits, followed by the long, nervous drive around the perimeter track to our waiting aircraft. As the over-laden Bedford wheezed and bumped its way ever nearer to our dispersal I felt rather than saw six pairs of eyes anxiously watching their new skipper for signs of nerves. What none of them knew, but I did, was that we were safe from 'the chop' until the 29th of March. I say 'we' but I had every intention of being safely back at home in 21st century Lincoln well before then.

In the circumstances I suppose it was inevitable that I remembered Samuel Johnson's famous quote, "Every man thinks meanly of himself who has not been a soldier." And in recalling these words, sitting in the chilly darkness with six frightened men, came the realisation that I was possibly the only man in history with the opportunity to learn at first-hand what it was like to face a battle in which others would die, safe in the knowledge that I would not. For a brief and shameful moment, I thought not of my crew who had just over three months to live, nor of the German civilians we would kill that night, but of the elation at the prospect of adventure to come. If only I had known the awful truth of the Faustian pact I had signed.

Just as on my previous mission, our aircraft joined the lumbering queue, like elephants trooping patiently to the water hole. Then our turn came to take off and for a moment, my cocksure certainty that no harm could befall me evaporated. What if Harrison couldn't be trusted? What if we were killed that night rather than in March? All that would change from the viewpoint of the 21st century would be a few entries in long-forgotten files and the dates on seven headstones. A steady green light from the runway controller's caravan broke my reverie and as I released the brakes I felt Boyle's hands below mine, pushing the throttles open to maximum boost, leading with the port outer throttle slightly ahead of the others to check the Lanc's natural tendency to swing left on takeoff. For all his swagger, Boyle seemed to know his stuff. Fully laden, O-Orange took what to me was an eternity to reach our takeoff speed, which at an all-up-weight of 65,000 lbs was 100 knots. As the end of the runway flashed beneath us, I raised the undercarriage and settled into a shallow climb, waiting for the safety speed of 140 knots before starting to raise the flaps.

We settled into the climb and once Boyle had reduced the RPM and boost, the noise levels in the cockpit became almost bearable. Hudson gave me a course change and we continued, one of countless fireflies, winking through the dark towards the south east. One by one, as they crossed the English coast, the lights went out and, had we not known otherwise, it would have been easy to believe we were the only crew airborne that night.

As we neared the Dutch coast, twinkling bursts of light showed us that German flak gunners were engaging the head of the bomber stream. A few minutes later, it was our turn to run the gauntlet and I double checked that Peters, the bomb aimer, was sticking to his briefed task of throwing out bundles of radar-deceiving "window" at the correct intervals. A hesitant stammer from Peters confirming that he was doing his job was interrupted by the voice of Grey, the mid-upper gunner. 'Flamer going down to starboard, skipper.' I looked across and saw a stream of orange flame split itself into two as the stricken bomber broke up in mid-air, scattering a cascade of red and green target markers as it fell.

'Captain to navigator, make a note of time and position of that one,' I said.

'Wilco, skipper,' replied Hudson. If he felt fear, his voice didn't betray it, not that I'd heard him express any emotion in the short time I'd known him.

Our course took us between the known hotspots of Antwerp and Breda and now that we were clear of the coastal flak batteries, night fighters were our big threat. By the time we reached our next turning point, just north of Eindhoven, Grey in the mid-upper turret and tail-end 'Charlie' Chester had reported four more bombers going down in flames. Twenty-eight men who wouldn't be coming back tonight.

The lack of survival instinct in some of the crews amazed me. Aircraft in the lower height bands of the bomber stream were creating vapour trails in the clear night sky, ghostly white fingers pointing the way for waiting German fighters. Their gunners or even the pilots themselves must have noticed, but appeared not to realise what deadly peril it put them in even when Lancasters and Halifaxes were falling all around them.

I had other ideas. By climbing at maximum continuous revs and boost, Boyle and I managed to coax O-Orange to a safer 24,000 feet, well above our briefed height, but where we left no tell-tale contrails to betray our presence. After Venlo, the stream turned onto a southerly heading, the Bomber Command route planners hoping to fool the German fighter controllers into thinking that tonight's target was Monchengladbach or even Cologne.

When we made our final turn towards the target there was no longer any need for Hudson to navigate. Ahead of us, Dusseldorf was a cauldron of target markers, flame and what looked like a solid red curtain of flak bursts over the city. Searchlight beams, blue and white, crisscrossed the sky as they sought out prey for the gunners. Above the flak bursts, fighter flares drifted down, silhouetting the lumbering bombers for the Luftwaffe night fighter crews. Just ahead and to the right an orange glow blossomed into an oily fireball, the funeral pyre of yet another crew.

Peters' voice came over the intercom. 'Christ, we're not going into that, are we, skipper?'

'Well, the rest of us are,' I replied. 'If you don't fancy it, you can get out and walk. Opening bomb doors now and descending. Bomb aimer, let me know when you have a positive ident of the aiming point.' A flak burst somewhere under the aircraft buffeted us, but without causing any apparent damage.

Four minutes into our target run there was still no word from the bomb aimer. Then at last, 'Th- th- thirty seconds to release, keep her steady,' Peters sounded as though he was on the verge of tears.

'Do you have the aiming point?'

Silence.

'For fuck's sake, man, can you see the aiming point?'

'I'm not sure, sir,' came the quavering reply.

I'd had enough. 'Make switches safe, bomb aimer. I'm closing the bomb doors and we're going round again. And we'll keep going round until you pull yourself together and do your job properly.' I knew I was being cruel to Peters by making an example of him in front of the others. Had I been less sure of my own temporary immortality, I would probably have been happy for him to drop the bombs somewhere within the urban area of Dusseldorf and then get the hell out as quickly as possible. Feigning courage like this was the worst form of dishonesty and I shudder when I look back on it. Events have paid me back a hundredfold for what I did that night – but more of that later.

'Navigator, give me a heading back to the run-in point.'

'Steer 315 for now skipper, I'm already working on a more accurate heading.'

For all his lack of charisma, Hudson was a bloody sharp navigator. Flying's like that to an experienced aviator – you can tell who the good guys are pretty much straight away. Boyle clearly knew his stuff too, but Peters was a liability. As for the two gunners and Wells the wireless op, I hadn't really seen enough to form an opinion.

Hudson's monotone broke my reverie. 'New heading, skipper. Steer three two five, that'll set us up two miles offset from the run in point to allow for the radius of turn. Five minutes twenty on that heading… Bomb aimer, give me a bomb-sight drift reading,' he added.

Peters' reply was barely audible. 'Ch- checking now.'

It was all I could do to restrain myself from climbing out of my seat, going down into the nose of the aircraft and throwing Peters out of the escape hatch. Helping the nav by using the bomb-sight to estimate wind speed, and hence the aircraft's drift, should have been second nature to him.

'I think I can see the lakes to the west of Kempen,' Peters said. 'The sight's giving me a wind velocity of 350 degrees, 55 knots. Estimating 345/50 at bombing altitude.'

Thank Christ for that, I thought, the dozy bugger's doing his job at last. To the west, I could see the glinting ribbon of what had to be the river Maas and beyond it, a pall of smog which marked the Dutch city of Venlo.

'Turn starboard now,' said Hudson. 'New heading 130.'

Once more, we were face to face with the inferno. Even though I knew we would come to no harm, fear gripped every ounce of my being. What it must have been like for Peters, alone in O-Orange's nose with his god's-eye view of the storm of high explosive and steel, I shuddered to imagine.

'I can see the harbour, skipper,' said Peters, his voice now firm and confident. 'Come port three, roll out

202

127 degrees. Steady, steady...' An eternity of waiting and then, 'Bombs gone, skipper!'

Freed of nearly six tons of ordnance, the Lancaster soared upwards. I held the nose down and waited the agonising thirty seconds for the photoflash to go off – if we didn't bring home a target photo, there was every chance that our efforts would not be counted against the allotted tally of thirty ops.

I reached my left hand down and pulled up the handle to close the bomb doors. No sooner had I done so than the whole aircraft was lit up brighter than day. We had been 'coned' and in an instant it felt like every searchlight in Dusseldorf was pointed our way. I pushed all four throttles wide open and overbanked, pulling the nose hard down until we were almost in the vertical. The glare was so bright that I couldn't even read the airspeed indicator, but I realised we must be close to the limit. Below us, Dusseldorf was ablaze from end to end and the thought of what its inhabitants might do to us if my confidence in our invulnerability was misplaced didn't bear thinking about.

'Help me pull her out,' I said, grunting under the g-forces forcing me down into my seat. Somehow I managed to get both feet on the instrument panel for more leverage, and with Boyle's help we managed to get the wings level on what I hoped was a northerly heading. At that point the searchlights lost us and I saw to my horror that we were at only 3,000 feet and doing over 400 knots, 100 knots faster than the aircraft's limit. If I really was the cat whose nine lives ran out on the 29th of March, I must have used eight of them getting away from those searchlights and I could feel the cooling sweat trickling down my spine. None of the crew spoke.

Fizzing with adrenalin and endorphins, I decided to show them I was on top of things. 'Right, that's half the job done. Gunners, keep your eyes peeled. Watch out for fighters creeping up underneath us.'

I had read the history books and knew all about the Luftwaffe's upward-firing *Schräge Musik* canons that were scything their way through the ranks of Bomber Command. The tactic was brutally simple – approach the bomber from below, keeping in the gunners' blind spot, slide into position underneath the wing (firing into the fuselage risked detonating the bomb load and immolating both hunter and hunted), fire a short burst of tracerless 20mm shells into the fuel tanks between the engines and break away before the victim knew what had hit him. Tragically, the RAF did not discover the truth about *Schräge Musik* until after the war.

I kept the aircraft low, skimming over occupied Belgium and France at 2,500 feet. Just below us was a solid blanket of cloud, perfect cover if we got jumped by a fighter. The crew remained silent, whether from a professional aversion to idle chat or struck dumb by fear I knew not.

Eventually, Hudson's voice crackled over the roar of the engines. 'Getting a radar paint on the coast, skipper. We're on track. Maintain this heading for now.'

As we reached the coast, I began a gentle climb to 12,000 feet and followed Hudson's instructions to turn right onto a northerly heading for base. Britain was still under blackout conditions and as we crossed the Thames at Reading, the cloud cover broke up allowing me a view of a country seemingly devoid of all human life except for the odd cluster of lights which marked the airfields open as diversions for bombers too badly damaged or too short of fuel to make it home. Here and there, bright, blueish-white columns rising vertically into the night sky marked the presence of the "Darky" searchlights that were used to guide stricken aircraft to one of these safe havens.

Heading further north and east the little patches of light grew so densely packed that in places they seemed to overlap, and as we got lower I could make out the navigation lights of hundreds of bombers waiting their turn to land, circling round each bright patch like moths around countless flames. Soon, it was our turn and I eased O-Orange into a gentle left bank to join the downwind leg of our approach, lowered the gear and flaps and then followed the Drem lights in a curving descent to the runway threshold at Leckonby.

At our dispersal the same WAAF driver who had driven us from the ops block what seemed like a lifetime ago, was waiting for us with her Bedford truck. 'Welcome back, sir,' she said. 'Hope you had a good trip.'

'Yes, it was ok I suppose,' I replied. We might as well have been chatting about a day trip to Skegness. The others said nothing, the two gunners drawing deeply on their first cigarettes of the new day.

As one of the first crews to return, we didn't have to wait long for our debriefing. The shiny-faced Flight Lieutenant was there, fussing around the trestle tables as we gulped our hot tea, strongly laced with rum.

And then, it was over. After all the hours of tension waiting for the green flare, the knotted stomachs full of butterflies, the surreal horror of watching bombers falling in flames while Dusseldorf burned beneath us and the anxious hours of the homeward leg where every shadow became a prowling night fighter, we were summarily dismissed to our beds. Not with a bang, but a whimper.

Two nights later we were back on ops. Once more, the nervous wait in the blue, smoky haze of the briefing room for the CO's arrival. Then the gasps as he drew back the curtain – this time the line of red ribbon seemed to go on for ever. Whitebait. The Big City. Berlin. For once there were no muttered curses, just a collective intake of breath at what was to come and the certain knowledge that some of us wouldn't be coming back.

Over one hundred silent prayers went up unheeded into the void. Please, God, let it be some other crew tonight, please let me live – three crews had failed to return to Leckonby from Dusseldorf – the law of averages meant that of the twenty-one men in the aircraft shot down that night, two – probably bomb aimers – would have survived. None of the grey, frightened faces gave voice to the unspoken prayer, but its effect was almost audible.

As with the Dusseldorf raid, I knew we would come through unscathed, but nothing could have prepared me for what happened that night. From landfall over occupied Denmark, all the way to the target and back, oily smears of orange fire across the night sky marked the funeral pyres of Bomber Command's young men. Even over the target itself, the night fighters continued to snap and tear at the bomber stream. Fighter flares dropped to illuminate us made it seem as though we were flying along a well-lit highway – slow-moving, fat black insects, inching their way across a floodlit tablecloth. Instinctively, I hunched myself up in the seat in a futile attempt to make myself a smaller target for when the inevitable happened. In the glare of an exploding bomber about a mile away to our left I saw the silhouettes of two parachutes. Given the stories of what Berlin's civilians did to downed airmen – we'd all heard the rumours of bomber crews hanged from lamp-posts – I shuddered at the thought of what might await them.

Berlin, as usual, was covered by eight-eighths cloud and the bombing accuracy was correspondingly sporadic. We'd been warned that the Germans lit decoy fires to draw bombers away from their targets, but with the Pathfinders' marker flares widely scattered and drifting downwind at over 100 knots, we picked what we hoped was the right one and as soon as the photoflash had gone off – no doubt showing that we'd bombed some pinpricks of light, somewhere above solid cloud – I swung the aircraft hard round to the right and held a westerly heading to make good our escape from the hornets' nest beneath.

Then it happened. A rapid series of bangs that I felt as much as heard, as though someone was attacking the aircraft with a pneumatic drill. 'Corkscrew port, skipper.' Chester's voice from the rear turret rose to a scream. I banked hard left and pulled the nose down below the horizon, hoping to turn into the threat and thus spoiling the night fighter's aim. O-Orange responded sluggishly to the controls – we'd been hit hard.

'Gunners, can you see him?' I grunted, struggling against the g forces that pinned me into the seat and made my head and arms feel like lumps of lead.

Sergeant Chester's voice came over the intercom. 'No, skipper. Keep turning, the bastard can't be far away.'

With difficulty, I rolled the wings level, reduced the power and eased the Lancaster out of the dive. We were now heading back towards Berlin and I needed almost full right rudder to keep the aircraft straight. 'Check starboard down,' I said, standing our long-suffering O-Orange on its starboard wingtip.

'Nothing seen,' replied both gunners, almost in chorus.

'Port outer's on fire, skipper. Feathering it now.' To my right, Sgt Boyle, the flight engineer was a blur of activity as he closed the port outer throttle, pressed and held the feathering button at the bottom of his console, switched off the engine's magnetos, leaned over the throttle quadrant to shut the left engine master cock and then reached down for the fire extinguisher button. I chanced a nervous glance to my left. The fire seemed to be out but we were still a long way from home with no idea how much precious fuel we might be losing from our damaged left wing. Temporary immortality was all very well, but this was bloody frightening.

Chester's voice crackled over the intercom. 'Rear turret's U/S, skipper.' Losing the port outer engine had robbed us of hydraulic power to the rear turret. 'Roger that. Keep your eyes peeled,' I replied.

With only three serviceable engines we were unable to maintain height and so began a weary trudge home at 10,000 ft and 130 knots. As the white runway lights of Leckonby appeared out of the drizzle at 500 ft on the approach I felt as though we had been airborne a lifetime. Then, as we turned onto our parking slot in the pre-dawn darkness, I realised that tomorrow would be Christmas day.

Chapter Thirteen

Low cloud and driving sleet meant that ops were cancelled for the night of the 24th of December. The glad tidings came just before lunch and, as one, everyone headed for the bars of their respective messes.

I had just ordered a pint when a female voice caught my attention. 'Glad to see you made it back. We were a bit worried when you were reported overdue.' I turned to see the WAAF signals officer who had briefed us for both the Dusseldorf and Berlin raids.

'Yes. It was a long flog home on three engines. The Flight Sergeant wasn't happy – says he won't let me use his aeroplane again if I don't take better care of it.'

She laughed and, hearing that welcome sound, I realised just how much I had missed female company since arriving at Leckonby – I was now twenty-four after all. I introduced myself and learned that she was called Betty Clark and had been studying classics at Newnham College, Cambridge before the war interrupted her studies and she had volunteered to serve in the Women's Auxiliary Air Force.

'So how does being a whizz at Latin and Greek help with signals?' I asked.

That tinkling laugh again. 'Everybody asks me that. Teleprinters, Morse, wireless, R/T they're just languages, that's all. Same as Latin or Greek.'

Intrigued, I let her do most of the talking. A solid, horsey, Home Counties background, public school and a scholarship to read classics. Way out of my league, of course, but I was flattered that she was taking the time to talk to me and was secretly amused at some of the envious glances our conversation was attracting from the other officers in the room. What was it Hudson had said about many being called but none chosen? Could I really be that lucky?

'It's Christmas Day tomorrow,' Betty said.

'Bit of a long way to go to play football against Jerry between the trenches,' I replied.

'No, it's not that. You see there's a dance on at the Assembly Rooms in Lincoln tonight. Frank Dey and his orchestra – I hear they're awfully good.' Then she paused. 'You do dance, don't you?' I nodded and she continued, eyes looking down as though embarrassed. 'I know this must sound awfully forward seeing as we've only just met, but you see, there's a whole gang of us going and we're a man short. Would you like to come?'

'You mean to the dance?'

'Yes of course, silly. Where did you think I meant?' That infectious laugh again.

'I'd be delighted to,' I replied.

We chatted for a few more minutes. Betty then left to catch up on overdue paperwork and I returned to the bar. A voice by my shoulder caused me to turn round. 'You don't hang about, do you?' said one of the other B-Flight pilots, standing uncomfortably close and glaring at me.

'What do you mean?' I asked.

He gave a laugh that sounded far from friendly. 'Muscling in like that. You've only been here five minutes and now you're off dancing with the only eligible popsie for miles. Bad show, y'know.'

I pinched him on the cheek and smiled. 'Well, old lad, you've either got it or you haven't.' He swatted my hand away angrily. Jealousy? Too much beer? Too

210

many nights over Berlin? I never did find out. In a few weeks he would be dead along with his entire crew.

**

Later that evening, Betty and I caught the train from Leckonby Junction to Lincoln. It was packed with all ranks, eager for the bright lights and for a few hours' welcome oblivion – a tinsel and fairy-light escape from the drabness of the fifth winter of the war.

We half walked, half ran the few hundred yards that separated the Assembly Rooms from Lincoln station, huddling under Betty's umbrella in a futile attempt to keep dry. For some reason we both seemed to find the episode hilarious and, giggling like maniacs, burst into the warmth and light of the foyer.

The evening passed in a blur for me. I had forgotten what little I knew of the etiquette of ballroom dancing and the arcane rules of how a dance card worked, but it seemed that within a matter of minutes of arriving, the Frank Dey orchestra was playing out with a waltz and, as my good luck would have it, I was the last man on Betty's card. The floor was packed and our attempts to dance were reduced to a slow-moving shuffle in the press of bodies orbiting anti-clockwise under the glitter ball high above us.

Betty fixed me with her pale blue eyes and I felt the awakening of long-forgotten desires. 'I've had a lovely time this evening,' she said. 'Thanks so much for coming along at such short…' As she spoke we collided with another couple, forcing the two of us into an intimate proximity which would have left her in no doubt about my state of arousal. Rather than pulling away, she stayed pressed against me and then slowly ground her hips against me before resuming the usual arm's length respectability of the waltz. The message was unmistakeable but her features displayed barely a flicker that anything out of the ordinary had happened. Just the trace of a smile told me she was enjoying the effect she was having on me.

We ran back to the station, feet splashing through the puddles on the pavements, and made the last train to Leckonby Junction with seconds to spare. Panting and laughing, we caught our breath as it clanked and wheezed into the blackout. Not for the first time I caught that cocktail of smells that was wartime Britain; cigarette smoke, polish, the camphor-based insecticide used to treat military uniforms, and the sour tang of sweat.

At Leckonby a sea of blue uniforms spilled out onto the platform. Still buzzing with the party atmosphere, everyone seemed to be speaking at once as we trooped down the steps to the buses waiting to take us back to reality. I barely had time to exchange more than a couple of words with Betty before she disappeared to round up some of her straggling WAAF charges who had clearly had one cherry brandy too many and whose virtue she considered under threat from an equally boisterous group of NCO aircrew who were trying to persuade them to board their bus instead of the one marked "*WAAF Personnel Only*".

***

The weather remained dismal and overcast. Christmas 1943 was mud-coloured rather than white, but at least it gave the crews of Bomber Command a respite and, for some, a few more precious days of life. Our reprieve was short-lived, however, and on the night of the 29th we set off once more to Berlin. We ran into icing over the Baltic which forced us down to below 10,000 feet. The target itself was covered by cloud and only a handful of scattered target markers showed where the Pathfinder squadrons had done their best to find the aiming point. There was no sign of intense fires below us, a sure sign that we were either in the wrong place or that the bombing had been so sporadic that no serious damage had been done. We bombed on what Hudson considered the most likely position of the city and then turned for home. By the time we reached a dank and dripping Leckonby, we had been airborne over 9 hours. We were so weary that even the prospect of the all-ranks dance on New Year's Eve could not fire us with any enthusiasm, and I wandered back to my room through the pre-dawn drizzle, careless of my own discomfort.

By default I had recently acquired a new room-mate, a talkative Canadian pilot from Winnipeg, fresh out of training – to my eternal shame I forgot his name as soon as he had told me it. Tonight's raid had been his first operation and I noticed with not too much concern that he wasn't back yet. When I awoke several hours later his bed was still untouched and a now familiar arrangement of wax seals and string across his locker door told me all I needed to know. I had been so deeply asleep that the effects team had been able to let themselves in to the room and had done their job without waking me.

Around mid-morning, night gave way imperceptibly to a lighter shade of gloom and, unable to sleep any more, I got up and splashed my way through the drizzle to the mess. I had only been there five minutes, reading an out-of-date magazine and sipping at a mug of stewed tea, when a tannoy broadcast broke the news that operations were cancelled for that night. Once more, time hung heavy on my hands and I realised the truth of the saying that war is made up of long periods of boredom punctuated by short intervals of sheer terror. That said, despite my current overcast of ennui, I felt deeply and wonderfully alive in a way that I had completely forgotten. Like the onset of winter, the fires of youth dampen so slowly that the victim never feels a thing – time's anaesthesia had neutered the old Bill Price, but now I felt like a young tomcat, ready to take on all-comers.

Chapter Fourteen

New Year's Eve dawned every bit as gloomy as the previous days, ending any speculation that the all ranks' dance might be interrupted by the war. The enforced idleness was frustrating, but at the same time it allowed the Lancaster crews of RAF Leckonby another respite.

Those of us not on duty helped put up decorations and by the end of the afternoon, a drab concrete mess hut had been turned into a passable imitation of a dance hall. Some resourceful soul had 'liberated' two Christmas trees which were now festooned with strings of cockpit instrument lights and garlands made from the aluminium strips of 'window' cut into patterns. A glitter ball had been made from papier mâché and milk bottle tops, and garlands of coloured paper streamers criss-crossed the metal roof trusses.

The festivities started at eight but my hopes of getting a dance with Betty were thwarted by the sheer weight of numbers. Men outnumbered women on bomber bases by over ten to one and the competition was too great, so I retreated to the bar where I bought drinks for my crew. Sgt Boyle, my flight engineer, was clearly no stranger to dance halls and he somehow managed to find a partner for almost every number. Peters, the bomb aimer, seemed to come out of his shell a little after a couple of beers, as did Wells the wireless operator who succeeded in monopolising the attention of a plump little WAAF corporal who barely came up to his chest. Neither of them could dance a step but that didn't seem to bother them as they tottered round in ungainly circles, clinging to one another like survivors from a shipwreck. Hudson, drank one half of shandy, made his excuses and left. Sgt Grey, my Glaswegian mid-upper gunner, emboldened by drink made innumerable attempts to find a dance partner but without success. And as for 'Charlie' Chester, our rear gunner, he was content to spend the evening drinking and watching proceedings with cynical detachment. My hopes of getting the crew to bond seemed as remote as ever.

Just before midnight I got dragged into a conga line which snaked its way drunkenly around a dance floor that was by now sticky with spilt beer. The air inside the hut had become almost unbreathable, a cocktail of cigarette smoke, beer fumes and stale sweat that caught in the back of the throat. Then came the obligatory tuneless bellowing of 'Auld Lang Syne' and the countdown to midnight. I had tried to enjoy the evening but had failed – this wasn't my party, I shouldn't even have been there and I desperately wanted to be anywhere else but here. I made to leave, but a woman's voice, raised in anger, made me stop. I couldn't catch what she was saying against the background hubbub of yelling and cheering, but something didn't seem right. I pushed my way through the crowd and a few feet away came across Betty in a clinch with the pilot whose cheek I had pinched in the mess bar a few days earlier. He was trying to kiss her but she kept pushing him away.

Her voice was slurred. 'Look, just stop it, will you. I've had a lovely time but I want to go to bed.'

He pulled her towards him again with a leer, 'Sounds like the best offer I've had all evening. Just give me a kiss first.' He was none too sober either.

She put up a hand to fend him off and accidently

caught him across the face.

'Prick-teasing little tart,' he spat, wiping a trace of blood away from his mouth with the back of his hand.

I had heard enough and pulled him round by the shoulder. 'Listen, old son, Section Officer Clark has said she wants to go to bed and it's clear you're not invited.'

He made to throw a punch but given that I was much taller than him, he thought better of it and instead, stumbled unsteadily to the door mumbling threats of what he would do the next time he saw me.

Betty's eyes were glazed and she shifted unsteadily from one foot to another. 'D'you know…? D'you know? I think that horrible little man was trying to get me tight,' she said.

'Looks like he did a pretty good job. Are you all right?'

This was clearly a difficult question and it took her a long time to answer. 'I *think* so, but I do feel a bit funny.'

'I'll see you home.'

On the way out Betty tripped on the steps and would have fallen had I not caught her. She seemed to find this hilarious, but after only a few paces she turned aside and threw up into a flower bed. Luckily, the blackout saved her the embarrassment of being identified in this state and eventually, after two more stops to be sick and then her loudly stated decision that she couldn't walk any further and would spend the night on the grass, I managed to get her back to the WAAF officers' block. After much fumbling, Betty found her room key, located the light switch at the third attempt and allowed me to steer her towards the bed. As she sat down, she suddenly put her arms around my neck and pulled me down on top of her.

'Do you know?' she slurred, her face pressed close against mine. 'I really liked it the other night when we were dancing and you got all hard.' She giggled. 'Are you all hard now?' She tugged at the waistband of my trousers.

'Betty, I really don't think this is a good idea,' I said, disentangling myself and standing up.

A pout and arms reaching out to me again. 'Don't you like me?' Then she frowned. 'You're not a pansy, are you?'

'I like you just fine,' I replied. 'And no, I'm not a pansy, but *you* are very drunk.' I closed the door behind me and crept outside, keeping to the shadows until well clear of the WAAF accommodation. The penalties for being caught there were biblical in their severity, even for a good-ish Samaritan who had come very close to yielding to temptation.

***

New Year's Day brought a break in the weather and those whose hangovers still clung to them had now to face the prospect of a night over Berlin. In clear skies, the Luftwaffe's night fighters cut bloody swathes through the ranks of the heavies and the following morning, two empty dispersals at Leckonby marked the loss of another fourteen men from 362 Squadron.

To everyone's dismay, we were 'on' again the following night – Berlin once more. The route to the target was trouble free and the gunners called only a single loss. However, over the target, not only was the marking sporadic, meaning that the RAF crews were unable to concentrate their bombing, causing bombs to fall in open countryside, but the night fighters fell upon us in droves. I lost count of the number of 'corkscrews' that the gunners called and all around us, greasy orange fireballs marked the pyres of crew after crew.

During January 1944 362 Squadron made seven more trips to Berlin at the cost of ten crews. It didn't take much to work out that the chances of a crew surviving a tour of thirty trips was now less than one in four. To my shame, I now revelled in the excitement of doing this job, safe in the knowledge that I was, literally, fireproof. One small piece of good came from my deception – at long last, my crew began to bond. Little, by little they started to show unmistakeable signs of confidence in their own ability.

It was over a week before I caught up with Betty again. We were in the officers' mess just before lunch. She pretended not to see me, turned away and found something absolutely riveting in a month-old magazine on the ante-room table. I looked over her shoulder to see an article on Land Army girls hay-making. 'Something I said?' I asked.

'You must hate me,' she said, blushing and turning away.

'Not a bit of it. You got tight, that's all – not that I can remember much, I wasn't exactly sober myself.'

For the first time in our exchange she made eye contact. 'That's very kind of you to say so. I'm terribly ashamed at getting so drunk. And…' she hesitated and then stopped.

'And what?'

She flushed bright red once more and lowered her

eyes. 'And, well… you know. Thanks for being so decent. There are lots of chaps who would've taken advantage of me.'

'All in good time,' I said with a conspiratorial wink. This seemed to break the ice and we chatted away amiably until the subject of tonight's op came up. Then the conversation clouded over. 'I take it you've seen the signals from Command and you know where we're going?' I asked.

She nodded.

'And you're not allowed to tell us of course.'

'That's right.'

I forced a smile. 'Full fuel load, has to be Berlin again, doesn't it?'

She looked away. 'I… I'm not allowed to say.'

'Don't worry. We all know it's Berlin. What we don't know for sure is who's coming home tomorrow morning and who isn't.'

She put her hand on my arm. 'Please make sure you come safe home, won't you, Bill?'

'Don't worry, I'll be all right.' Now it was my turn to feel embarrassed. Sailing under false colours has never been my strong point. What's more, to add to my feelings of guilt and shame, it was pretty obvious, even to one as tone-deaf to these matters as I am, that Betty was becoming fond of me.

Serious relationships between WAAF and RAF personnel were strictly forbidden and we both risked being posted away to other stations if it became too obvious we were a couple.

***

A particularly hair-raising slog to Berlin was followed the next day by a planned raid on Essen. To everyone's great relief, bad weather meant the operation was cancelled at midday, and as luck would have it, Betty was off shift too. We caught the bus to Boston and spent the evening dancing at the Gliderdrome. According to Betty, my dancing had improved from dreadful to merely bad, but that evening something between us finally clicked into place and as we walked arm-in-arm back to the bus stop it seemed the most natural thing in the world to kiss her.

'I thought I was going to die waiting for you to do that,' she said when at last we surfaced for air. 'Talk about *Time's wingèd chariot*, Bill.'

I finished the quotation. '*The grave's a fine and private place, but none, I think, do there embrace*. Isn't that how it goes?'

'Something like that,' she said in a way that made me stop and look into her face. Her eyes wouldn't meet mine. 'I worry about you, Bill. You know, when you're on ops.'

I thought for a moment as we stood, sheltering in the lee of a hedge while the last of the evening traffic splashed by along the road towards the Town Bridge. This talk of death and the folly of not seizing the moment made my decision for me. I had to tell her, the need to share the knowledge of my plight with someone was overwhelming. I took a deep breath. 'Do you believe in premonitions?'

She shook her head. 'No. No premonitions, no God, no ghosts. All stuff and nonsense.'

This wasn't going to be easy. I tried another tack. 'What about the blokes who know they're for the chop?

We've both seen that often enough.'

A tone of anger entered her voice. 'Self-fulfilling rubbish. They give up, stop trying, that's why they get killed – nothing's pre-ordained. If you're trying to tell me you think you're for the chop, you can forget it. You and your crew are going to finish your thirty ops or I'll kill you myself!'

I raised my hands in surrender. I had tried to explain, but I'd funked it. Then, as the conversation continued I gradually awoke to the reality that Betty and I ending up in a clinch had been engineered by her alone.

***

The next night saw us out mine-laying – "gardening" as it was known – in the waters of the Kattegat. Down at low altitude we were buffeted by gales and driving sleet – a four hour trip with the ever-present risk that the slightest navigation error might take us right over a flak battery on the coast of occupied Denmark, our black mood made worse by the knowledge that "gardening" missions only counted as half an op towards the thirty that made up a tour.

It was our last trip for a week. The moon period intervened to give 362 Squadron's crews a welcome respite. The moon parties were still held but sadly, the pianist and the members of the "Sod's Opera" had all been killed, so we contented ourselves with drinking too much and tuneless bellowing of rude songs. Someone fetched a rugby ball and we cleared away the mess furniture and divided ourselves into two teams. Early in the fray I tried to tackle a Canadian wireless operator twice my size and as he mowed me down my ankle turned over. Even with the anaesthetising effect of the alcohol in my system, the pain was sickening. I hobbled to the sidelines and sat down to inspect the damage. Already, my ankle had swollen to what seemed like twice its normal size and any attempt to put weight on it send vivid jags of pain up my leg.

Hung-over and sheepish, I reported to the Medical Officer the next day. He prodded and poked at my ankle, pronounced it sprained rather than broken, told me not to fly for a week, strapped me up with adhesive bandage halfway to my knee and sent me to collect a walking stick from the dispensary. I had no intention of opening myself up to an inevitable tide of banter and ridicule by hobbling around, propped up on a walking stick, but after a few agonising steps down the corridor leading away from the MO's consulting room, I realised that I desperately needed the bloody thing.

I skulked behind a newspaper in a corner of the mess ante room for the rest of the morning, my invalid's stick hidden next to my armchair. I was on the point of dozing off when a familiar voice shook me out of my reverie.

'What are you doing hiding in here?' It was Betty. She looked down to where I was trying to hide my bandaged leg under the table in front of me. She spotted the carpet slipper on my swollen foot and stifled a giggle. 'Did you drop your beer glass on it?' she asked.

'No. I did it playing mess rugby, if you must know. Off flying for a whole bloody week.'

'Now, now. No need to be grumpy. Come and have lunch. I've got some news too.'

I struggled to my feet and with the aid of my hated walking stick, hobbled along towards the dining room. A barrage of catcalls followed me and I did my best to smile and go along with the joke. Betty was invited to join one of the A Flight crews for lunch and so it wasn't until later that I managed to catch up with her.

'So what's the scoop?' I asked.

'I've got the whole of next weekend off. Imagine that. A whole weekend.' Her face wore the look of a child who'd just been told Christmas had come early.

'We could go out somewhere,' I said. 'That is, if it wasn't for my stupid leg.'

She laughed. 'It doesn't have to be a hiking trip. They do have things called buses and trains these days. Where did you have in mind?'

I thought for a moment. 'How about a day out at the seaside? Skegness is supposed to be "bracing" – according to the posters anyway.'

'More like freezing at this time of year,' she replied.

There are times when my mouth becomes completely decoupled from my brain, and something else, often far baser takes over. 'I'd keep you warm,' I said. 'We could go for the whole weekend.'

For a moment I thought I had completely overstepped the mark and that she was going to slap me, but instead she looked me in the eye and asked, 'Are you suggesting what I think you're suggesting?'

I gulped. 'Yes. You were the one who quoted Marvell, remember. *The grave's a fine and private place, but none I think do there embrace.* That was it, wasn't it?'

'You do realise they'd court martial us if we were caught?'

'That'd be a blow,' I replied. 'You mean I'd have to give up being shot at over Germany every night?'

'No,' she said, her features suddenly grave. 'They'd

224

remuster you as a private soldier in the PBI and send you off to get killed somewhere else like they do with the LMF cases.'

And so it was that on a clear but bitingly cold Friday evening we caught the train to Skegness. I had managed to find one of the few boarding houses in the town that had not been requisitioned for military use. The landlady of the Dunnottar Castle Hotel was a fearsome Scot who eyed us with a suspicion born of many years' successfully thwarting the plans of would-be fornicators and adulterers. Betty had taken the precaution of slipping her signet ring onto the third finger of her left hand and twisting it so that the thin part of the band was uppermost. This and her oblique references to "my husband's leg wound" seemed to do the trick and the hotel's blue-rinsed Cerberus was well and truly duped. So much so that as a special treat she found us an electric fire to heat our room, but on strict instructions not to put both bars on at once. 'There's a war on, you know,' she chided us.

'So they tell me,' I replied, earning a dig in the ribs from Betty and a look of Siberian froideur from the landlady.

Our bedroom was equally glacial. In a wrought iron grate we found a small pile of cheap coal splinters. Had it not been for a page from last week's Skegness Standard, the fragments would have all fallen through the bars into the ash pan. We plugged the electric fire in and defiantly switched both bars on, huddling together to keep warm. Neither of us spoke. Finally, Betty broke the silence. 'I'm nervous,' she said, her eyes downcast.

'You needn't be,' I said, stroking her hair and kissing her on the cheek.

'So you've done this with lots of girls then?'

My ignorance of how this game was played by 1940s rules left me scrabbling for an answer. The best I could manage was, 'No I haven't. And how would *you* feel if I asked you how many other men you've been to bed with?'

'Sorry. I didn't mean it like that.'

'I know. I was only joking.'

She helped me to my feet and we kissed, just as we had done on the way home from the dance in Boston. We stayed pressed close together for what seemed a delicious eternity until, by an unspoken mutual consent, we made our way to the bed where I gently began to undress her.

At first, Betty proved to be a timid and almost passive lover, but by the time we finally turned off the light, it was clear that the shock of the new was no longer a restraint. We clung together in the darkness.

'This is wonderful, Bill,' she whispered, nuzzling my neck. 'I never want it to end.'

'Nor do I,' I said as a tear rolled down my cheek. 'Nor do I.'

The following morning, after breakfast, along with the other guests, we were chivvied out of the Dunnottar Castle Hotel with strict instructions not to return before five o'clock. Our collars turned up against the wind we walked along the sea front. A squad of recruits from the nearby naval base, HMS Royal Arthur, marched past, with cold-blued hands trying not to lose hold of the heavy rifles sloped over their shoulders. On each face was etched a picture of abject, frozen misery. We waited for them to pass and then crossed over to where the railings above the beach had been reinforced with coils of barbed wire.

My ankle was feeling a little less tender, so with Betty holding my arm and with the aid of my stick, I managed to hobble the hundred yards or so to the entrance to the pier only to find it barricaded and its steel doors welded shut. A sign proclaimed it, "*Closed for the duration of hostilities.*" From the roof of the ticket office, a seagull turned a beady yellow eye on us, squawked and then flew off.

'I think he was laughing at me,' I said.

Betty laughed. 'Well then, run him over next time you go flying. That'll teach him.'

Our naive hopes of a walk on the beach were dispelled by the presence of more barbed wire and the fact that the sand was littered with anti-invasion obstacles, hung with mines, even at this late stage of the war.

The cold drove us to seek shelter in a café where we found a corner table and made one pot of tea last us until lunchtime while we talked about everything and nothing.

'You've never told me what you're going to do when this is all over,' said Betty, tangling her fingers with mine.

I looked down into the tea leaves at the bottom of my cup, but as to my future, they remained mute. 'I don't know any more,' I said.

'What do you mean?'

'You wouldn't understand.'

Betty wasn't to be diverted so easily. 'Try me,' she said.

The pain of having to lie to her went deep. 'Well, before I joined up I had all sorts of ideas. Thought I'd try Australia or maybe somewhere like Kenya. You know, see the world, get my knees brown. Do something a bit different.'

I felt her pale blue eyes see right through my charade. 'So what's changed? Why did joining up put you off the colonies?'

'A couple of things really,' I said, again, failing to meet her gaze.

'Such as?'

'Such as the fact that my chances of surviving thirty ops are about nil. You know that as well as I do.'

She wagged a finger in my face. 'Now stop that at once. The bloody Germans won't get you… they won't… they can't… I won't let them…' she broke off and turned away, dabbing away a tear with the corner of her handkerchief. I took her hand and held it tight while she composed herself. 'Listen, Bill,' she continued. 'If you do come through this and you do go off to Timbuktu or wherever, could I come with you?'

The tension eased a little. 'Of course. How are you with lions?' I asked.

She snapped her fingers, 'Putty in my hands.'

Not for the first time since my arrival at Leckonby, I inwardly flinched at the unforeseen consequences that my deception was having on others.

'I'd love to see Africa one day,' she said, putting her hand on my arm. 'And when you're back on ops, you will be careful, won't you?'

"You will be careful, won't you?" Hearing those words again cut through me like a knife and I hastily changed the subject.

We had lunch – Brown Windsor Soup followed by gristly lamb – at the Grand Hotel on North Parade and

228

then spent the afternoon in the cinema, leaning close together in the flickering darkness, our fingers entwined, lost in a make-believe world where the good guys wear white hats and the bad guys black ones. For a few brief hours we were travellers in a land that didn't smell of floor polish, carbolic soap or stale sweat and where the curvaceous Jane Russell could pass herself off as a gunslinger. No flak, no nightmares, no empty seats in the briefing room, just wonderful escapist nonsense where the hero gets his gal and they ride off into the sunset together on the same horse.

At just before five, we joined a huddle of our fellow guests in the lee of the privet hedge outside the hotel, stamping our feet and blowing into cupped hands in an attempt to keep warm. The nets twitched. The old bat knew we were out there but still took what was probably only a few minutes – but seemed like an eternity – to open the door.

The temperature inside our room was almost indistinguishable from that outside on the sea-front, so we turned on the forbidden second bar, lit the pile of coal scraps and huddled together under the sheets fully dressed until we were warm enough to take our clothes off.

***

Whoever christened Skegness's Ritz hotel after its namesake in London's Piccadilly clearly had an over-developed sense of irony. Dinner was even more indigestible than the lunch we had suffered at The Grand and we were insanely grateful to swap the smell of drains and overcooked cabbage for the biting cold of the

Grand Parade.

The Locarno ballroom had seen better days. Inside, dark blue Royal Navy uniforms outnumbered RAF blue and the atmosphere around the bar seethed with menace. Outside, the presence of uniformed police patrols from both services gave warning that come throwing-out time, the rivalry between the two services was likely to boil over.

Despite the nagging pain in my ankle, I managed to hobble round in circles on the dance floor while propped up by Betty.

'When the war's over we can do this every weekend,' she whispered as we danced.

This sounded like a bad case of wedding bells in the ears. 'I hear the Locarno in Timbuktu is quite the place these days,' I said, trying to lighten the tone.

'I don't care where it is, so long as we can be together.'

I so longed to tell her I felt the same.

Tired and happy, we made it back to the Dunnottar Castle Hotel just before the ten thirty curfew. The landlady fixed us with a Presbyterian scowl and another admonishment not to put the second bar on.

All night we talked and loved. Sleep could wait. These moments were too precious to lose.

***

The following afternoon we caught the train back to Leckonby. We found a compartment to ourselves and Betty dozed, her head on my shoulder, while I gazed at the flat monotony of the Lincolnshire countryside. As the train clattered over the points just after Little

Steeping station, Betty woke up and slid her hand into mine. Then came the words I'd been dreading. 'Bill, you do know I love you, don't you?'

'Yes I do.'

'And?'

'And I wish you didn't.' I saw her features crumple and the tears well up in her eyes. I pulled her to me. 'It's not that I don't care for you, Betty. I do. Desperately. I just don't want you to be hurt when one night I don't come back.'

'But you will come back. You will. I know it.' Her tone was petulant, like an angry child.

Once more, my moral courage failed me. 'Listen, the last thing I want to do is hurt you –'

She pulled away from me. 'You've got another girl, haven't you? That's what it is.'

'No. There's no other girl. Just you. If I finish this tour in one piece, then we'll talk about the future. I just don't want to see you hurt.'

'A future together you mean?' She was persistent, if nothing else.

'Yes. Together. For always.' I hated myself for what I had just said.

Chapter Fifteen

Even now, I can recall almost every second of those first weeks of operations at Leckonby – the fear, the night fighters, the six uncongenial strangers with whom I shared an aircraft on those nights, and worst of all, the searing red fireballs that marked the loss of so many young airmen, so many hopes and dreams snuffed out before their time. It all jarred so horribly with the few precious hours of solitude that Betty and I managed to snatch – furtive, desperate couplings and evenings spent close to one another on the dance floor, savouring her touch and the smell of her hair as she buried her head into my neck.

Back on the ground it was impossible to explain to anyone just what it was like to be on operations night after night – not even the intelligence staff who debriefed us after every trip could ever come close to understanding the reality of our words that they so patiently transcribed into official terms. How could they possibly know what 'heavy flak' or 'vigorous night-fighter opposition' actually looked and felt like? Not even Betty could realise what the bomber boys went through, waiting in line, dry-mouthed, stomach full of butterflies, for the green light from the runway caravan that told you it was your turn to take off, possibly for the last time. And in my turn, I could never fathom the depths of courage shown by the aircrews who did not share my blessing, or if truth be told, my curse, of knowing when they would die.

Whether as close friends, crew-members or mere acquaintances that war had thrown together, all bomber aircrew faced the vast gulf between two realities – on one hand, the nightly terror of violent, agonising death in the skies over occupied Europe, and on the other, the prosaic rhythm of life on a hastily constructed airfield in rural Lincolnshire. Some sought solace in drink, others in dances, socials and similar distractions, whereas a few turned in on themselves, reading, walking alone and shunning the noise and sweat of the crowd. The members of this last group were usually the first to die.

After our weekend together in Skegness, the relationship with Betty had turned into something neither of us had planned. I longed to stay with her, yet I knew that I would be returning to the twenty-first century before the end of March – something that I could not explain to anyone without being certified insane.

So it was with some relief that in February, along with the rest of my crew, I was granted a week's leave. I told Betty that I would be going down to London to see my parents, then I broke the news to Harrison. 'I suppose you want to go back?' he asked. I nodded in reply. 'Well, that's fine,' he said. 'Just so long as you don't get any silly ideas about going AWOL.'

'Perish the thought,' I said.

'Good. Just let me know when you're leaving and I'll come to the Ferryboat with you.'

'Tomorrow evening.'

'I'll see you outside the station at seven,' he said, as though the prospect of arranging my return was no more than popping down to the corner shop. And then he added ominously, 'You never know, we might bump into one another in Lincoln.'

Harrison was waiting for me the following evening. At first, all I could see was the glow of his cigarette as he sheltered from the raw east wind in the lee of the station building. Without a word, he emerged from the shadows and nodded towards the Hobbs Bank Drain. As we clambered to the top I could see that the landlord of the Ferryboat Inn was already waiting for us, his boat nodding and rolling on the waves stirred up by the wind. Without speaking he motioned me to sit at the stern while Harrison climbed aboard. Hard pellets of sleet peppered us as we rowed across and followed the path from the jetty. Leading the way, the landlord opened the door and pushed aside the blackout curtain. As he did so, a warm, soupy fug of beer and cigarette smoke welcomed us and I stood blinking in the unaccustomed brightness. He motioned me to the door next to the counter and I followed him down the same corridor I remembered from my arrival. My God, that seemed a lifetime ago. Then, he paused by the back door, looked towards Harrison who nodded in reply, opened it and ushered me outside into the cold and dark. The door closed behind me with a bang. All was black as pitch. I turned back to look at the pub – nothing, no Ferryboat Inn, just a vague mound in a field beside the canal bank and the sting of sleet against my face.

***

The first thing I noticed when I awoke the following morning was how different everything smelled. No more floor polish, cigarette smoke, drains, stale sweat and boiled cabbage, just the fresh smell of clean bed linen against my face.

I made to swing myself out of bed, but forgot that I was no longer twenty-four, but fifty-six with knees that had been twice round the clock. The effort of standing up made me wince and my back joined in the protest at my sudden movements.

I pulled on my dressing gown – that too smelled almost overpoweringly perfumed to my coarsened senses – and padded through to the kitchen. While the kettle was boiling I leafed through the pile of mail that had accumulated in my absence and turned on my PC. I had just taken my first sip of tea when it happened – a movement on the kitchen worktop caught my eye. The ginger cat was back. It treated me to a look of contempt, tiptoed round the sink with the grace of a ballerina and then disappeared through the wall next to the microwave. After my earlier mistake of trying to leap out of bed like a twenty-something, the cat was yet another unwelcome reminder of the reality to which I'd returned. I swallowed a couple of pills and stared at my PC screen, willing my hallucinations to stay away.

I turned once more to the 362 Squadron Operation Record Book for February and March 1944 to see what awaited me. A list of familiar names; Berlin (several times), Magdeburg, Frankfurt, Augsburg, Schweinfurt, Leipzig – 362 lost five aircraft out of eighteen sent on that raid and now, all thirty-five names had faces. The list continued through March with the same dismal butcher's bill of young lives until I got to the date that interested me most – the 29th of March. Depleted by so many losses, 362 Squadron could only muster twelve aircraft for the raid on Brunswick. Bomber Command's loss rate was catastrophic – thirteen percent of the aircraft sent out that night failed to return – the forecast cloud en route never materialised and, under a bright moon, the Luftwaffe's night fighters wrought terrible destruction. By a ghastly twist of fate, of the twelve Lancasters that took off from Leckonby that night, not one returned. My aircraft, I knew, had crashed shortly after takeoff, three others crash-landed in southern England after being badly damaged and the remaining eight, including Press-on Preston's crew, were shot down. Of the fifty-six men in these aircraft, only ten parachuted to safety to become prisoners of war. The entire squadron had been destroyed in a single night. However, the RAF's training machine had evidently churned relentlessly on, because by the end of the following week, 362 Squadron was already getting back to strength with a new CO, Flight Commanders, three crews recalled from leave and ten new crews, two of which were starting their second tour of ops.

A few months earlier I would have scoffed at such a notion, but now I understood how the horror of this loss had seeped into the very fabric of RAF Leckonby and why it was still manifesting itself today. That thirteen percent of the Lancasters and Halifaxes despatched to Brunswick had failed to return was just another grim statistic in the audit of Bomber Command's war and in the same way, 362 Squadron's losses that night were nothing more than an unlucky roll of the dice.

A further search on the Commonwealth War Graves Commission's website showed me that of the 362 Squadron crews who had been shot down over Germany, the majority had their final resting place in one of three cemeteries. To me, these names were now more than statistics, they had faces, personalities, some of them I counted as friends. I had no intention of sharing their fate, but I reasoned that the least I could do was to make my own small act of homage by visiting their graves, starting my visit at the CWGC cemeteries at Reichswald and Rheinburg, both near the Dutch border. It took me only a few mouse clicks to make the bookings and I found a flight from Humberside to Weeze airport, an airfield I had visited many times when it was called RAF Laarbruch. It seemed only right that I should fly to Germany on the evening of the 29th of March.

At around ten I phoned the Lincoln Post's office and told them I'd be coming in. Bennett, the editor, welcomed me back and accepted without demur my story that I'd been too ill to work. I then drew an envelope out of my jacket pocket and handed it across the desk to him. He opened it and read my resignation letter to the end. He then looked at me over the top of his glasses and said, 'Well, I can't say I'm surprised, old son, just hope you find enough to keep you occupied.' He then trotted out the ritual platitudes about 'dropping in to see them if ever I was passing', ignoring the fact that anyone walking down Lincoln High Street couldn't help but pass the newspaper's front door.

So it was with a sense of relief that I headed out once more into the gloom of a damp February morning and set off to buy some food. I had only gone a few paces when I became aware of a figure walking in step by my side. Harrison. 'Why can't you leave me alone?' I hissed out of the corner of my mouth. 'I've said I'll come back and I will.'

'Just making sure you're all right,' he replied. 'Don't be surprised if you have visitors.'

'Stop talking in bloody riddles, man,' I said,

stopping in my tracks, all earlier feelings of contentment now destroyed. I turned towards him, hands on hips, but all I saw was a middle-aged woman shopper who looked at me very oddly and hurried on, crossing the road to put as much space between herself and the local madman as possible. I took one of my pills and dismissed Harrison's appearance as a hallucination.

What happened that evening showed me I was wrong. I had just finished clearing away the supper things and was about to settle down in front of the TV when I heard a tapping at the window. At first I ignored it as the product of tiredness and an over-active imagination, but then it came again – tap, tap, tap. I pulled the curtains aside. What I saw made me reel back in shock. The courtyard outside my kitchen was full of people, not just any people but aircrew from 362 Squadron. Some were maimed beyond recognition, others horribly burned while a few looked almost normal save for a greenish, unhealthy pallor to their skin.

The sound of a cough inside the kitchen made me let go of the curtains and spin round in alarm. It was Harrison, dressed in his usual tweed coat and sitting, perfectly relaxed, at my kitchen table. 'Evening, Bill,' he said. 'Told you there might be visitors, didn't I?'

For a second I considered killing him but then realised that would be impossible. 'How the hell did you get in here?' I shouted.

'Come now, Bill,' he replied with a sneer. 'You should know better than to ask silly questions like that.'

'And what are *they* doing here?' I jerked my thumb towards the kitchen window.

'Who?'

238

'You know bloody well who. Them. Your precious sodding visitors. You can bugger off and take them with you.' I marched across to the window and pulled the curtains aside. The courtyard was empty. Then the breeze blew and a bare branch of Wisteria knocked gently against the window. Tap, tap, tap. 'If this is your idea of a joke…' I made to grab at Harrison but there was nobody there. Just the sound of a man's laughter fading into the distance.

When eventually I got to sleep that night, my dreams were haunted by visions of dead aircrews and the sound of Amy's voice calling to me for help. As a result I felt tired and irritable when at last a yellowish-grey dawn broke over Lincoln. Worse still, I realised that I had absolutely nothing to do – no work, no deadlines, no reason for so much as putting one foot in front of the other.

Why I did it, I'll never know, but I finally decided I had to visit Leckonby again, to see for myself whether the modern age had finally blotted out the horrors of the past.

During the weeks since my last visit the old airfield had changed beyond recognition. The new estate had an unmistakeable Sunday morning feel to it as I drove along what was still just recognisable as the line of the south-westerly runway. Front lawns were newly turfed and proud owners were washing their cars on the driveways of identikit houses. The first daffodils were out. On the eastern side of the site, work was still going on and I parked the car to see if I could locate any of the buildings that were now so familiar to me. All had been erased and as I picked my way along a muddy track, the setting would have been tranquil were it not for the whump, whump, whump from the wind turbines which now lowered from the crest of the Wolds. Everything was perfectly normal, wonderfully, boringly normal, but the sense of relief I was so hoping for eluded me. Seeing Leckonby transformed like this left me mourning for my other life – a life where I was young and, for six more weeks anyway, immortal. I turned and started to walk back to the car. As I felt in my pocket for the keys, a movement in the next field the other side of the lane caught my eye – a tall, elderly gentleman was striding along the hedgerow and at his side gambolled a black Labrador. The man stopped and looked directly at me. Colonel Cavendish – this was the final straw, I had to go back.

When I got home I went from room to room calling Harrison's name, but as I had come to learn, people who turn up unbidden are never around when you need them. After ten minutes of calling him I lost patience, grabbed my coat and set off on foot down the hill to the High Street. I hung around for a few minutes outside the Lincoln Post's offices – no Harrison. Next I tried the coffee shop round the corner – still no sign of him. After an hour of fruitless trudging the streets of Lincoln in the raw chill of the east wind, I gave up and went into the bookshop, scene of my earlier embarrassment. I was browsing half-heartedly at the history shelves when a familiar voice came from behind me.

'I understand you're looking for me.'

'Yes. Where the hell have you been?'

'Berlin, since you asked,' replied Harrison. 'Anyway, last time we met you told me to bugger off. So I did.'

The sweat was forming on my brow and I checked

240

over my shoulder to make sure nobody could see me talking to thin air. 'Look, I don't care about that. I'll come back, just call the dogs off, will you? I've got a few days' leave and then I come back to die. Is it too much to ask to leave me in peace?'

'No. It's perfectly reasonable,' he replied with that annoying bloody nonchalance of his. 'Just wanted to make sure you'd got the message.'

I snorted at this. 'Oh I've got the bloody message all right. And I could've done without you conjuring up Colonel Cavendish and his loveable sidekick this morning.'

Harrison frowned. 'Believe me, Bill. I have nothing to do with Cavendish. He comes and goes as he pleases and if it's any consolation he scares me shitless too.'

I shuddered at the thought that even Harrison went in fear of Cavendish. 'So how do I get back?' I asked.

'Come to the Ferryboat at seven on Sunday evening. I'll be waiting for you.'

***

Driving February rains filled the dykes of Lincolnshire to the brim that year. Trapped indoors by the weather with no company and nothing to do, time hung heavily on me once more. The normality I had craved now felt dull after my brief dalliance with early 1944, I missed Betty terribly and I longed to return. However, what would happen to me after I dodged my fate on the 29th of March still nagged at me like a bad tooth.

Chapter Sixteen

The rain continued to fall in stair-rods as I made my way along the side of the Hobbs Bank Drain in the dark. Even the cows and their calves must have been under shelter because I saw not a single living thing until I reached the Ferryboat Inn. I knocked at the back door. Footsteps approached and then I heard the sound of the bolts being drawn back. The landlord's face appeared briefly around the door and without a word he beckoned me inside. I followed him along the dimly-lit corridor and he nodded towards the door leading into the bar.

As promised, Harrison was waiting for me and a few minutes later we were both huddled in the bow of the rowing boat, trying to keep dry under the pouring rain. Once more he had borrowed the CO's car and he drove us back to the mess.

When I reported to the B Flight offices the following morning, there were almost as many new faces as familiar ones. The squadron had been back to Berlin the night before and three more of its aircraft had been lost – another twenty-one men gone and another twenty-one to take their place on the abattoir conveyor belt. My own crew seemed better for their leave. They were now over half way through their tour having seventeen trips to their credit with me lagging two trips behind. Hudson, my mute navigator, actually instigated a conversation and Peters now spoke with the confidence of an old hand. The unspoken belief seemed to be that they might just be the first 362 Squadron crew in nearly a year to survive their tour of thirty ops. I longed to tell them what fate had in store but my courage failed me.

***

The rain turned to heavy snow and it wasn't until the night of the 15th of March that we restarted on operations with a raid on Stuttgart, a city 362 Squadron had bombed twice in the previous few weeks. Of the twenty-seven bombers lost that night, none were from Leckonby and there was even talk that our run of bad luck might have ended. I knew differently. Three nights later, we were part of a mass raid on Frankfurt which left the city a boiling cauldron of flame. One of our aircraft failed to return.

On the night of the 24th word came back from the squadron's engineers of full fuel tanks and a lighter than usual bomb load. We all knew what that meant – Berlin. Our run of good luck had come to an end. The forecast winds were hopelessly inaccurate, but thanks to Hudson's skill as a navigator, we were one of the few aircraft to find and bomb the city centre. Peters did well too, confidently assuring me that the target markers were way to the south-west of the briefed aiming point. Out of the eighteen Leckonby-based Lancasters taking part, two of our crews failed to come home. Virtually none of the men I had met in December were still alive.

It was to be my last operation. By now I desperately wanted to stay – the crew of O-Orange were at last working as a team, I was in love with Betty and distraught at the thought of leaving her. But leave her I must, so, without a word to anyone, on the night of the 28th of March I took my crew for a drink in the Ferryboat Inn. I bought the first round, carrying a tray bearing seven pints of foaming bitter back to our table by the

243

fire. I took a couple of sips and then excused myself. Without pausing, I made my way into the now familiar corridor and in a few paces, my hand hesitated over the handle of the door that stood between a life I had come to love but must forsake, and the grey reality of what was little better than an existence. I took a deep breath, opened the door and ran out into the darkness, crunching over the frozen slush. After about fifty yards I turned round. The Ferryboat Inn had gone. Against the glow from the streetlights of the new housing estate I could just about make out the mound that marked where the pub had once stood.

Chapter Seventeen

The following evening I loaded my suitcase into the back of the car and set off for Humberside Airport to catch the flight to Weeze in Germany.

We were taken by bus from the terminal to an Anglia Airways twin turboprop airliner where I took my seat two rows back from the front of the cabin on the left hand side and settled down to read my book. The other passengers trooped on but I paid them no heed. I thought we were about to start up but the captain's voice came over the PA system, apologising for the delay, saying there were six more passengers still to board but they would be arriving shortly on a second bus.

I was vaguely aware of headlights outside on the ramp and then the sound of men's voices, chattering and bantering as they climbed the short steps to the aircraft. I don't know what made me look up, but what I saw was not possible. The first man was in his late twenties, short, of stocky build and with a broken nose. I blinked and rubbed my eyes, staring at him to make sure. He was the double of 'Charlie' Chester, my rear gunner from 362 Squadron. An unsettling experience, but as I told myself, just a coincidence. Moments later, my confidence was shattered when I saw the next of the latecomers – thin, boyish, with pinched, whippet-like features. Grey, my mid-upper gunner. I gawped at him in disbelief as he walked past but he seemed entirely unaware of my presence. Close behind him strode a tall individual whose pale features were heavily freckled and topped with a mop of badly cut orange hair – Wells, the wireless operator. By now I was frozen with terror, dreading what I knew must come. It did. Hudson, my navigator took the seat just behind mine, shortly followed by Boyle, the flight engineer, who took the seat to the right of mine across the aisle. Last of all came Peters, my bomb aimer. He too completely ignored me and took the seat in front of mine. For a moment I considered jumping up and running off the aircraft but it was too late. The cabin crew had already shut the door and the left propeller was turning. I tried to steady myself. Logic told me that these were nothing but six ordinary passengers and my misfiring subconscious had transformed them into something they were not. I grabbed the pill bottle from my pocket and swallowed two tablets.

A few minutes later, the pilot swung the aircraft onto the runway and the dull thrum of the engines rose to a roar as we began the takeoff roll. The wheels thumped home and a few seconds later the lights of Lincolnshire disappeared as we entered cloud.

At first, it was no more than a gentle lurch in yaw and I put it down to the autopilot engaging, but then it came again, more strongly, and then moments later…mayhem. An appalling detonation and the aircraft slewed violently to the left as shards of metal blasted through the aluminium skin and into the cabin. It had to be a bomb. Terrified screams. Darkness. Falling luggage as the aircraft lurched into a 60-degree bank to the left. Then light, but this time orange and menacing, coming from the left wing. A plume of bright flame streamed back from the engine housing which was now at an angle to the wing, tilted outwards and upwards. Through gaping holes in its outer casing I could see stationary turbine blades that should have been spinning at thousands of RPM. But where was the propeller? As the crew managed to roll the aircraft wings-level and the emergency cabin lights came on, it dawned on me. No bomb. A propeller blade must have come adrift and sliced into the aircraft. The massive centrifugal forces generated by the destabilised propeller disc had almost torn the engine from its mountings, twisting it at a crazy angle to the airflow. Worse was to come. The cockpit door opened and on hands and knees, bleeding from gaping wounds to his left arm and face, the captain struggled into the passenger cabin. One of the cabin crew tried to help him to his feet. He attempted to speak. 'Help us. For God's sake, help us. I can't see. I can't see…'

With difficulty I got to my feet. Icy needles of cold air were gushing into the cabin through holes in the side of the aircraft. Whatever malign chance was operating against me that night I wasn't going to let it win. I shut the flight deck door behind me and climbed into the captain's vacant seat, flinching as the still warm blood from his headset ran down my cheek. To my right, the co-pilot had the control yoke hard over to the right. The intercom was still working. 'You need more right rudder,' I said, gesturing at the slip ball which was parked at full deflection to the right.

'Can't,' was all he said.

I looked more closely and saw that his right leg had been almost completely severed and bright red arterial blood was pumping out in regular but weakening spurts.

'I have control,' I replied, taking the yoke. I had instructed on turboprops during my time in the RAF. This one was bigger than the King Airs I had flown, but I saw enough that was familiar to give me a fighting chance of getting us back on the ground in one piece. To my relief, I was able to trim out most of the yaw and with only gentle pressure on the right rudder pedal, managed to get the aircraft flying in what passed for a straight line. 'Right, I'll fly the aircraft. Shut the left HP cock, turn off the engine master and fire the extinguisher. Make a mayday call, transponder to emergency and get us a heading to the nearest airfield.' No reply. I looked to my right and saw the co-pilot's head had slumped forward onto his chest.

I carried out the emergency drills myself and then took stock. We were in dense cloud at 5,000 feet heading roughly south. The co-pilot was beyond saving but I didn't know how many passengers and crew were injured, nor did I know how long the port wing would last, so we needed to get back on the ground quickly. I keyed the transmit switch to make the mayday call. Silence. No side tone, nothing. The damage to the aircraft had clearly taken out the radios. The primary flight instruments and all the navigation displays had failed, so I was reduced to using the standby artificial horizon, airspeed indicator, altimeter and compass. To have a chance of getting us all back on the ground in one piece I desperately needed to know where we were – one of the oldest and wisest sayings in flying is that in an emergency you need to do only three things: 'Aviate, Navigate and Communicate.' In other words; first, fly the aircraft, secondly, don't get lost or fly into high ground, and, finally, tell someone who can help you that you've got a problem. To navigate and to have a hope of communicating, I needed to get the stricken aircraft's electrical systems back on line. The starboard engine was still working, so in theory it should be providing power to its generator. That was the theory. Try as I might, the aircraft remained electrically dead. All I had was battery power, and with no heating to the aircraft's speed and altitude sensing systems they would soon ice up. Then we would die.

Lincolnshire is pretty flat and mostly rural so I reasoned that as long as I stayed away from the Wolds and the Belmont transmitter mast, I could risk a gentle descent even if it meant landing wheels up in a field. I tried not to think about electricity pylons, hoped our luck would hold, and with sweating, clammy hands, turned onto a northerly heading, lowered the nose and reduced power on the good engine. The die was cast.

With no radio I had no further need for the captain's blood-soaked headset and was about to take it off when to my amazement I heard a voice. Weak at first, crackly with static but distinct and familiar. 'Battery level critical, skipper, bad fuel imbalance… all the transfer pumps are out.' Boyle. I turned to my right. In place of the co-pilot was a figure clad in a fur-lined Irvin flying jacket, his head covered by a leather flying helmet and his features, save for his eyes, hidden by an oxygen mask. This was a hallucination. It had to be. I knew that stress can bring them on so that had to be it. Of all the bloody times for this to happen. Sod it, I thought. If I ignored him, Boyle would go away.

Then another voice. Hudson's. 'Descending through 3,000 feet, skipper. Estimate we're somewhere between Sleaford and Boston. Can't be more precise without a fix.' Again, my first reflex was to ignore him but what the voice had said seemed about right given that we'd been on a southerly heading since the prop came off and were now heading roughly north.

The cold in the cockpit was getting to me now. The sweat of fear had condensed and icy rivulets ran down my back. Trying hard to concentrate, I timed our rate of descent – 300 feet per minute. Gentle enough for me to cobble together a landing if we came out of cloud. We were descending through 1,500 feet when I saw it – just below us, a green light and then slightly offset to the left, a white one. Seconds later I saw a red light. We had almost collided with another aircraft and I swung the yoke hard over to the right. Only fifty yards separated us but all I could make out was the three lights, the darker mass of a fuselage and the starboard wing, tipped by its green navigation light. Like us, the aircraft was descending, presumably to land. All I had to do was follow and we would arrive at an airfield where I could force land on the grass next to the runway. It wouldn't be a comfortable landing, but it would be survivable. We were going to make it.

Then disaster. A patch of thicker cloud and for agonising seconds I lost sight of the stranger. All my previous training screamed at me to break away but instead I increased the power, edging towards him, tensing against the mid-air collision that I so feared would come if I misjudged our closing speed. There it was. A flicker of green. Gone. No, got it again. Thank Christ for that. A last glance in at the artificial horizon, heading, height and speed, before transferring my attention to formating on my unknown rescuer. Night formation flying is difficult at the best of times – my lack of practice started to tell and at first I overcontrolled in my attempts to hold a stable position in an aircraft that was doing its best to fly sideways. I chanced another glance inside at the instruments – a 600 feet per minute rate of descent. Spot on for a 3-degree glidepath at this speed. He was definitely on his final approach to land. I fumbled for the undercarriage handle and activated the emergency gravity release. Three satisfying thumps as the gear locked down were confirmed by three green bulbs glowing at me from the instrument panel. With damage to the trailing edge of the left wing I didn't dare lower the flaps for fear of generating an uncontrollable roll to port if the left hand flap was damaged or didn't deploy.

Then, as the cloud began to thin, I got a better look at him – four engines, black fuselage, twin tail fins, one at the end of each horizontal stabiliser… a bloody Lancaster, battle letters CD-O… this wasn't possible. No time to think, lights coming in to view. A tapering funnel of white, evenly-spaced, wonderful lights. Height 300 feet. A runway. Thank Christ for that. Then realisation as we broke fully clear of cloud. No sign of the Lanc. Not a runway but instead, a long straight road. Houses. Streetlights. Full power. Got to go around. Mustn't hit the houses. I raised the nose. Control yoke hard over to counter the roll. Full right rudder… but no good. Not enough control authority at this speed.

The port wingtip hit the ground first. I was aware of the aircraft cartwheeling and then the searing brightness and heat of a terrible explosion.

Then nothing.

Chapter Eighteen

The national media covered the accident at Leckonby. Here is the report that appeared on the front page of *The Times*, the following day, the 30th of March.

Forty-nine passengers and crew are feared dead after an Anglia Airways flight from Humberside airport to Weeze in Germany crashed onto a housing estate near the village of Leckonby in Lincolnshire last night. Wreckage was strewn along the newly-built Lancaster Way where fourteen homes and over twenty cars are reported to have been damaged. The emergency services have confirmed that four people on the ground have been treated for shock and minor injuries at local hospitals.

The Civil Aviation Authority have opened an enquiry into the accident which unofficial sources are blaming on the disintegration of a propeller shortly after takeoff. Wreckage, believed to be from the left engine of the stricken turboprop airliner, has been found in a field near the village of Habrough to the north east of Humberside airport. Cont'd page 3...

The Lincoln Post also covered the story. On its inside pages in the personal column, it carried a brief obituary of Miss Elizabeth Clark, former wartime WAAF officer, who "passed away in her sleep" at Hobbs End Hall Retirement Home, Leckonby on the night of 29th March, aged 98.

***

So now you know everything. I had hoped to find rest, but even that is denied me. Sometimes I am visible to the living, at other times not – it is something beyond my control. My ability to interact with the physical world is failing and even the effort of pushing a pencil across the pages of a notebook to record these last few words has taken every ounce of strength still remaining to me.

I ask not for pity, merely that you understand the human frailty that led me, like a moth to a flame, to meddle in things that ultimately destroyed me. I am now condemned to wander this shadow world – for how long, I have no idea – where even the quiet eternity of the grave is denied me.

THE END